D1732879

WRECKS OF KEY LARGO

AJ BAILEY ADVENTURE SERIES - BOOK 12

NICHOLAS HARVEY

HarveyBooks

Copyright © 2022 by Harvey Books, LLC

All rights reserved. This book or any portion thereof may not be reproduced or used in any manner whatsoever without the express written permission of the publisher except for the use of brief quotations in a book review.

Printed in the United States of America

First Printing, 2022

ISBN-13: 979-8830363747

Cover design by Wicked Good Book Covers

Cover photograph courtesy of Shutterstock

Author photograph by Lift Your Eyes Photography

This is a work of fiction. Names, characters, businesses, places, events and incidents are either the products of the author's imagination or used in a fictitious manner unless noted otherwise. Any resemblance to actual persons, living or dead, or actual events is purely coincidental. Several characters in the story generously gave permission to use their names in a fictional manner.

DEDICATION

This is for my older brother Michael.
Much older.
Okay, eighteen months, but you're still older.

Every time I've ever needed you, you've been there.

Well, except for a few occasions when we were kids.
Like the time you left me with my feet stuck in the mud by that mucky pond off Elmer Road.
Although, we might be even.
I did knock a big rock off the breakwater on the beach down Sea Lane and cracked your head open.

Regardless, you've almost always been there for me.
Lots of love from your far younger brother.

PREFACE

It was a big decision to take AJ away from the Cayman Islands, and I assure you it's only a temporary visit. My wife, Cheryl, and I had visited Key Largo many times in the past, and subsequently have called the town home since the beginning of 2020. As we built our memories here, I knew a story would soon emerge, and AJ would return to the place where her professional diving career began.

Key Largo boasts the best warm-water diving North America has to offer, and while the reefs are struggling compared to many Caribbean destinations – more on that in the novel – they are still incredibly beautiful and full of fish life. But for me, the big draw is the wrecks. Outside of Truk Lagoon and Scapa Flow, the Keys sports some of the most diverse and fantastic wrecks. Many are artificial reefs deliberately sunk for fishing and diving, but many more are ships which fell foul of the shallow reefs, weather, or collision. Each has its own personality and unique attraction.

The USCGC *Duane* is a favourite of Cheryl and mine. The prolific coral growth and common Goliath grouper and shark sightings make it a treat every dive. Sister ship to the *Duane* is the *Bibb* which lies on its side, making it a completely different dive despite the ships' commonality.

But the crown jewel is the magnificent *Spiegel Grove*; a 510-feet long behemoth of a ship, you could spend a lifetime exploring. Initially guided by local friends, I began venturing deeper into the labyrinth of passageways and rooms of the magnificent wreck, and over time, it became more and more familiar. So when *Wrecks of Key Largo* started taking shape, I immediately knew where AJ should explore in the story.

Needless to say, I do not recommend the dives described in this fictional work without the proper training and experience, but in the course of writing the book, I ventured to, or close to, each destination mentioned. They are as described, with very few embellishments for the sake of the story.

With me, on every dive, often filming with our trusty GoPro, was my amazing wife and dive buddy, Cheryl. AJ Bailey isn't based on any one person, she's a fusion of the many incredible people I've met over the years diving, partly me, partly the person I wish I was, but mainly, she's based on Cheryl. And... my wife is quick to point out she had purple highlights and tattoos before I ever put pen to paper and created AJ!

I hope you enjoy this novel. I tried to weave many of our favourite spots into the story and reflect the ambiance of life in the Keys. I also snuck a few friends into the plot, some in their actual roles, and some in a more amusing light. I thank them all for the friendship and good humour!

MAP

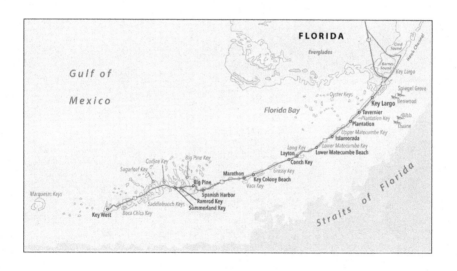

1

TUESDAY

If it wasn't for early mornings being a great time to fish, Rosie would consider his line of work perfection. As it was, most of the tourists who chartered his services weren't partial to getting up before dawn on their holidays, so his alarm rarely went off before sunrise. Unless he chose to cast a line before daybreak. Like today.

The sun was about to break above the horizon with orange hues already painting the water and lower eastern sky. Two good-sized mutton snappers already graced the fish well. Rosie had weighted the Carolina rigs with 10 oz egg sinkers and if a couple more took the ballyhoos wriggling on the hooks a few feet off the bottom, then he'd be enjoying breakfast by 8am.

He enjoyed the peace and quiet of early mornings on the water; it was the getting out of bed while it was still dark he disliked. But stunningly beautiful dawns, like the one he was savouring, soon made him forget the comfort of his berth below. He had no need for conversation, no mindless banter to spoil the calm; just the sound of the ocean gently slapping the boat, and a good cup of coffee.

Rosie's boat, and the second love of his life, *Reel-Lee Hooked*, was a 34-foot Glacier Bay 3470 Ocean Runner. He'd replaced the original 225-horsepower Honda outboards with more efficient Yamaha

250s in 2015, and the 17-year-old powered catamaran still ran like a Swiss watch. She was a little dinged up around the edges, and the interior, which doubled as Rosie's home, showed her age, but the love affair was still in full bloom.

Trolling slowly along, he checked his 9-inch fish-finder screen, which showed a depth of 79 feet. Rosie had intended to make for deeper water, but once the *Reel-Lee Hooked* had cleared the slope past the *Benwood* wreck, he'd slowed and thrown a pair of lines in the water. Not a minute later, the first line went taught and Rosie hauled the catch aboard. He hadn't seen the need to move too far afterwards, as the second line began running as he dropped the first mutton snapper in the well.

With the wind blowing from the east, as it most commonly did in the Florida Keys, the sound of boat engines reached him before Rosie saw the vessel. He looked up from the dashboard and scanned the waters off his bow and starboard side. Well out to sea, he picked up a boat but couldn't tell the direction it was heading. Letting his eyes adjust as he stared into the direction of the sun peeking above the Atlantic Ocean, he realised a second boat was trailing the first. He glanced over at the cockpit and nodded his head out to sea.

Rosie reached for the VHF radio and turned up the volume, which he'd lowered once he'd begun fishing. Tuned to the general marine channel 16, he heard a Coast Guard boat urgently hailing someone to stop. Taking his binoculars from the cabinet under the helm, Rosie focused on the distant boats.

"Someone's day has turned to shit early," he muttered.

The first boat looked like a Sea Ray with its distinctive swept-forward hardtop supports. It appeared to be running wide open, and Rosie guessed it was one of the SLX models, perhaps the top-of-the-line with triple 400s. Hardly a drug-running cigarette boat, but certainly capable of outrunning most vessels it would come across. With the exception of a Coastie's rigid inflatable boat, or RIB, with with its own set of triple outboards, which was currently closing from behind.

Rosie forgot about his lines for a moment, transfixed by the high-speed chase across the glassy morning water. They were close enough now that he put the binoculars down and could make out two figures on the Sea Ray. One at the helm, and the other gamely trying to hang on in the cockpit as he frantically worked on something Rosie couldn't see.

The Coasties made it alongside, choosing starboard, which put them on the far side of the Sea Ray from the *Reel-Lee Hooked* as the two boats passed by, 200 yards to the north. Suddenly, the Sea Ray throttled back and turned hard to port and the second man dropped something over the side while their hull shielded them from the Coast Guard boat. Slowing, they passed Rosie on the inland side, still a few hundred yards away, and the two men on the Sea Ray held up their hands, surrendering themselves.

Rosie dropped a pin on his GPS and took a compass reading of the direction in which he figured the mystery package had gone in the water. He wondered what it could be. Too small to be any quantity of weed or coke for any smuggler to bother with, but maybe it was recreational, and the two rich guys on the Sea Ray didn't want to get a possession charge. Best to stay out of it, he told himself.

One of his lines whirred as the reel spun out and he quickly remembered he was supposed to be fishing. With one eye on the Coasties boarding the Sea Ray, now half a mile or more away, Rosie fought his fish for a while, letting it run itself tired. By the time he'd finally pulled the largest mutton snapper he'd ever caught aboard, the other two boats were leaving with officers at both helms. Whatever those two guys were up to, they were being taken to the Islamorada station for further investigation.

Rosie dropped the snapper in the fish well and admired his morning's work. One more would look good next to the three. He re-baited the hook and dropped the line in the water, setting the rod in its holder. Back at the helm, he made a wide arc to backtrack along the path towards the *Benwood*. He was in 90 feet of water. Ahead, the GPS plotter showed the pin he'd dropped. Looking over his shoulder, Rosie checked his lines. They were both trolling straight, no bites.

Over his fifty-one years, Rodney Lee – Rosie to anyone who'd spent more than a few minutes with him in the past 25 years – had decided life was a series of curiosities and adventures. Of course, this spirited attitude had landed him in hot water more than a few times, but an inquisitive nature required constant food for the hungry mind. Two minutes later, his lines were reeled in.

With the *Reel-Lee Hooked* sitting over his GPS pin, Rosie aimed the bow on the compass heading he'd taken and eased into the throttles. His biggest struggle would be judging the distance to travel along his heading. Distance across the ocean is notoriously hard to judge by the human eye, but a man who'd spent much of his adult life on the waters of the Florida Keys had a better chance than most.

Taking his best guess, Rosie throttled back and checked his fish-finder sonar. Thirty-two feet of depth over what appeared to be mainly sand. He took both engines out of gear and released the windlass, dropping the anchor to the sea floor. Letting the gentle waves move the Glacier Bay, he felt the anchor drag and take a bite into the sandy bottom. After another 70 feet of rode played out, he locked the windlass and shut off the engines.

In the far distance to the south, Rosie could see a few charter boats making their way out for their first dives. He didn't have much time. Not that anyone would know what he was up to, but he'd found it best to slide by unseen whenever possible. He unhooked a dive tank from the gunwale in the cockpit, with his buoyancy control device, or BCD, the jacket-like piece of gear divers wear, already strapped to the tank. His regulator was also attached, so he opened the tank valve and checked the pressure gauge. He had 2100 psi, which was just over two-thirds of a full tank. Enough to spend 45 minutes at this depth if he didn't work too hard.

Collecting fins and mask from below deck, Rosie made sure the *Reel-Lee Hooked* hadn't moved while he was getting ready.

According to the GPS, the anchor seemed to be holding firm, but he'd follow the line to the sea floor just to double check. He peeled off his shirt and geared up on the swim step, which extended between the two outboards, and lowered the ladder for his return. With a final gear check and an okay signal in the air, Rosie took a giant stride, dropping into the balmy water.

Visibility was good, over 50 feet he guessed, and his anchor was indeed in the sand, well away from any coral heads or reef. The sea floor was strewn with patches of seagrass and occasional boulders of old dead coral. Satisfied his Danforth anchor was deeply embedded, Rosie quickly moved on with his search.

Back on the boat, he'd known he was facing a needle in a haystack, but now, looking across the vastness of the ocean floor, it hit home. Taking out his compass, Rosie set off along the same heading he'd used to arrive at the spot, and arbitrarily decided on three minutes of kicking until his turnaround boundary. Scanning to either side, he made long, efficient strokes with his fins, keeping his arms wrapped tightly around his midriff, relaxed and streamlined.

At three minutes, he turned 90 degrees to his right, made ten fin strokes before turning 90 degrees right once more. Offset from his first pass, Rosie began the three-minute swim towards the Glacier Bay.

A discarded tyre, several beer bottles, a length of rope, and a couple of sections of scrap metal caught his eye, but nothing worthy of further investigation. After a little under three minutes, his own anchor came into view and Rosie turned again, going ten fin strokes past his marker. With another 90-degree right turn, he began the next run along the same heading.

His fruitless search continued for another eighteen minutes, before the sound of a boat engine and prop droned through the water. He never saw the hull, but he guessed it was one of the dive boats heading for the Christ of the Abyss statue to the north-east, or the USS *Spiegel Grove* wreck in deeper water to the east. Regardless, more would soon follow and he didn't need all the captains seeing

Reel-Lee Hooked in the area if something more came of that morning's incident with the Sea Ray.

Finishing his current run back towards the boat, Rosie turned to make the forty fin strokes to the anchor. The moment he took his eyes from his compass back to the sandy bottom, he saw a shiny dive weight. Nothing stayed shiny for long in the ocean. Tethered to the dive weight was a small, black, watertight container, the kind people used to keep their mobile phones and wallets dry. The air in the container made it bob like a balloon above the weight, nestled amongst willowy strands of seagrass.

Rosie didn't waste any time. He gathered up the weight, added air to his BCD to compensate for the additional ballast, and kicked like crazy towards the *Reel-Lee Hooked*. He couldn't hazard a guess what was in the little box, but it was important enough to ditch before the Coasties nabbed them, so it had to be interesting – or more to the point, valuable.

Arriving at the stern, Rosie surfaced and clung to the drop-down ladder of the Glacier Bay. He pulled his mask down around his neck and studied the container in his hand. He wondered what could be so incriminating, and yet so small?

Reaching up, he gave the weight and the container to the extended hand of his friend.

2

WEDNESDAY

Annabelle Jayne Bailey sat in the passenger seat of the old Land Rover driven by her friend and mentor, Reg Moore. They bounced along the road towards the airport, each jolt a reminder that the dampers were long overdue for replacement. She checked her watch for the twelfth time and glanced at her rucksack in the back once again.

"Your passport ain't jumped out of your bloody bag," Reg growled in his deep, voice. "You're making me nervous with all your twitching."

"Oh, hush up," she retorted. "Are you positive you won't need Carlos over the weekend?"

Reg shook his head. "Still sure. Haven't changed my mind since the last time you asked, five minutes ago."

AJ rolled her eyes behind her bamboo-framed sunglasses. "I've never been away from the business before. You can't blame me for being worried."

Reg grunted behind his thick beard. "You'll be back Monday. I think we can manage till then."

"I know, I know," she muttered. "I'm glad you're staying here... well, I wish you were coming too... that's not to say I didn't want you to come along… but I'm glad you'll be here to keep an eye on things… Bugger, you know what I mean."

Reg chuckled as he pulled up to the kerb by departures at Owen Roberts International Airport, which was 50 yards from arrivals, as the Grand Cayman airport was a nice building, but hardly expansive.

"Go on, get along with you," Reg said, grinning. "I better hurry back and see if the lads have sunk your boat yet."

AJ opened the creaky door to the old Landy and stepped out. "Hilarious. You're a regular Benny Hill," she replied, before smacking the door closed. She opened the back door and grabbed her rucksack, slinging it over her shoulder before dragging a roller bag along the back seat until it dropped to the pavement. Reg's laugh finally faded when she closed the door.

He leaned over to the passenger side and unwound the side window. "Have a good time. Don't worry about things here."

AJ paused by the window. "I will, and I will, but I'm sure you'll take care of everything. I'll text when we land."

With a quick wave, Reg set off, and AJ headed for the terminal building with her bag in tow. She was barely through the automatic sliding doors when a fellow Englishwoman bellowed across the check-in area, turning a sea of surprised heads.

"Come on, Bailey, we're going on our hols!"

A short blonde woman in bright green sunglasses – meaning shorter than AJ's five feet and almost four inches – waved enthusiastically from one of the lines. At least half the people in the terminal were arrivals, making their way out towards shuttle buses, hire cars and taxis. For them, the idea that anyone would leave the Cayman Islands to go on holiday was like carrying coals to Newcastle.

AJ hustled towards her friend Emily Durand, her cheeks glowing red with embarrassment as everyone watched her. Emily was oblivious to the attention and threw her arms around AJ once she reached her.

"I'm so excited!" she squealed. "Feels naughty running off without the boys, and I love it!"

AJ grinned. Emily's ridiculous zeal and energy were infectious. She and her boyfriend, Boone, ran a dive operation on Little Cayman, one of the sister islands 80 miles north-east of Grand. They'd spent the last few years moving around a variety of islands in the Caribbean, savouring the different cultures and diving before finding the next venue to set up shop.

"I feel awfully guilty leaving Jackson to do all the work while I'm gone," AJ admitted. "I've never left the business for more than a day off before."

Emily lifted her oversized sunglasses. "Are you barmy? They'll be fine," Emily assured her. "Lean into the Thelma and Louise vibe we've got going, AJ!" She gestured triumphantly towards the front of the line. "Don't give a toss for what's behind you, only what lies ahead!"

"Uhh… that was plunging off a cliff to their deaths, if you remember?"

Emily waved her off. "Details, details. We're heading for exotic locales, boundless adventure, and fruity cocktails."

AJ laughed, and the businessman ahead in line gave Emily a confused look.

"I think that's actually what we're leaving," AJ pointed out. "Where we're heading is a conference in Florida."

"But it's Key Largo!" Emily countered.

"I think that's still in Florida, Em," AJ chuckled.

They kicked their bags forward as the line moved.

"Florida makes it sound like retirement communities, snow-birds, and mosquito-infested swamps," Emily claimed, with unfettered fervour. "Key Largo is far more romantic."

"Well, the breeze keeps the mosquitos down most of the time, but I'm afraid you'll still find plenty of retirees in the Keys. Although the snowbirds will be long gone this time of year."

"See? Exotic, fruity and boundless!" Emily repeated as they shuffled the rest of the way to the check-in counter. "And the

African Queen, don't forget we have to take a tour on the *African Queen.*"

AJ rolled her eyes. The old prop from the movie still ran people down a canal and out to the ocean, where it promptly turned and chugged back, driven by a small outboard hidden beneath a cover. She had no intention of paying for the privilege, but maybe they'd get a picture next to the old boat by the dock.

The flight from Grand Cayman to Miami International was an hour and a half. Emily kept AJ distracted from her worries with endless chatter as the two caught up on all their goings-on since the last time they were together at Christmas.

"Who is it we're staying with?" Emily asked, after a brief lull while a flight attendant offered them beverages.

"My friends Cass and Rosie," AJ replied. "Cass is picking us up in Miami."

Em swallowed her mouthful of orange juice. "They're a couple?"

"Yeah," AJ answered, and then thought about her friends again. "Well, not really."

"They live together, but they're not *together* together?"

"No, they don't live together, exactly," AJ replied.

"So, are we staying with Cass, or Rosie? I'm confused."

"If you'd hush up a second, I could explain," AJ retorted, grinning at her friend.

"Righto." Emily drew her fingers across her lips like a zipper.

AJ laughed, knowing the zipper wouldn't hold for very long. "Cass lives in the house and Rosie lives on his boat, which is kept at the house, as they're on a canal."

"Wait, his? Rosie's a bloke?"

"Oh, yeah, I probably should have explained that," AJ said sheepishly. "His real name is Rodney Lee."

Em laughed. "That's brilliant! Rosie Lee, like the rhyming slang for tea?"

"Yup. Cass is from London and when they met, she started calling him Rosie," AJ explained. "All his mates thought it was hilarious, so it stuck. You'll find anyone who actually knows him calls him Rosie."

"He didn't mind?" Emily asked.

"I think he was too besotted with Cass to care. She's pretty fit."

"But now they're separated, or divorced?"

AJ thought for a moment again. "I don't think they ever divorced, but they decided it was better if they didn't live together all the time. Well, Cass kicked him out for the umpteenth time one day, and told him that was it. He wasn't coming back in. Rosie stayed on the boat while he figured things out. That was 14 or 15 years ago, back when I was living in Key Largo. I guess he's still contemplating his next step, 'cos he's lived on the boat ever since."

Emily raised her eyebrows. "That has to be a bit awkward when... you know... one of them has a friend over for a bit of nookie!"

AJ shook her head, grinning. "I bet they still have the same arrangement they'd come up with when I was here last. Anytime Cass feels like overnight company, she walks down to the end of the garden and hops on the boat. Rosie knows Cass is the best thing that ever happened to him, and he's the one who screwed it all up. He'll take anything she'll give him."

Em giggled. "If we hear Cass sneaking out in the middle of the night, we'll know where she's going, then."

"I'm sure Rosie will join us for dinner or drinks one evening. He's quite the character," AJ said fondly. "Lovely bloke, he just... makes poor decisions sometimes."

"He put his thingy in the wrong wife?" Emily asked with a frown.

AJ laughed. "Not to my knowledge. I'm pretty sure Cass would take a fillet knife to his goolies if he did."

Em winced.

"No, it's more his decisions on ways to make income," AJ continued. "He runs fishing charters and dive trips, but he's also been known to transport a little square grouper. When a really nice big-screen telly showed up, she realised it must have fallen off the back of a lorry, and that was the final straw."

"Did she turn him in?"

"No, I think she rather liked the telly, and besides, she still loved the silly bugger. This all sounds bad, but wait till you meet Rosie. It's hard not to like him. At least he's a fun drunk."

"Bloody hell, AJ, he's an alky too?"

"He was," AJ admitted. "He used to drink a bit too much. Well, a lot too much. You can see how it all added up."

"Too right. And what about now?"

"He just drinks a lot now, which is better than before," AJ said with a grin. "I'm guessing he's kept his hands clean on the other stuff, or he'd either be in jail or Cass would cut his dock lines and her relationship with him for good."

Emily held up her plastic airline cup of orange juice, and AJ tapped her water against it.

"Cheers," Em declared. "I think I'll like them both."

"Bottoms up! You will. They really took care of me when I was in the Keys. Rosie sounds like a wanker when I hear myself describe all his troubles, but you'll see, he's a lovable wanker."

They both took a swig and finished their drinks as the flight attendant swept by with a black plastic bag, reluctantly gathering rubbish. The captain announced their descent into Miami International airport and Emily grabbed AJ's hand.

"We're going to have such a giggle, it's going to be brill!"

AJ smiled. "It's never dull with you, Em."

3

WEDNESDAY

AJ and Emily dragged their rolling bags of dive gear behind them to the kerb. The heat under the covered arrivals area was stifling, with a constant stream of vehicles adding to the triple-digit heat index Florida naturally provided. Of course, they'd just left a similar climate, but a constant ocean breeze helped the islands feel a whole lot cooler.

A horn honked somewhere back in the line of traffic as the parade of oversized SUVs shuffled along, searching for their passengers. After a few more honks, a faded red 1979 Volkswagen Beetle Cabriolet appeared from behind the mass of large black vehicles, with a hand waving above the windscreen.

"I used to have a Beetle! But that's nearly as decrepit as Boone's Thing," Emily said, laughing.

"Do what?" AJ questioned with a stunned look.

"Hi there!" came an Englishwoman's voice from behind the wheel as Cassandra Lee pulled to the kerb and put the manual gearbox in neutral. The old air-cooled engine spluttered and complained, but kept running.

"You're a sight for sore eyes!" she yelled, rushing around the car to hug AJ.

"Hi Cass, you look amazing as always," AJ managed mid bear hug.

"A few more wrinkles and some parts are further south than they used to be, but I'm doing alright," Cass replied, releasing AJ and throwing her arms around her next victim. "You must be Emily!"

For once, Emily was dumbstruck, but she grinned from ear to ear.

AJ laughed. "You could be sisters, huh?"

"I love her already," Em replied as Cass opened the bonnet of the bug.

"Not much will fit in here, but maybe one of the dive bags," Cass declared, then looked back and forth from the luggage to the limited space in the front of the car. "Hmm... maybe not. Shove your rucksacks in here and the dive gear can go on the back seat."

AJ took their smaller bags and wedged them behind the spare tyre, which looked like the tread had seen a few too many miles to be of much use. Emily tugged on the passenger door handle, but it didn't budge. She tried the door lock pull, which was already up.

"That door's a bit sticky, love," Cass said, waving a hand. "Just hop over and climb back there."

Emily did as instructed and clambered her tiny frame over the door, onto the passenger seat, then stepped into the back, quickly followed by the first bag heaved over by AJ.

"Stand them on end, Em."

With Emily wedged between the luggage in the back, and AJ wrestling with the old-style non-retractable safety belt, Cass put on her indicator, ground the bug into first gear, and waved to an SUV driver who honked his annoyance as she barged in line.

"I can't believe you still have the Love Bug," AJ said.

"You can't rely on men or the weather, but this old beauty never lets me down," Cass enthused. "Which reminds me, let's hope it doesn't rain, 'cos the convertible top has jammed up and dear ol' Rosie hasn't found his way to mending it yet."

AJ looked up at the blue sky, knowing clear skies were no guarantee a pop-up shower wouldn't soak them on the way. "How long has it been broken?"

Cass looked thoughtful. "What's today? Wednesday?"

"Yeah," AJ replied, looking behind at Emily fending off a bag of dive gear as they rounded a corner onto NW 12th Drive towards the Dolphin Expressway.

"About three years then," Cass said, followed by a raucous laugh. She glanced up at Emily in the rear-view mirror. "Alright back there, love?"

"Tip top!" Em replied, stiff-arming a bag and grinning.

Cass drove on, taxing the 1600 cc engine up to 70 mph, which still left them the slowest vehicle on the southbound lanes of the Ronald Reagan Turnpike.

"How's Rosie doing?" AJ asked over the wind noise and what she guessed to be a leaky exhaust.

Cass looked at her with a crooked smile and waved a hand in the air. "Same old, same old. I don't suppose anything much has changed since you were here last." She ran a hand through her wavy auburn hair – a habit AJ recalled of her friend when she felt self-conscious. "Silly bugger never changes. Still as daft as ever."

AJ wanted to ask more, but it felt invasive, especially so soon after arriving. She'd see for herself over the next few days, or bring it up over drinks one evening. AJ cared deeply for them both. She was only eighteen when she'd first landed in Florida, fresh out of dive instructor training, and thrown into the deep end with a busy dive op.

Cass and Rosie were well known in the diving community and AJ had rented a room from them for a while. They'd helped steer her through the early months when she was eager, energetic, and relatively clueless. Scuba diving was like many adventurous sporting industries: margins were thin, pay was terrible, and hours were long and tiring. Companies relied on a steady turnover of keen, young employees who'd accept the lousy wages in return for working in their dream job.

Inevitably, most quickly grew tired of sharing rooms in crappy apartments and eating ramen noodles to survive. They'd move on and use their college degrees for better paying 'real jobs'. Or continue diving in a new exotic location, using the industry to tour the world.

Cass and Rosie were the main reason AJ stuck around for three years before moving to Grand Cayman to work for Reg. Especially Rosie, who encouraged AJ to continue her diving education. Taking his advice, she trained in technical mixed gas diving and cave diving in central and northern Florida, all of which helped her become a versatile and confident diver.

When AJ arrived at Reg's doorstep, the man who'd first taught her to dive on a family holiday, she was an experienced instructor with an impressive skill set for a 21-year-old. It was a path which eventually led to Reg and AJ's father helping her start Mermaid Divers.

"Not sure where the dopey sod has got to this week," Cass added. "Haven't seen him since Monday."

"Oh?" AJ questioned, worried Rosie might be drinking again... or more accurately, excessively drinking again.

"Boat's there, but his truck's gone. Probably crewing for someone on a delivery, or maybe a Bimini run," Cass said, putting AJ's mind at ease. "He was around Tuesday, 'cos the boat was gone when I left for work, and back when I came home."

Emily leaned forward from the back seat. "What did you say we're doing tomorrow?"

"Nice try, sneaky," AJ replied. "It's called a surprise for a reason."

Em rolled her eyes behind her sunglasses. "How do I prepare myself if I don't know what we're doing?"

"Like I already told you the twenty-three times you've already asked, bring your dive gear and be ready to work."

Emily slumped back into the seat. "If we're scrubbing barnacles off hulls, I'm never going on holiday with you again."

Cass and AJ looked at each other and chuckled.

"I wish you could come with us, Cass."

"Me too," AJ's friend replied. "But the doctor wants me to keep my ear dry for another week."

"What happened?" Emily asked, peeking between the front seats again.

"I was playing silly buggers with the neighbour's dog and he smacked me upside the noggin with a giant paw. Guess he got me just right, 'cos my ear rang, and I got all dizzy. Still felt weird the next morning, so I went to the doc's. Perforated eardrum, he says, but it's a small pinhole and should heal itself."

"Blimey, what kind of dog is it?" Em asked. "I mean, I'm sorry about your ear, but I do love the pooches."

"His name is Admiral, and he's a bloody great big Alsatian. Scares the crap out of anyone who doesn't know him, but he's just a big softy. Plus, he's the perfect pet for me."

"I thought you said he was the neighbour's?" Emily questioned.

Cass smiled. "Exactly. I go by and enjoy some play and lovin', then leave him for the neighbours to feed him and scoop up his poop. Kinda like nieces and nephews."

"It'll surprise you to know Cass doesn't have any children," AJ pointed out.

"Ghastly messy little things," Cass confirmed. "Expensive too."

They chatted and drove south with the wind whipping their hair and the Florida sunshine beating down on the little Beetle. When they hit The Stretch – the 18-mile section of Highway US1 connecting Florida City to Key Largo – AJ felt a flood of memories return with the familiar terrain.

She'd enjoyed her time in the Keys. It was a far cry from the southern coast of England, and her first taste of living away from home. Everything about the place was exciting and starkly different from where she'd grown up. Scenery, weather, culture, and of course, the diving.

Passing Gilbert's Resort, they rose 65 feet above the water on Jewfish Creek Bridge spanning Lake Surprise, before making the right curve into the town of Key Largo. From there, US1, known as Overseas Highway, reached another 106 miles down to the tip of Key West. Like all the towns along the way, Key Largo is narrow, perched on ancient coral limestone, and peaking an average of 8 feet above the water.

As Cass drove south, AJ looked around and commented on businesses and restaurants she noted were new, or missing since her last trip, which was before Hurricane Irma in 2017. The storm had caused catastrophic damage throughout the Keys.

"Did you get your tattoos here?" Emily asked as they passed a sign for South of Heaven Tattoo. She was equal parts obsessed, and scared, to get a tattoo, ever since she'd met AJ, who had full sleeves on both arms.

"Deano Cook did mine. He's actually in Atlanta," AJ replied. "Deano's the best in the world for underwater scenes. He's a diver and photographer as well as an artist."

"South of Heaven is superb too," Cass added. "They did my upper arm. Want me to see if you can get an appointment while you're here?"

AJ grinned at Em, who looked around nervously. "Hmm... I'm not altogether sure what to get just yet."

AJ pointed out the left side of the Beetle. "The Fish House is still here, thank goodness!" AJ yelped. "We have to eat there before we leave, Em."

"Now that I'm up for," she replied, glad to move the subject away from her indecision over body art.

4

WEDNESDAY

Cass stopped in the left turn lane at the light for Atlantic Avenue. Ahead, Overseas Highway split either side of a broad central reservation, wide enough to accommodate businesses. While stationary, the blazing summer heat and humidity would be suffocating to most, but the three women were used to the tropics.

Turning left on green, Cass took the first right, then left on Ocean Bay Drive. The scenery switched from the business-lined dual carriageway of US1 to scattered residences between dense stands of buttonwoods. A quarter of a mile along Ocean Bay, a small marina appeared on the left, home to a mixture of pleasure craft and private fishing boats.

AJ excitedly pointed out the Coral Restoration Foundation building and Pilot House Restaurant, Emily's head whipping around to see as they drove by. On the far side of the marina, commercial fishing boats docked before a series of buildings signed Key Largo Fisheries.

"They sell fresh fish straight off the boats," AJ explained as Cass made a left on Ocean Way. "They also have their own restaurant, as well as supplying most of the others in town."

On their left were short canal-lined cul-de-sacs ending at the main channel leading to the ocean. Cass turned on Mahogany and slowed halfway up at the fourth house. It was a typical Keys home, raised on pilings, painted a soft yellow with blue accents, and surrounded by crushed limestone with concrete pathways. It looked just as AJ remembered.

The neighbourhood was a mixture of small, older homes, similar to Cass and Rosie's, with larger, newer, and more extravagant houses squeezed into the lots. Cass parked underneath the house, sheltering the Beetle from the sun and rain, and they piled out of the car, dragging their bags with them.

Potted palms and pretty flowers were spaced between the pilings, adding colour amongst the gravel and concrete, and half the ground level looked like part of the house, but was in fact storage. The home had been built thirty years ago before building code dictated living areas had to be raised above Base Flood Elevation in the area, but Rosie had made sure the structure was raised anyway, having endured several hurricanes.

Steps ran up the side to the front door on the south-facing wall, where a walkway continued to a deck overlooking the canal. Em dropped her bag and rushed to the railing, taking in the view.

"This isn't half bad, is it?"

Cass and AJ joined her in the shade of the overhanging roof.

"Is Rosie home?" AJ asked, looking down at the *Reel-Lee Hooked*, snugly moored in the dock, notched into their backyard.

"Boat's been here, but his truck is still gone," Cass replied. "Could be we've been missing each other, but I usually hear him coming and going."

The Glacier Bay looked buttoned up with no visible light inside and AJ wondered again if Rosie was okay, or if he'd fallen foul of his weakness once again. Cass didn't appear to be overly worried, so she didn't want to fuss over it, but it was hard not to be concerned.

"Have you tried calling him?"

Cass thought for a moment. "I sent a text this morning reminding him I was picking you up." She took her mobile from a hip pocket of her black Capri leggings. "Nothing," she mumbled, looking at the screen. She speed-dialled her husband's number. A moment later, Cass ended the call. "Straight to voicemail."

She continued staring at her mobile for a moment before shrugging her shoulders. "He's a big boy. I'm sure he's fine." She looked up and smiled. "How about lunch on the deck?"

"I'm famished," Em replied, looking at her watch.

AJ nodded, but her concerns hadn't diminished, and she saw the same in Cass's eyes.

The three women ate their late lunch, then stayed on the deck chatting and getting caught up. Before they knew it, 5:30 pm rolled around, and Cass jumped up.

"Bollocks, I have to be at work at six. You can drop me off if you'd like to take the car and roam about. I'm sure you have other people to see."

Em looked at AJ and shrugged her shoulders. "I'm along for the ride, yeah?"

AJ thought for a moment before standing up and gathering her wine glass and empty crisp bowl from the table. "We'll come with you. I bet most of the people I wouldn't mind running into will be where you're going."

"True," Cass replied, and they cleared the table before heading into the house to change.

The drive took all of four minutes to reach the canal-side bar and restaurant where Cass worked. Sharkey's was at the north end of Port Largo, a large warren of man-made waterways lined with homes, varying from little Keys cottages to extravagant ocean-front mansions.

The restaurant had mostly outdoor seating next door to one of the largest dive operators in town. The food was reasonably priced, the atmosphere casual, and the booze flowed freely. Clientele varied from tourists staying at the nearby hotels within easy walking distance, divers coming in from a day on the water, to locals who gathered most evenings for an after-work beverage.

Right around 6:00 pm, the divemasters finished prepping the boats for the next day and rowdily descended upon the tables adjacent to their work. Some had a quick drink before heading home, and others often wound up spending the evening and nursing a sore head the next morning.

Cass waved goodbye with a smile as she pushed through the crowd while AJ was quickly recognised at the first table. The scuba diving industry was a migratory business, but there were always the few who settled in one spot and watched the youngsters come and go.

"AJ Bailey!" called an older man, unshaven, with a tanned complexion showing wrinkles from sun and age. He was slight in build with a soft, almost musical voice, and a crooked grin. "You missed me so much you've come back!"

AJ gave the man a hug. "Captain David, I can't believe you're here."

"I have to check my mail every once in a while," he replied.

"This is my friend Emily," AJ said, stepping back so they could shake hands. "Captain David lives on his sailboat. He's usually sailing around the Bahamas or somewhere fun."

"The wind is free, but I do have a few bills to pay," the old man said. "So I stop in and captain a boat for a month or two in between."

"Sounds like a brilliant life," Em enthused. "My manservant, Boone, and I are rather nomadic ourselves."

"They have a dive boat and set up operations on an island for a while, then move on to another when the urge takes them," AJ explained.

"Sounds like you have it figured out," David commented. "You still on Grand Cayman?" he asked, turning to AJ.

"I am, and business is doing alright. I can't wait to tell Reg we ran into you."

"How is that old sea dog?" David said with an even broader smile. "Or more importantly, how's that lovely wife of his?"

AJ laughed. "They're both great. Pearl still plays at our local a few times a month."

"She's really good," Em added. "I heard her play over the Christmas hols."

The Captain introduced them to the others at the table, bombarding AJ with names she'd never be able to remember. They were all young and enthusiastic.

"Didn't you discover that U-boat a few years back?" one girl asked. AJ thought her name was Gaelen, but wasn't positive. AJ nodded, always embarrassed when her accomplishment was brought up.

"I had a lot of help."

The young woman smiled. "But weren't you on your own when you found it?"

AJ sighed. She'd broken a bunch of recreational diving rules in her search for U-1026, and she'd taken heat in some of the press. "I didn't set a very good example, I'm afraid."

"Well, it was really cool," Gaelen said. "Crazy brave."

Others at the table joined in their praise, and Captain David looked like a Cheshire cat, enjoying the scene.

"I read about it in the dive mags when it happened," Gaelen added. "It was inspiring. I always remember because I was just certified, back when I was a sophomore in high school."

Emily chuckled, and AJ elbowed her friend. Gaelen was just being nice, but AJ didn't need the reminder she was no longer one of the twenty-something crowd. Captain David was laughing too.

AJ rolled her eyes and quickly switched topics. "Did you know Emily starred in a movie?"

All eyes shifted to Em, who was always eager to chat about her brush with stardom.

"It's called *Man O' War*, and they haven't released it yet..." Em began, and AJ stepped away, looking for Cass.

She spotted her at a small round table by the railing, talking to a man. AJ walked over and Cass saw her approach them.

"This is Phil Giles," she said, still looking at the man. "He and Rosie often fish together. I was just asking if he'd seen him lately."

Phil shook his head and waggled a finger. "I've not seen him," he replied in a monotone voice, which sounded more like a slurred groan. AJ realised the man was deaf.

"Text?" Cass asked, taking her mobile from her pocket and tapping the screen.

Phil shook his head again and shrugged his shoulders. His brow knitted in concern, which was clearly growing in Cass's mind.

"Thanks, Phil," she said and squeezed his arm before turning away. "He's a good bloke, Phil. Rosie's been spending more time with him since he lost his missus, poor bugger. Cancer," she added in a whisper.

"How sad for him," AJ responded.

"It's been over six months now and he's still having a hard time. They had this dream of taking off to Tahiti and living out their days in a hut near the beach. Lately, he's been saying he might take her ashes with him and finally go. Rosie says he's been saving, which has never been one of ol' Phil's fortes, but maybe he'll make it happen after all. Rosie will really miss him."

"I can't imagine how hard that would be."

They both stopped and thought a moment before AJ shifted the subject back to Cass's missing husband.

"Is there anywhere I could have a look for Rosie while you're working?"

Cass considered the idea. "Nah. I'm on breakfast shift in the morning while you two go diving. We usually get a few of the captains and fishing guides come in early. I'll ask around then."

The idea of waiting longer didn't sit well with AJ. She was too impatient. But it was Cass's husband, and no one knew him better than she did.

"Alright, but if he still hasn't shown up when we get back at lunchtime tomorrow, I think we should report him missing."

"To the coppers?"

AJ was surprised at Cass's reaction. "Yeah. I mean, they're the best ones to find a missing person."

Cass leaned in closer and took AJ's arm. "Rosie would have my guts for garters if I went to the Old Bill."

"I thought you said he'd straightened out his ways?"

"His ways are straighter than they used to be," Cass whispered in reply. "But he wouldn't want them sniffing around. Besides, you don't know who to trust around here. Most of the coppers are all right, but there's always one or two in the pocket of some smuggler or politician."

"Really?"

"Really," Cass reiterated firmly.

5

THURSDAY

AJ and Emily ate breakfast at Sharkey's, as Cass had to be at work well before the dive boat was leaving. When AJ had lived and worked in Key Largo, it had been Ocean Divers located adjacent to the restaurant, but a few years back, Rainbow Reef had bought them out, adding to their already impressive fleet of Newton custom dive boats.

Despite Emily's constant pestering, AJ wouldn't let on any more than the fact that they were going diving. Her curiosity was finally sated when they checked in at the upstairs office and Gaelen, the young woman they'd met the night before, confirmed them both on the Coral Restoration Foundation boat.

"What do we get to do?" Em badgered AJ as they walked down to the boat. "Do we help, or are we just observing? I want to plant some coral. Do you think they'll let us plant some new coral?"

AJ grinned and let the barrage continue until they reached the assigned boat, where Captain David greeted them.

"Good morning, I'm afraid I'm your captain today, so no one will have any fun. Come aboard and my first mate will find you a tank. If you're lucky, there'll be air in it."

They carried their gear on board, laughing all the way, and were guided to a rack of tanks. The 46-foot Newton was the big brother version of AJ's dive boat in Grand Cayman, so she was familiar with the layout. A young woman, Madeleine, introduced herself and explained she'd be guiding the dives, and pointed out two other CRF volunteers on the boat. Emily immediately set upon the fresh source of information, leaving AJ setting up gear.

The ride out to the dive site took less than thirty minutes, almost a third of that spent in the canals between the dock and the open ocean, which was all no-wake zone. AJ held her breath when they passed the *African Queen* trundling along with a pair of tourists aboard, but Em was fortunately too busy to notice.

Madeleine took the time to explain what they'd be doing on the first dive, and handed out the tools they'd be using. Eight divers, including AJ and Emily, had volunteered their time and paid the dive op to help with the coral restoration project.

Moored up to a buoy, they were soon in the water, where Madeleine led the group to the coral nursery. In a little over 20 feet of water, the nursery appeared out of the distant blue water like the saplings at the edge of a forest. Tethered to pins driven into the bedrock below the sandy floor, plastic tubular 'trees' hung like ghostly frames in the water column.

Bobbing six feet below the surface, clear of passing boats, buoys tied to the tops of the trees pulled the tethers tight. Swells and currents rolled through the nursery, bringing nutrients to feed the growing coral sprigs, individually tied to the plastic branches with monofilament line.

Madeleine kept the divers in pairs and assigned them to a tree, where their job was to clean and scrub the limbs, keeping the unwanted algae and barnacles at bay. Using wire brushes, AJ and Emily started from the top on opposite sides, and scrubbed away, careful to avoid the delicate sprigs themselves.

The coral, mainly staghorn – named for its antler-like growth – formed small fragments of a larger colony. The offcuts, under the right conditions, could continue to flourish and would begin to branch out themselves, starting a new colony. Once the sprigs were large and healthy enough, they'd be removed from the nursery and replaced with new fragments to start the process over. Their second dive would reveal the next step.

Residents of the coral nursery soon gathered round, snatching pieces of organic matter as quickly as the cleaners knocked them from the plastic. The oddly clothes-iron-shaped trunkfish and their boxfish family cousins, the cowfish, were especially keen, hovering closely by the divers' masks with their pouty lips eagerly feeding.

Once they'd cleaned one tree from top to bottom, Madeleine led them to their next one, followed closely by their new fish friends. The process continued for almost an hour, until the first member of the group reached 750 psi of tank pressure and Madeleine led them all back to the boat. Behind them, they left a cleaner nursery and some happy fish.

While the guest divers had been cleaning, the other two volunteers from CRF had been gathering fragments they deemed ready for transplant. Several buckets of the sprigs sloshed in seawater as the Newton made its way towards Pickles Reef.

Madeleine stood by the table towards the stern of the boat, reserved for cameras, and spoke passionately to the group. "Here in the Florida Keys, the magnificent reef system which helps protect the shoreline and provide an ecosystem for the large and varied population of fish, began its decline decades ago. Poorly regulated run-off from farmland, factories, and housing development in southern Florida led to devastating effects in the Everglades and the offshore reefs. Climate change has piled on the pressure to the delicate balance, causing temperature-related bleaching and increased ocean acidification."

AJ could tell she was reading from a memorised script, but the young woman delivered the speech well, and had everyone's attention.

"Finally, to top off the coral's problems, stony coral tissue loss disease first reared its head in 2014, and has caused widespread damage ever since. We believe it to be caused by bacteria; it's still not clear, but the disease is transmitted to other corals through direct contact and water circulation."

Madeleine took a pause before delivering the statistics. "Estimates conservatively show over 90% loss of coral coverage in Florida since the 1970s. What you're helping with today may feel like a band-aid for a severed limb, but it does make a difference, and it's better than watching the whole reef disappear."

Moored once again to a dive buoy, the group prepared for their second dive. This time they'd be using hammers and marine epoxy to adhere the new fragments to dead colonies of the reef. They splashed in and followed Madeleine to an area where the old coral had almost completely died, and their new growth was beginning to take hold.

Fragments had been 'out-planted', as the team called it, in different sections over several years, so the area was an example of growth versus time. Some of the oldest colonies were beginning to cover the limestone. The area they would be working in was thinly populated with small sprigs.

Using the technique the volunteers had shown them on the boat, AJ and Emily chipped small indents in the limestone, forming three good anchor points. The epoxy felt like putty between their fingers, and shoving a bubblegum-sized piece into each divot, they stuck the new fragment in place with three points of contact.

It was slow going, making sure the sprig was securely seated in the epoxy. The seas were calm, with one-foot swells, but where they worked at fifteen feet underwater, the subtle surge back and forth was enough to make them feel like they were working from a swinging rope. It was easy to see why conditions had to be perfect to out-plant. Until the epoxy set, a strong wave could sweep all their hard work away.

As dive professionals in great shape, AJ and Em were both outstanding on their air consumption, so they were both disappointed when the group was rounded up and guided back to the boat. In fifteen feet of water they could have stayed down there a lot longer and kept planting, but once back aboard, Madeleine pointed out that between everyone they'd secured all the fragments they'd brought.

"Let's go get some more," Emily declared.

Captain David grinned. "I like that idea, but the folks waiting at the dock for their afternoon trip on this boat won't be so keen."

"Joy vacuum," Emily retorted with a big smile.

"You've been talking to my wife," David came back, without missing a beat. "Everyone have a good time?" he asked, quickly moving on. He was rewarded with an enthusiastic cheer. "On behalf of Rainbow Reef and the Coral Restoration Foundation, I'd like to thank you all for your help today in keeping our coral reef around for many years to come. Now strap down your gear 'cos we're heading back in, where you'll kindly get off my boat." With that, he scurried up the ladder to the fly-bridge to another round of cheers and laughter.

AJ and Emily spent the ride back chatting with Madeleine and the other volunteers. By the time they'd reached the dock, Emily had a plethora of new best friends and an invitation to spend the afternoon at the CRF building. AJ declined as she'd volunteered there in the past and felt she should spend the free time with Cass, who'd taken time off work while they were visiting.

She thanked Madeleine and gave Captain David a hug, before popping a generous tip in the jar for the hard-working crew. She knew better than anyone how tough it was to make ends meet on a divemaster's salary, and how they relied on tips.

They carried their gear off the boat and met Cass walking down the dock towards them.

"Are you off work?" AJ asked.

"Yup. My friend, who's covering the afternoon shift, showed up early, so I clocked out once I saw you pull in. How was it?"

"Brilliant," Emily beamed.

"Em's ready to abandon Bubble Chasers and volunteer at CRF," AJ joked.

"Not quite, but we have the Central Caribbean Marine Institute on Little Cayman, and I've been meaning to contact them about volunteering. They do coral restoration too."

"That's perfect," AJ said. "The Cayman Islands have just started seeing cases of stony coral tissue loss disease, so anything to help keep it at bay would be good."

"Hungry?" Cass asked.

"Bloody starving," AJ responded. "We just have to kick Miss Social Butterfly out on the way home."

6

THURSDAY

After dropping off Emily and arranging for her to call when she was finished with the CRF folks, Cass drove AJ to the house. They were both ready for lunch. Cass ran upstairs to prepare food, while AJ quickly washed down their dive gear and hung it over a rack under the house.

Hearing a thud, AJ looked towards the canal. The sound appeared to have come from the *Reel-Lee Hooked*, moored in the notched-out dock. Relieved to hear activity, she walked across the backyard to the Glacier Bay, ready to greet Rosie.

"About time you showed up to say hello," she called out from alongside.

Any movement inside the boat had stopped and AJ waited, but no one appeared. She couldn't see through the Eisenglass with the sun glinting, and began to wonder if the noise had come from somewhere else.

"Lunch is ready," Cass announced from the deck. "He home?" she added, seeing AJ by the boat.

"I thought so, but I might have been hearing things."

The boat rocked, and a man pushed the flap in the soft enclosure aside. He was in his late thirties, wore dark grey trousers, a tan button-down shirt, and a brown sport jacket. He rolled his broad shoulders and forced a smile.

"Hey there, I'm looking for Lee. Seen him today?"

AJ was awkwardly aware she was in her bathing suit as the man's eyes looked her over. She wished she'd put her T-shirt back on after washing down the gear.

"You'd better tell me who you are and why you're on his boat first."

The man's eyes narrowed, but he refocused on appearing pleasant, and managed another smile. "I'm a friend of his."

"The hell you are!" Cass shouted, pacing across the backyard.

The man quickly stepped on the gunwale and over to the concrete dock. He was taller than he'd seemed in the cockpit of the *Reel-Lee Hooked*, and nimble for his size. AJ took a step back, moving herself out of reach. The man lost his smile and slid one side of his jacket back to reveal a gun under his left arm in some kind of holster.

"Stay where you are and everything will be fine," he said in a low voice. He had the eerie calm of someone who'd been in this kind of situation plenty of times before. AJ had not, and hated guns. Especially the kind directed her way.

Cass stopped next to AJ with an arm protectively across her friend. "What do you want?"

"Where's Lee?"

"I don't know," Cass replied. "I haven't seen him all week."

"We thought he might be back, but it was you breaking and entering," AJ added, pointing out the crime.

"You his wife?"

Cass nodded and AJ wondered whether revealing the fact was a smart move.

"You?" the man asked, looking at AJ again, his eyes lingering at bikini-top level.

"A friend," she responded, giving him as little information as possible.

"How can you not know where your husband is all week?" the man asked, switching back to Cass.

"We're sort of separated. He lives on the boat. I live in the house."

The man raised an eyebrow and looked back and forth between the Glacier Bay and the home.

"What the hell do you want with him, anyway?"

"He has something that doesn't belong to him, and my boss wants it back."

"Well, as you can see, he's not here and we don't know where he is, so you can leave."

A smirk crept across his face. "Tell you what. I'll leave for now, but tomorrow at this time, I'll be back. I'm either taking my boss's property with me, or you."

"I've got nothing to bloody well do with... whatever shit this is," Cass snapped back.

"Apparently you're missing the point, sweet cheeks. I don't care, and my boss, I guarantee, cares even less. You'd better start finding your hubby, or you'll be coming with me. Then we'll see how separated you two really are."

He took a step forward, Cass screamed, and AJ quickly dodged in front of her. He briskly swiped AJ aside, knocking her to the ground, and grabbed Cass, spinning her around and covering her mouth with his hand. AJ groaned from the concrete dock where she'd bashed her elbow and backside.

"Don't make this difficult," he growled, looking around to see if anyone had seen the scuffle. "Tomorrow. Our property, your husband, or you. I'll be leaving with one of them. Which one is up to you."

His left arm pinned Cass's arms tightly to her sides, while his right hand remained over her mouth. "And if you go to the police, I'll know. Got that?"

Cass nodded as best she could.

"Are you going to stay quiet?"

Cass nodded again, and he finally released her.

"You'd better be here tomorrow. If I have to go looking for you, it will not be fun when I find you," he said with a sneer. "And believe me, you'll be much easier to find than your husband. I'll be watching."

AJ was picking herself up as the man now towered over her with a strange look on his face. Deciding her best defence was offence, she popped up faster than he was expecting, and delivered a punch to his groin. The thug staggered backwards, holding his crotch and groaning. AJ and Cass backed away, unsure whether to run, jump in the water, or try for another punch. To their surprise, he straightened up and managed a brief smile, which quickly returned to a grimace.

"I had a feeling you had some fire in you. I'm gonna give you that one, 'cos I pretty much deserved it, but come tomorrow, my forgiving side won't be showing up."

The two women gave him plenty of room as he made his way across the backyard and past the VW under the house. His walk wasn't quite as bold as AJ imagined it had been upon his arrival. The world didn't need him reproducing anyway, in her opinion, so she hoped she'd made a contribution.

A white SUV that she hadn't noticed before waited for the man to reach the street. He got in the passenger seat and the vehicle quickly pulled away, the windows heavily tinted to conceal the occupants.

"Are you okay?" Cass asked, fussing over AJ.

She brushed her away. "I'm fine. Hitting the ground just knocked the wind out of me." AJ looked at her friend, making sure she couldn't see her grazed elbow. "What on earth was that all about?"

Cass shook her head. "That stupid bugger must have got himself into some kind of mess again."

"That guy wasn't your everyday small town thug, Cass. He talked about his boss like a drug lord or mobster."

"Bet he talks with a high voice for a few days though," Cass replied, and managed a grin.

"That was pretty stupid of me. He could have shot us both."

"It was pretty ballsy of you, if you ask me. But this time tomorrow, we'll be shoved in the back of that fancy car of theirs, I reckon."

AJ chewed on her lip for a moment. "We'd better find Rosie so we can sort it out."

"Rosie shouldn't be worried about Sore Balls finding him," Cass said, putting her hands on her hips. "It's me he wants to worry about. I'll string him up by his goolies and smack him senseless."

The idea made AJ shudder. Cass sounded serious. "Let's check the boat."

They stepped onto *Reel-Lee Hooked* and pulled the flap back. He'd pulled the cushions from the L-shaped couch in the pilot-house, and every cabinet and drawer was open. AJ went down the narrow opening to the port-side stateroom. Clothes, toiletries and personal effects lay strewn across the berth, with drawers and cabinet doors hanging open. Nothing appeared broken, but the place was ransacked. AJ went back up and met Cass coming up from the starboard berth.

"What a bloody mess," she moaned. "I'm not cleaning it up for the silly sod."

"I wonder what Sore Balls was looking for?" AJ pondered, unable to hide her grin at Cass's nickname for the thug.

"I don't think it's as simple as a VCR."

AJ laughed, slapping her own backside and instantly regretted it. Her bum was going to have a nice bruise.

"I know, I know, but whatever people have these days instead of a bloody VCR," Cass said.

"Netflix?"

"Hush up smartypants. I actually know what Netflix is. And Hulu."

They both looked around and AJ couldn't help picking up the cushions and putting them back in place. The disarray was too distressing.

"Must be relatively small from the places he searched. No point looking in the medicine cabinet for an outboard," AJ said, turning to Cass. "What about going to the police now? I know he said not to, but they always say that, right?"

Cass shook her head. "I can't. Whatever Rosie's into is obviously dodgy, and you heard Wobbly Bollocks. He'll know if we go to the police. I'm telling you, AJ, there are still a few bent coppers down here."

AJ sighed. "Fine. Then we'd better find Rosie before he does. I get the feeling he'll keep looking rather than rely on us."

"What's this 'us' business?" Cass said, pushing the door flap aside and stepping out to the cockpit. "This has nothing to do with you, and I don't want you more involved than you've already been."

AJ followed through the flap Cass held open. "I'm not leaving my friend to deal with this on her own."

Cass zipped the soft enclosure. "Still as stubborn as ever, I see."

"And hungry," AJ replied. "You were threatening lunch before we were rudely interrupted. How about we eat and come up with a plan?"

Cass put an arm around her friend. "Fine. But you're not missing your conference over Rosie's shenanigans."

7

THURSDAY

AJ glanced at her watch. "Isn't it a bit early to be checking the bars?"

Cass looked over at her from the driver's seat and raised an eyebrow. "How long have you been gone from here?"

AJ nodded. "Right, I guess a while now."

"The tourists start drinking when the boat leaves the dock," Cass reminded her. "The locals start drinking when the boat is back at the dock. Seeing as the *Reel-Lee Hooked* has been home since Tuesday, there's no telling what bar the idiot is bellied up to."

They'd already stopped by the Pilot House across the marina from home, and Cass had called Sharkey's, but no one had seen Rosie today, or earlier in the week. She'd driven south and now pulled into the Tavernier Towne Center car park. The retail park, or strip mall as the locals called it, had nothing to do with the centre of town, and was somewhere between remodelled and run down. She parked the Beetle in front of Dillon's Sports Bar.

A late lunch crowd filled a handful of tables and various sports games played on a plethora of flatscreen TVs mounted anywhere they'd fit in the room. Cass made for the long, dark wood bar where a cute twenty-something brunette in a scoop-neck white T-shirt briefly looked up before continuing cleaning glasses. Her big-tipping clientele were not usually a pair of women.

"Excuse me, love," Cass began, sensibly ignoring the bartender's chilly demeanour. "We're looking for someone, and he often comes in here. Do you know Rosie Lee?"

The young woman paused. "Rosie Lee is a guy? That's weird."

"I take it you don't work evenings."

"Weekdays, lunch through happy hour," the bartender replied. "I have things to do in the evenings and on weekends."

Cass took out her mobile and pulled up a picture of her husband she'd thought to have ready. "This is him," she said, holding the phone over the bar.

The woman sighed and looked briefly at the screen. "Yeah. I've seen him from time to time."

"This week?"

The bartender shrugged her shoulders. "You know how many people come through this place every week?"

"Take one more look and try to remember, please," AJ said, noting Cass's body tense and sensing she was about to run out of patience. "It's important. He could be in trouble."

The young woman took another cursory glance. "Maybe. Tuesday I think. Or it could have been last night. He was with a couple of other guys. It was happy hour, so we had two bartenders working. They weren't my customers."

"Which night makes a big difference," Cass persisted.

The woman let out a sigh. "You know, guys don't come by the bar expecting me to tell their wives what they're up to. I do good on tips. I don't need that changing."

AJ quickly put a hand on Cass's arm. "Like she said, he could be in trouble. It has nothing to do with another woman. We think he might be in danger."

The bartender shook her head and thought for a moment. "It was last night."

"You're sure?"

"Richard was working, so yeah, it had to have been last night," she replied, and turned away, returning to her cleaning.

"Thanks for your help," AJ said, as she knew Cass wasn't about to.

"Smarmy little trollop," Cass muttered as they walked outside into the bright mid-afternoon sunshine.

"That's something," AJ said as they got back in the VW. "Who would the other two blokes be?"

Cass turned over the engine, which finally started after AJ was beginning to think they'd be walking.

"You know Rosie. Could have been some mates he came in with, or his new best friends he'd just met at the bar."

"But it wasn't Phil, the chap from Sharkey's," AJ commented. "He said he hasn't seen Rosie."

"That's what he said," Cass muttered.

She drove them over Tavernier Creek bridge and made a left at the first break in the centre reservation, then another left on Old Highway. A hundred yards north, she parked in front of some older buildings housing small retail shops. AJ recognised the spot. She followed Cass through a covered walkway with shops on either side, to a canal front at the other end. On their left was Mar Bar, a hidden gem serving fresh crab legs and oysters, along with cold beer. The place was small, outdoors, under the shade of an over-hanging roof, and popular with the locals.

"Hey Cass, what's cookin'?" a woman around Cass's age asked from behind the bar. She had long blonde hair and the tanned, slightly weathered look of a local who'd spent plenty of time on the water.

"Hi June, this is my friend AJ. She runs a dive op in Grand Cayman."

AJ waved a greeting over the heads of several men sitting at the bar.

"Hey," June responded. "You look familiar. Have you been here before?"

"I lived in the Keys for about three years, and I remember

coming here a few times," AJ replied.

June pointed to AJ's arm. "I'll admit I couldn't have come up with your name to save my life, but I remember the tats." She switched her attention back to Cass. "Drink? Something to eat?"

"I could murder a cocktail, but I'd better not. We're actually looking for Rosie. Have you seen him lately?"

June grabbed a cloth and began wiping the bar. "Been a few days, I think."

AJ noticed she made a quick glance up at one of the men, who sat hunched over, keeping his head turned away. Cass must have seen the same.

"Poppers, is that you?"

The man raised a hand but didn't move. "Hey there, Cass. How's things?"

Between his gravelly smoker's voice, the extra pounds he carried, and his salt and pepper tangle of hair, AJ guessed he was a fisherman who'd split his time between the water and the bar. Probably in equal measure.

Cass moved around the end of the bar to get a better look. "What the hell happened to you?"

The man finally turned, and AJ saw the shiner around his left eye.

"Ain't nothing," he replied. "Smacked myself in the face with a cabinet door."

AJ caught a scowl, this time from June.

"You should be more careful, love, can't mess up that pretty face of yours," Cass said, and the other men at the bar cracked up laughing. AJ could see enough to know 'pretty' wouldn't be how she'd describe Poppers.

"You seen Rosie?" Cass asked.

Poppers shook his head. "Not for a few days, I suppose."

"I see," Cass responded casually. "So over at Dillon's then? What was that, Tuesday? Or was it last night?"

The man shifted uncomfortably in his seat. "Could have been either, Cass. You know me, I ain't the best at remembering details."

"Who else was with you?" Cass persisted, sounding friendly, but it was obvious to all she was grilling him for information.

Poppers shook his head. "Hell, I don't remember. Could have been someone came and went throughout the evening, but I couldn't tell you."

Cass glanced back and forth between June and Poppers, both of them avoiding her glare. "Seriously? You're not going to tell me anything?"

Poppers made himself busy with his beer, but June looked up. Her eyes were sympathetic. "What's your Rosie got himself into this time?"

"That's what I'm trying to find out, isn't it?" Cass snapped, then calmed herself down. "I'm really worried, June. Something's not right."

"Have you checked with his other buddies?"

"Phil hasn't seen him," Cass replied, and June's brow furrowed.

Cass rolled her eyes, then glared at the side of Popper's head. He refused to look her way. She looked at the boat side-tied to the dock. "Maybe I should check your bloody boat, Poppers? He hiding on there?"

AJ noted the centre console and wondered where a man would hide on the boat.

"You silly buggers and your bullshit he-man code," Cass vented, before turning tail and stomping away from the bar.

AJ jogged to keep up. They both got into the VW and Cass smacked the steering wheel with her hand.

"What's this code rubbish?" AJ asked.

Cass groaned. "You know what a conch is, right?" she asked, pronouncing the word as 'conk' rather than the British English version, 'con-ch'.

"I presume you mean the person, not the shell."

"Exactly. Anyone born and raised in the Keys." Cass turned the ignition key and the engine eventually fired after several seconds of strenuous work by the starter motor. "Especially the male fishing crowd. They have this stupid code of keeping secrets, no matter what. Fishing spots, cheating on their wives, dodgy deals, whatever. You get the point. They'll rat on an outsider in a heartbeat, but they'll never tell on a fellow conch."

"Would you mind turning the air conditioning on?" AJ asked.

"Oh, yeah," Cass replied. She backed out of the parking spot and drove down Old Highway, getting air moving over the cabriolet.

"But surely you're considered a conch by now?"

Cass shook her head as she made the U-turn onto Overseas Highway north. "I am and always will be a freshwater conch. I think you gain the title after seven years living in the Keys. But unless you were born here, you'll never be a fully fledged conch."

"Well, they both knew more than they were saying, that's for sure."

Cass nodded. "No question about it, but my idiot husband must have told them not to say anything, so they won't."

"June did mention Phil. Isn't he the deaf chap I met last night?"

"And that would make three, like twinkletoes at Dillon's told us."

Reaching the north end of Tavernier, Cass pulled into a small car park in front of a single-storey building signed Sunrise Cafe Cubano. The place looked like it had stood the test of time, and probably a few storms. Along the front, above the windows, were big picture signs of various Cuban dishes, and to the left, a walk-up window.

"Blimey, I'd forgotten about this place," AJ said with a smile as they walked up to the window.

"*Dos cortaditos, por favor*," Cass said to the young woman at the counter, who didn't reply but went about making the espresso drinks.

"Where now?" AJ asked as they waited.

Cass thought for a moment. "I'm thinking we go home."

The young Cuban woman placed two small, lidded cups on the counter and AJ quickly handed her a five-dollar bill. The woman rang up the sale and handed AJ two dollars and a few coins.

"*Gracias*," AJ said with a smile and left the coins and a dollar bill, then scooped up the little cups. The woman nodded her thanks.

"I was going to buy them," Cass complained.

"Nonsense, you're putting us both up. The least I can do is buy you some coffee and a meal or two."

Sitting back in the car, they both knew better than to try and drink the piping hot coffee for a few minutes, so Cass got back on the road.

"Shouldn't we keep checking places for Rosie?" AJ asked, looking at her watch. It was 3:15pm. "We could try the marine supply shops. Maybe someone has seen him."

"We could, but we'll probably run into the same tight-lipped bullshit everywhere we go. Besides, I'm guessing no one has seen Rosie since last night."

AJ considered that for a moment. "If it was last night he told his mates to stay quiet, you're thinking he's been hiding somewhere since then?"

Cass looked over and nodded. "That's my guess. He must know Sore Balls and his boss are after him for whatever reason, so he's slipped off the radar."

"I wonder why he wouldn't take off on *Reel-Lee Hooked*? Surely it would be easier to hide on the water than in town."

"Unless he was scared to return to the house," Cass pointed out.

"Good point. So, what are we going to do back at home?"

"Sore Balls wants his stuff back, right?"

"Right."

"So, if we can't find Rosie, we'd better find whatever it is he took of theirs."

"And you think it's in the house?"

Cass shook her head. "No way he'd hide something dodgy in the house, he wouldn't want to put me at risk. We're gonna look on the boat."

"But Sore Balls already searched the boat."

Cass smiled. "Yeah, but he didn't know where to look."

8

THURSDAY

Emily texted AJ to say she had finished her visit with the folks at the Coral Restoration Foundation, so they stopped by and picked her up on the way home. Emily was effervescent about the program until she realised the other two were being rather quiet.

"What did I miss?" she asked as Cass parked the Beetle under the house.

Between them, AJ and Cass explained the events of the afternoon and Emily fired a hundred questions their way, most of which they wished they knew the answers to, but didn't.

The three women walked across the backyard to where *Reel-Lee Hooked* sat innocently and serenely at the dock.

"Be careful," Emily said as Cass stepped aboard. "You know, in case that bloke is poking around again, yeah?"

"I doubt he'll be back here until tomorrow," Cass replied. But she tentatively unzipped the soft enclosure. "Anyone aboard?" she yelled before venturing inside.

AJ followed, and Emily was about to do the same when she heard a vehicle pull up to the house.

"Hey, you two. Somebody's here."

Cass and AJ rushed back out.

"Is it a pickup truck?" Cass asked hopefully.

"What colour is Rosie's?" Emily said from the dock, still looking towards the house.

"It's green and silver," Cass replied. "Mixed with a fair amount of brown rust."

"Not him then," Emily confirmed, and Cass and AJ hopped up to the dock to join her.

"It's a bloody police car, Em," AJ pointed out. "Why did you ask what colour?"

Emily shrugged her shoulders. "I was curious."

"Oh bugger," Cass mumbled, hurrying in the direction of the policeman, who was getting out of his car. "Oh, Rosie…"

AJ and Emily rushed along behind her, realising a visit from a law enforcement officer could be the worst news anyone could ever hear. A death notification.

"Is Rodney Lee home, ma'am?" the officer asked and AJ watched Cass stop and put her hands on her knees. Fortunately, in relief instead of grief.

"Everything okay, ma'am?"

Cass stood up straight as AJ and Em reached her side. AJ put her arm on her friend's shoulder.

"Yeah, I'm fine. Just gives you pause when a panda car shows up. I'm sure you get that a lot."

The officer wore a dark green uniform, the obligatory aviator sunglasses, and a confused expression. "Panda, ma'am?"

"Sorry, yeah, it's what we call police cars in England."

"You're visiting, ma'am?"

"No, I live here," Cass explained. "I'm Rosie's wife. I mean Rodney's wife."

The officer nodded slowly, but still looked unsure. "Is Mr Lee home, ma'am?"

"No, he's not, I'm afraid."

"But he does reside here?" he asked, looking up at the house.

"Not here, no."

"Okay. Can you give me an address where he currently resides?" The officer took out a notebook from his chest pocket.

"Well, that would be here, but it's in the boat out back, not in the house, you see."

The policeman paused, notebook in hand, and peered at Cass. "Let's start with your name, ma'am."

"Cassandra Lee, Officer..?"

AJ noticed the man didn't have a name badge on his uniform.

"Officer Reid," he replied. "Now, let me see if I have this straight. Rodney Lee lives at this address, but in the boat, not in the house, in which you, Cassandra Lee, do in fact reside. That about right?"

"That's correct, and why is it you're looking for my husband, Officer Reid?"

"I'll get to that in a moment, ma'am." He looked at AJ and Emily. "May I ask who you two ladies are?"

AJ was about to answer, but Cass beat her to it. "They're friends of mine from out of town. They're visiting for the weekend."

He paused for a moment, then let the point go. "I'm looking for Mr Lee because we've found a vehicle registered to him. It's been broken into."

"Oh..." Cass stammered.

"Where did you find it?" AJ asked, letting her friend digest the news.

"Harry Harris Park in Tavernier. A ranger noticed it had been there a few days and took a look. Saw the passenger window was smashed and called it in. It was considered abandoned as there's no overnight parking at Harry Harris, so we've towed the truck. Your husband will need to collect it from the tow company."

"Okay," Cass said, unsure what to ask next.

"When did you see your husband last, ma'am?"

The question woke Cass out of her confused daze. "Couple of days back," she replied vaguely.

"Well, tell him to hurry up and come get it. Impound runs up a steep bill if it sits there too long. He'll owe for the towing too."

"I'll be sure to tell him," Cass replied.

The officer looked past the women to the Glacier Bay. "Nice cat, but that must be tight living quarters."

Cass glanced over her shoulder at the boat. "He seems to do fine." She checked her watch. "We have to get going I'm afraid, Officer Reid, but thank you for coming by and I'll be sure to tell my husband about his truck."

The policeman took the hint and put his notebook away. "Thanks for your time, ladies. Have a good afternoon."

They watched him walk back to his car as they went to the stairs leading up to the house. Once he'd left, they stopped their pretence of going inside and started back towards the boat.

"He seemed nice enough," AJ commented.

"Most of them are," Cass replied.

"Odd he didn't have a name badge."

"I noticed that too," Cass said, pausing by the boat.

"You think he wasn't a copper?" Emily chimed in.

Cass looked towards where the police car had recently sat in her front yard. "No, he was a copper alright." She returned her attention to the boat and stepped into the cockpit. "The question is whether he's a bent one or not."

AJ followed Cass into the cramped space of the starboard hull. Forward was a guest stateroom, which was ingeniously designed to double as a small office space. All the cushions had been removed from the berth, leaving it dedicated as an office, with the surrounding berth platform acting like a wide shelf. They stood in the narrow galley, careful not to tread on anything, looking at the mess of paperwork and books strewn around the stateroom.

"What a bloody mess," Emily commented, peering from the step.

Cass sighed. "Could have been a lot worse. Maybe we stopped him before he started ripping cushions and forcing panels open."

AJ bent down and began picking up cutlery and packets of food. "Why would Rosie's truck be at Harry Harris Park?"

Cass started clearing a path into the stateroom, piling the

many books on a shelf and stacking paperwork on the desk. "I can't figure that out. He was either meeting someone there, in which case, where did he go? Or he was being picked up at the pier."

"Which begs the same question, yeah?" Emily added, stepping down and helping with the clean-up.

"Exactly," Cass replied. "Or he was with someone launching a boat as they have a ramp there."

"We were talking about him hiding on the water," AJ said. "Maybe that's what he's doing, but with someone else, or at least on someone else's boat."

Cass let out a long sigh. "Maybe. Can't imagine whose boat that would be. All his mates are fishermen who make their living with their boats. None of them can afford not to work for a week. You met Poppers. They're all about like him."

After another fifteen minutes, they had the starboard hull in reasonable shape, with everything put away or thrown away if it had spoilt from the fridge.

"Right, so where's this super-secret hidey-hole?" AJ asked as the three of them stood in the claustrophobic confines of the galley.

Cass stepped into the stateroom and took hold of the upholstered stool seat, which sat upon an adjustable-height pedestal mounted to the floor. Pulling up on the lever, she slid the seat post off its base and flipped it over. The post was fixed to the underside of the seat by four wingnuts, holding a welded top plate against the wooden bottom of the seat. She unscrewed the wingnuts and revealed a compartment between the false bottom and a second wooden base, several inches deep.

"That's a bit trick!" Emily exclaimed.

"I'd say," AJ agreed. "If anyone ripped the cushion apart, they'd find the wooden base as expected. Doubt they'd think to remove the post."

Cass grinned and reached her fingers inside the compartment. "I dread to think what Rosie's hidden in here over the years."

After a few moments searching around, Cass pulled out a single piece of notebook paper, torn from a spiral-bound pad. "What the hell's this?" she mumbled, setting the seat aside.

The three huddled around to look at the note.

Cass - just in case!

$2/4$ $9/29$ $1/7$ $11/1$ $15/13$ $6/6$ $11/2$ $9/42$ $1/1$ $7/17$ $5/2$ $13/4$

$11/9$ $3/2$ $16/6$ $6/4$ $20/11$ $21/25$ $8/12$ $19/2$ $22/21$ $12/1$ $8/6$ $18/3$ $1/2$ $5/8$

$21/8$ $2/5$ $6/8$ $19/1$ $18/4$ $9/15$ $20/4$ $9/5$ $6/11$ $15/3$ $21/5$ $9/4$ $8/6$ $16/5$

$13/9$ $2/17$ $19/3$ $15/8$ $13/5$ $5/22$ $17/10$ $21/27$ $7/7$ $11/11$ $9/17$ $22/33$ $1/5$ $21/8$ $12/2$ $19/7$ $17/8$

If you're not Cass - Piss off!

"What the bloody hell does any of that mean?" AJ asked.

Cass shook her head. "Got me."

"He obviously knew you'd find it."

"I like his security warning at the bottom," Emily commented with a chuckle.

Cass sighed. "Yeah. When... well, *if* you get to meet Rosie, all will become clear. He's a silly bugger, but he's a loveable silly bugger."

"It's *when*, Cass," AJ said reassuringly. "He'll show up."

Cass shook her head. "I'm getting more worried with every step of this fiasco."

"Well, let's try to figure out what he's attempting to tell you," AJ said, hoping she sounded more positive than she felt.

"They look like fractions," Emily volunteered. "But don't ask me to figure any of it out. Maths was never my favourite subject."

Cass leaned against the berth, which acted as a shelf. "Of course, this could be donkey's years old. We've got no way of knowing if it has anything to do with what's going on now."

AJ looked around the stateroom. "Did you see a spiral-bound notebook anywhere?"

Cass thought for a second. "Yeah, I did actually." She opened the cupboard at the back of the desk and dragged out the piles of paperwork she'd just put away. "Here," she said, holding up a notebook which was the same size as the paper. She handed it to AJ, who thumbed through to the first blank page. She didn't have to go far. There were only three pages with writing, which all looked like budget calculations for living expenses and boat maintenance. Little remnants of paper lay in the spiral binding, indicating a page had been torn away.

AJ held the blank page up to the overhead light and tilted it back and forth. She could see indentions from the previous pages of writing, which matched the paper they'd found.

"Can't say how recently he wrote this, but I can tell you it was the last thing he used that notebook for," AJ declared.

"Ooh, I've seen that in the movies," Em said excitedly. "Where's a pencil? We have to shade over the pad and the writing will show up darker."

"We already know what the page says, Em," AJ pointed out.

"Oh, right. But if we didn't, that's how we'd find out!"

Cass stared at the numbers on the piece of paper. "So now we have to figure out this gibberish."

Emily reached past Cass and plucked a book from the shelf behind her. "Perhaps this will help." She held up the cover for the other two to see: *Codes, Ciphers, Steganography & Secret Messages*, by Sunil Tanna.

Cass groaned. "Rosie and his bloody war books. He always fancied himself as a spy or an undercover agent."

"Maybe he is," AJ said.

Cass rolled her eyes. "Not bloody likely."

9

THURSDAY

The three women moved to the cockpit, where they sat around the table with several books and the piece of notepaper. The Glacier Bay was connected to shore power, so the air conditioner attempted to keep the temperature below tolerable, but the sunshine through the Eisenglass had the cockpit steaming. They gathered up their research and headed for the cooler house. And wine.

Emily thumbed through the code book, while AJ searched the internet for clues and Cass gathered up a bowl of crisps and three glasses of wine.

"I don't really know what to search for," AJ complained. "If I just put these numbers in, I get a page full of serial numbers to various products."

"Try searching for 'simple ciphers'," Cass suggested.

"I'll try, but I'm not sure it's a simple one."

Cass laughed. "You do remember Rosie, right? Believe me, he could only handle a simple one."

"I've got something," Emily declared, waving a hand in the air as though she were in a classroom.

"Go ahead, Miss Durand," AJ said with a grin.

"I remember seeing this in a film, too. The first number is a page, and the second number is the word or letter on that page. Says here it's called a 'book cipher'. The sender and recipient both need a copy of the same book. Well, actually, they have to be exactly the same edition of the same book, so every letter is in the same place, yeah?"

AJ and Cass moved around to look over Emily's shoulder.

"You're right, that could be it," Cass said.

"Yeah, but which book?" AJ asked, looking at the four books on codes they'd brought upstairs with them. "Could be any one of these, or the other dozen or more books we left on the boat."

They all stared once again at the numbers on the paper.

"The first numbers only go up to 22. I wonder if that's significant?" AJ asked.

"Maybe he only had to go as far as page 22 to get all the letters needed in the text," Emily suggested.

Cass stood up and threw her arms in the air. "Text to what? We don't know if this is just some silly project Rosie was working on. It could be page references to the latest copy of *Playboy*, the West Marine catalogue, or any of these bloody books. We have no idea, and we could spend from now until tomorrow lunchtime chasing our tails."

AJ put an arm around her friend. "I'm up for whatever you think is the best way to go, Cass. We can hit happy hour at the bars and see if we get lucky, if you like?"

Cass leaned her head on AJ's shoulder. "No, I'm convinced he's either hiding out somewhere, or he's... you know... we're too late."

"You can't think that way, Cass. Until we have proof to the contrary, he's alive and well. We have to do all we can before lunchtime tomorrow, and if we can't figure it out before then, I suggest we're somewhere else when Sore Balls comes back."

"That's a good point," Em commented. "Why would he think you'd hang around so he could haul you away?"

Cass shrugged her shoulders. "Maybe he figures we'll show up if we have his stuff, and if we don't have anything, he doesn't care anyway."

"Holding you is only an incentive for Rosie to show up if he knows you're being held," AJ surmised. "I think it's safe to assume Sore Balls and his boss don't have Rosie, and don't know where he is or how to reach him. So, yeah, he probably just threw out the threat pressuring you to come up with their stuff. But I still don't think it's a great idea to hang around at the house tomorrow."

Cass took a long sip of wine. "I'm gonna have heart failure before tomorrow lunchtime."

"We don't have a better plan right now, so let's work on the book cipher theory," AJ said, conjuring up an optimistic tone. "If we start with a book each, we can see if the code makes sense in any of them. We'll know after five or six letters if they're making an actual word."

"Righto!" Emily said. "We'll need a notepad each, and some pens."

Choosing a book each, they all set to work, and after ten minutes, Emily was the first to decipher a word.

"I've cracked the code, ladies!"

"That was quick. What have you got?" Cass asked, waiting expectantly.

"Does 'locolue' mean anything to you?"

"Loco-what?"

Em turned her notepad around and showed the other two the word she'd come up with. L-O-C-O-L-U-E.

"Good work, Em," AJ said, chuckling. "You've converted gibberish numbers into gibberish letters."

"Yeah," Emily said, tossing her pad down on the table. "I don't think the book cipher is the answer."

Cass went back to her notes. "Hang on, though. That's probably just the wrong book. Let's keep going."

Emily grabbed the fourth code book on the table and started over as the others finished the first word using the books they'd picked. Ten minutes later, after no one had come up with anything that made sense, they headed downstairs to retrieve the rest of Rosie's collection.

"Are you counting punctuation?" Emily asked as they walked to the boat.

"I am," Cass replied.

"Yup," AJ agreed.

"I was too," Em confirmed. "Maybe we shouldn't be?"

"What did the cipher book say about it?" AJ asked.

Emily thought for a few moments. "I don't think it mentioned anything."

"When we get back upstairs, try yours again without counting any punctuation," Cass said, deciding the matter.

Em wrinkled her nose. "Brill. Me and my big mouth just got me extra homework."

With a fresh stack of books in front of each of them, the three women quietly set to work. By 5:45pm they were several books into their search and still nothing made sense.

"Be handy if he'd given us a clue to which book he meant," AJ complained, grabbing the next one from her pile.

"I'm beginning to think it's not a book cipher after all," Emily said dejectedly. "Sorry if I led us down a dead end."

They all sat back and Cass reached for the wine bottle to top up their glasses. Hers was the only empty glass. AJ and Emily had barely touched theirs.

"How many books does he have in total?" AJ blurted, leaning forward and counting.

They all joined her.

"Twenty-one."

"Agreed," Cass and Emily both confirmed.

"Look at the codes," AJ continued. "Didn't you say the highest first number is 22?"

"If you're thinking it's all of the books, we're one short." Cass pointed out.

"The boat was ransacked," AJ said thoughtfully. "We could easily have missed one."

"So they'd need to be in some kind of order, yeah?" Emily pointed out.

"Bloody hell, you might have something here," Cass chimed in. "Rosie always had his books arranged in alphabetical order. He's a slob over some things, but fastidious about others. It would drive him bananas if I rearranged his books."

AJ grinned. "And you did, didn't you?"

Cass laughed. "When he was still in the house and I was mad at him for doing something... you know... Rosie-like. I'd take one book from each shelf and move it to another one. Everybody in Key Largo knew when he'd spotted what I'd done."

"By author, or title?" Emily asked, standing up to begin sorting books.

"Author's surname," Cass replied.

Setting the books in a row, they arranged them by author, using the book's title if several were by the same author.

"Okay, so now what are we using for the second number?" Emily asked.

"Could be the first letter on the corresponding page number," AJ suggested.

Cass read off the first number in the top line of code, and AJ selected the appropriate book. It was *Run Silent, Run Deep* by Edward L. Beach. She thumbed to the page matching the second number Cass gave her.

"The page starts with 'command', so letter 'C'."

Emily noted it down and AJ returned the book to its spot in the order.

"Book 4, page 29," Cass said.

AJ pulled *The USS Swordfish – The World War II Patrols of the First American Submarine to Sink a Japanese Ship* by George J. Billy from the selection, and turned to page 29.

"'Reau'," AJ said, flicking back and forth between pages. "It split the word 'bureau' across two pages, so I guess we go with 'R'"

Next up was *Around the World Submerged: The Voyage of the Triton*. Another book by Edward L. Beach.

"Page 7 begins with the letter 'A'."

"This looks promising," Emily announced. "C-R-A, it's starting to look like a real word."

"Book 10, page 1," Cass read from Rosie's note and AJ picked up *Escape from the Deep* by Alex Kershaw.

"Hmm. Do we use the chapter title, the subtitle, which in this case is a date, or the first word of the chapter itself?"

"Chapter title," Cass said, while Em declared, "First word."

'Okay, what are the three options?" Emily asked.

"'T' if it's the title or the first word. 'A' if it's the subtitle."

"Then 'T' it is as 'A' wouldn't make any sense."

"Book 15, page 13," Cass said, moving on.

AJ selected *Wahoo: The Patrols of America's Most Famous World War II Submarine* by Richard H. O'Kane.

"That's another 'C'."

Emily groaned. "C-R-A-T-C. That's not going to make a word."

"Bugger," Cass growled, shaking the note in her hand. "Bloody stupid cipher codswallop. Why couldn't he just tell me to look behind the cereal box in the larder?"

AJ stared at the books on the dining room table.

"How about titles?"

"What do you mean?" Emily asked, looking at the covers.

"The second letter could be referencing the whatever letter in the title."

"Book 2, letter 4," Cass read out.

"'S.'" AJ returned.

"Book 4, letter 30."

"'P.'"

Once the seventh set of numbers was deciphered, completing what they hoped would be the first word, Emily read it back to them with a big smile.

"S-P-I-E-G-E-L. *Spiegel!*"

For the next minute, all they could do was babble excitedly, hug each other, and soak up their hard-won success. Located six miles from the Key Largo coast, in 135 feet of water, lay the former United States Navy Thomaston-class dock landing ship, the *Spiegel*

Grove. Five hundred and ten feet long, the enormous vessel had been sunk as an artificial reef in 2002.

"The second word must be 'Grove'," Cass said when they finally settled down.

"Probably, but we should check to be sure," AJ replied, picking out the ninth book in their alphabetical order. She traced her finger along the title of *WAR Beneath the WAVES – A True Story of Courage and Leadership Aboard a World War II Submarine* by Don Keith.

"'L'."

"Huh?" Em grunted. "That's not going to be 'Grove' then."

AJ deciphered the next four letters, which Em wrote down, then held up her notepad for the others to see. "'Lathe'?"

"Blimey," AJ whispered. "We have a location."

"We do?" Emily asked with a furrowed brow.

"Machine room on the *Spiegel*, hidden somewhere around the lathe," Cass explained.

AJ walked over to the sliding door and looked beyond the deck at the late afternoon sky. She checked her watch. 6:25pm.

"We better get our arses into gear."

Em got to her feet, "What about the other ciphers?"

"No time if we want to make a dive tonight before dark," AJ replied.

"We're going tonight, then?" Em asked.

"Why not?" AJ replied as she hurried towards the front door.

10

THURSDAY

Once clear of the channel, the eight-and-a-half-mile run to the wreck site aboard the *Reel-Lee Hooked* took less than twenty minutes. Cass had the nimble catamaran running at 25 knots with the twin 250 hp Yamahas singing all the way.

One to two-foot swells gently rolled in from the south-east in four-second intervals, making the ride out a breeze for the dual-hulled boat. AJ and Emily had their gear set up and double checked before they were halfway there, using a pair of air tanks they'd pulled from the storage room under the house. Both were full. AJ would have preferred to use Nitrox – a breathing gas with a higher oxygen content – but as they planned on only making one dive, their bodies' nitrogen build-up shouldn't be a concern. She left the Nitrox tanks she'd seen for whatever surprises the ciphers still had in store.

Cass coasted up to the 'number six ball', a buoy tethered to the superstructure on the port side of the sunken ship. The *Spiegel Grove* is so large, the Florida Keys National Marine Sanctuary, who installed and maintain the mooring buoys, have eight on the wreck. AJ used a boathook to grab the line and fed a rope from the Glacier

Bay through the loop, securing it to a second cleat at the bow to hold them in place.

Sunset was less than an hour away, and the light was already dimming across the water. AJ and Emily pulled their 3 mm wetsuits up and helped each other with the back zippers. Cass had taken down the soft enclosure on the ride out, and peered over the side from the helm. The *Reel-Lee Hooked* had slowly taken up the slack in the mooring line and gently tugged on the buoy. A good indication there was a little surface current.

"I can rig a wreck line if you'd like?" she offered.

AJ looked over the side as Cass had just done. A wreck line would run from the mooring line at the bow, along the side of the boat to the swim platform at the stern. In a strong current, divers could haul themselves along the line instead of trying to swim against the powerful water. It was standard practice for recreational dive operations in the Keys, where they also insisted customers use the mooring line as their descent and ascent guide.

All it took was one diver not paying attention, or thinking they had the current figured out, and before they knew it, they were pulled clear of the boat. Many incidents had started in that fashion, and some had ended in tragedy.

The *Spiegel Grove* was a big, exciting wreck, with endless places to explore. But it was also a potentially deadly dive. On average, one diver each year lost their life on the wreck, and trips to the recompression chamber were not uncommon. The upper decks had plenty of access and egress points cut into the side of the ship, but the lower decks were a labyrinth of passageways and rooms at over 100 feet deep. A recipe for disaster, waiting for the unprepared.

"Just a tag line will be fine unless you see the current kick up," AJ replied.

She'd briefed Emily on the way out, so once they'd slipped into their BCDs and performed their final safety checks, they stepped to the narrow platform between the outboards.

Cass threw a small buoy attached to a line off the stern. It was tied to a cleat and would drift behind the boat, a 'tag line' the divers could grab hold of on their return.

"Good to go, Em?"

Emily beamed a broad smile and gave her the okay sign. "This is a bucket list dive for me. I can't wait to tell Boone about it."

"You mean gloat to Boone about it," AJ quipped.

"Exactly!" Em replied, then held up her hand. "One other question."

Cass and AJ both looked her way.

"What are we looking for?"

AJ laughed. "Your guess is as good as mine! Something small enough to fit in a cabinet on this boat, waterproof, and valuable to bad people."

"Probably not a garden gnome then," Emily joked.

"Probably not," AJ agreed. "But if you do see a garden gnome, bring him along and we'll put him somewhere else."

"Huh?" Em paused, about to put the regulator in her mouth.

"Someone placed a garden gnome on the wreck years ago," Cass explained. "Now he moves around the ship. If you come across our little friend, take him for a swim and place him somewhere else."

"That's brilliant! I'll keep an eye out."

Emily pulled her bright green mask in place, and the two divers each took a giant stride into the deep blue of the Atlantic Ocean. Swimming alongside the Glacier Bay, they gently kicked their way to the mooring buoy, where they paused and slowed their breathing.

"Okay," AJ began, giving a final reminder. "Just remember, if anything goes sideways, get out of the machine room and go back along the passageway until you see an opening out of the ship. There's plenty of cut-outs, but there'll be a room between the passageway and the opening. The doors to the rooms are all removed or open, but it'll feel super dark in the passageway. Make sure you look to port and you'll find your way out."

Emily was an extremely experienced and capable divemaster,

but there was no substitute for familiarity, and AJ had lost count of the dives she'd made on the *Spiegel Grove*. "I'll leave my spare light outside the door to the machine room when we go inside. It'll get silted out in there if we have to rummage around."

"Lead the way, I'll be nippin' at your fins," Em replied with a grin, before sticking the regulator in her mouth and dumping the air from her BCD.

Dive map courtesy of Reef Smart Dive Guides

Water clarity was good, but the sun, low in the western sky, had turned the dimmer dial down, so the mooring line disappeared below them into a deep bluish-green gloom. They passed a large school of young barracuda at 30 feet, loitering menacingly in the water column, curiously tracking the divers.

Once AJ was confident the current was minimal, she released the line and kicked away, slanting at an angle down and to their right. The upper deck of the vast ship slowly took shape like a ghost rising from the deep, and at 60 feet down, the immensity of the vessel became clear. In every direction before them, steel structure filled their view as far as visibility allowed.

AJ hoped Emily's first glimpse of the *Spiegel Grove* struck her with the same awe AJ had felt on her own first descent to the wreck many years before. The sight of the magnificent ship brought back another flood of memories; mostly good, but some she wished she could forget. Body recovery dives weren't something easily erased from the mind, and she'd made a couple.

Leading the way, AJ eased over the railing at the back of the superstructure and continued descending to what appeared to be lower decks extending back like steps. Every surface was covered in coral growth, without a patch of bare metal showing. Sponges and sea fans grew from railings, reaching out into the water, picking up nutrients flowing by.

Ahead, a small metal hut, known as the pre-flight shack, sat at the rear of the second deck down, a large American flag billowing softly from a pole on the roof. AJ glanced back at Emily, who gave her an okay sign, her eyes wide with excitement behind the lens of her mask.

Beyond the shack, the ship's belly appeared to have been scooped out, revealing a massive cargo hold. AJ dropped to the next deck where a railing fronted a walkway running across the ship with several open doors leading into the superstructure. Below that, the cavernous hold continued underneath the superstructure towards the bow.

The *Spiegel Grove* had been built to carry and deploy amphibious vehicles such as military hovercraft, its designation LSD-32 standing for 'landing ship, dock'. A huge ramp at the stern could be lowered, and the hold – called the well deck – flooded, allowing amphibious vehicles to be launched. Two massive 50-ton capacity cranes, just beyond AJ's visibility, were staggered on either side of the ship for loading and unloading from a dock.

She finned towards the port side, locating the last doorway into the superstructure, scattering a school of French grunts. With a quick check to make sure Emily was ready, AJ turned on her dive torch and entered the dark interior of the ship.

Within 20 feet of penetration, the passageway felt like a blacked-out tunnel. The coral growth thinned, giving way to a light coating of algae. AJ stayed well above the deck where years of silt had accumulated, waiting for a stray fin to kick up a cloud and blind the divers. She passed a doorway on the port side and could see through the room to an access hole cut in the side of the ship. AJ waved her torch in a circle on the floor, then flicked the beam through the doorway, pointing out the egress point to Emily.

Arriving at the second doorway available on the starboard side of the passageway, AJ paused and shone her light around the room. Her torch provided the only light to the machine shop, where large pieces of metalworking equipment remained where they'd resided since the *Spiegel Grove* was built in 1955.

Taking her back-up torch from her BCD pocket, she switched it on and rested it on the deck, pointing into the room. A small cloud of silt and particles wafted all around the torch. AJ checked her wristwatch-style Shearwater Teric dive computer. They'd been down ten minutes. She had 2495 psi of air in her tank, and they were 88 feet below the surface.

Where they were in the passageway was slightly beyond the limits of advanced recreational wreck penetration, which stopped at 130 feet combined distance from the surface, while maintaining sight of the exit. Their next step, into the pitch-black machine shop, would take them well beyond.

11

THURSDAY

AJ used the edge of the doorway to pull herself inside the machine room, keeping her fins still to avoid kicking the passageway wall behind her. Her torch cast eerie shadows from the equipment and cables hanging down from the ceiling. Some of those shadows flitted about the room, further confused by the second beam of light following the first. The fish quickly darted through a doorway in the far wall, escaping the strange bubble-making creatures intruding upon their refuge.

To AJ's right as she entered was a workbench and along the backside of the passageway wall were racks for metal stock, long since removed when the ship was decommissioned. To her left, in the middle of the room, a fuzzy brown covering of algae and debris hung from every surface of a large pillar drill, and on the far side, a milling machine was decorated in a similar manner.

Beyond the pillar drill, a lathe masked in the same drab coating extended from the left-hand wall into the centre of the room, its huge chuck still easily identifiable. AJ carefully ran her torch beam back and forth along the chip tray and the guide-ways, looking for anything unusual. She quickly spotted something out of place. The dead-straight and perfectly round, man-made shapes of the machine gave way to a lumpy section below the carriage.

AJ hung in the water as still as she could manage, playing her light around the edges of whatever it was she'd seen. It matched the dull colour of the muck covering the metal, but something was odd. She wondered if it was an old towel or rag stuffed underneath many moons ago, but surely it would have disintegrated by now?

Emily moved over the top of the lathe, careful not to bump the steel beams above, and joined her light beam with AJ's. That was enough for the octopus, who'd been camouflaged and hiding, waiting for nightfall. The eight-limbed mollusc scooted from the chip tray and shot past AJ, disappearing into the darkness at the back of the room. A huge cloud of silt billowed from the tray and the divers' lights were quickly subdued behind a thick brown haze.

"Bugger!" AJ groaned into her reg as she tried to stay still and patiently wait for the fog to clear. The swirling cloud around her was thoroughly disorientating and, within seconds, her equilibrium was thrown adrift. She'd flinched in surprise when the octopus had bolted, and now wasn't sure which way was up in the underwater environment which masked gravity.

AJ reached out and felt the tool post of the lathe. It was farther away than she'd expected, but as long as it was indeed the object in her mind, she was right side up and still facing the lathe. After what felt like an hour, but was more like two minutes, the haze cleared enough for the search to resume. AJ tapped her mask and pointed to the backside of the lathe, indicating for Emily to search there.

Starting where the octopus had called home, AJ checked all the nooks and crannies in the chip tray, under the carriage, and around the feed screws. Nothing. Emily's light danced around the backside until she popped above the machine, shone her light at herself, and shook her head.

AJ swept her torch beam around the machine room, looking for another lathe, or something that Rosie may have mistaken for a lathe. Particulate still hung in the water, but she could see well enough to know there was only one lathe in the room. Rosie was a guy who'd spent his whole life around boats, engines and mechanical things. She was confident he knew a lathe from a mill.

Returning her attention to the machine before her, she breathed out and waited a few beats before slowly drawing in her next breath. Evacuating the air from her lungs, she began dropping towards the deck until her next inhalation levelled her out, just above the floor. AJ shone her torch between the two large bases supporting the lathe. Emily had already looked underneath from the other side, but it was worth double checking. Nothing.

Then she noticed the algae and grime rubbed away from a small spot on the base below the headstock. She touched the spot and felt some kind of indented pull at the edge of a panel. Hidden by the even texture over the surface, a parts cabinet was built into the base. She pulled hard on the edge of the panel, and reluctantly the door opened a few inches. How the hinges had remained functional was a testament to the US Navy's attention to lubrication.

Reaching her fingers inside, she fumbled around, nudging something which moved. She prayed the cabinet was sealed and whatever it was inside didn't bite. Wrenching on the door, AJ was able to open it another inch, enough to slip her hand inside. Now she was able to grab what felt like a metal tube and pull it from the cabinet.

AJ held up the cylinder and illuminated it with her light so they could both see. It was red, approximately two inches in diameter and four inches long, with what appeared to be a cap at one end which screwed to the body. Its most outstanding feature was its lack of dirt, growth, or any evidence of time underwater.

Emily gave AJ an enthusiastic okay sign and AJ nodded in return. She shoved the door closed again, using a fin against the wall to gain leverage, stirring up more silt. Using the torch beam in the doorway as their guide, the two divers slipped out of the machine shop and back into the passageway. AJ checked her Teric. They'd been down 25 minutes, she had 1430 psi of air in her tank, and they were still at 88 feet below the surface. She had ten minutes remaining of 'no-deco' time – before the point at which the body became saturated with nitrogen from the compressed breathing gas, and required 'decompression' stops on the ascent.

Apart from a slight scare from an octopus, who was probably more shocked than she'd been, the dive had gone as planned. They'd figured out Rosie's cipher, and found his hidden cylinder. Whatever it contained, they could hand it over to Sore Balls and move on with their lives. AJ felt pretty good, and rather than beat a hasty retreat, she decided to show Emily something few got to see.

She tapped her Teric and pointed at Em, then gave her the okay sign. It was a question, and Emily answered by making a circling motion around her own Shearwater dive computer then holding up nine fingers. She was replying that she had nine minutes of no-deco time left. Plenty of time for what AJ had in mind.

Continuing down the passageway towards the bow, they soon came to a corner. On their left was an opening in the floor where steps used to be, leading to a lower deck. The passageway turned 90 degrees right and ahead was a doorway with debris piled midway up the opening. A faint light could be seen in the large room beyond.

AJ turned right and continued down the passageway towards the starboard side of the ship. Halfway along, she paused and fanned her hand across the floor below her, brushing away a light layer of silt. She then made a circling motion on the deck with her torch beam before finning forward, signalling for Emily to take a look.

The faded paint had lost much of its vigour, even in the bright light of her torch, but the ship's nickname 'Top Dog' could still be made out, with a caricature of Snoopy riding a shark. Em wriggled excitedly and clapped her hands together, her torch beam flashing around the passageway. AJ laughed into her regulator and the creases in her cheeks made her mask leak.

AJ led them to the starboard end of the passageway, where she passed over the railing for another stairwell in the floor. An opening on the far side led to a small room and a large cut-out in the side of the ship, where they exited and angled up and back towards the stern. Kicking across the top of the superstructure, AJ realised the sun must be finally setting, as the dimmer had been turned further down underwater. Not quite enough to require their lights, but if they'd stayed much longer, it would rank as a night dive.

Halfway over the broad top deck, she began ascending, continuing an angle towards the port side. Just as it seemed like they were swimming off into the deep, dark blue of open ocean, the mooring line appeared out of the gloom about the same time as the wreck disappeared from view below them.

Hanging on the line at 15 feet, the two divers studied the cylinder while they performed their safety stop, allowing their bodies to reacclimatise to the lower pressure, and 'off-gas' some of the accumulated nitrogen. AJ was bursting with curiosity. What could be so important, or valuable, to warrant threats of violence? The container certainly wasn't large enough to contain a worthwhile quantity of cash or drugs.

But the bigger question weighing on her mind was how her friend Rosie Lee had got himself involved in this mess.

12

THURSDAY

Under the deck light on the *Reel-Lee Hooked*, the three women stared at the red aluminium cylinder laying in a bucket of fresh water on the deck. They'd been rushing to open the container until Emily asked, "Exactly what are we expecting to find?" Now they were worried.

"I suppose it could be anthrax, or some chemical weapon," AJ said nervously. "The next virus to sweep the world?"

"Come off it," Cass responded. "Remember who put the bloody thing down there."

"Maybe Rosie is saving the planet," AJ said, but couldn't keep from grinning.

"Yer daft bugger. Open it and let's see."

AJ fished the cylinder out of the bucket and dried it with a towel.

"If it's another set of codes, I'm throwing it back in the water," Emily joked.

AJ handed the container to Cass. "You should do the honours."

Cass took the cylinder from her. "You just want to see if I fall over, so you two can hop in the water and swim to safety."

AJ laughed and Emily looked over her shoulder, sizing up her escape route while Cass tried unscrewing the lid. It wouldn't budge.

"Silly sod probably cross-threaded the damn thing," she complained.

AJ handed her the towel to see if she could get a better grip. The lid still wouldn't loosen.

"Probably the pressure," AJ commented. "The water pressure at 90 feet was trying to crush it. Even though it's back at atmospheric now, if it became even slightly distorted down there, it would make the threads tight."

Cass offered it up for the others to try, so Emily grabbed the cylinder. With her face contorting into strange expressions, she groaned with the effort until it finally released. Em quickly handed it back to Cass for her to undo the top the rest of the way.

"You really don't want to sniff this, do you?" Cass laughed, turning the lid until it came free. She tipped up the cylinder and a clear, viscous liquid poured out, carrying a soft, black, velvet-looking pouch. Cass yanked her hand out of the way and the pouch dropped to the deck in a puddle of fluid. She rubbed her fingers together with some of the liquid and sniffed her hand.

"Doesn't seem to be melting my skin."

AJ dabbed a finger in the liquid on the table and Em looked at them both as though they were mad.

"I bet it's glycerine," AJ said. "He needed something heavier than water in the cylinder replacing the air, or it would float. You can buy glycerine at any local chemist."

Cass set the cylinder on the pilothouse table and pulled the drawstring open on the soggy pouch. Turning it over into her hand, a large red gemstone dropped out.

"Blimey!" AJ exclaimed. "That's a huge ruby."

The stone was an emerald cut, over three-quarters of an inch long.

"Give it a quick sniff," Em encouraged and the other two looked at her as though she was mad this time, shaking their heads.

"What? Can't be too careful these days."

They returned their attention to the stone, and Cass let out a long sigh. "Oh Rosie, Rosie, Rosie. Where on earth did you come up with this?"

"From Sore Balls's boss, I'm guessing," AJ replied.

"S'pose so," Cass agreed.

They sat in dumbfounded silence for a few moments as Cass handed the red gemstone to each of them for a closer look.

"We are idiots," AJ finally announced.

"I think that's a fair statement," Cass responded with a frown. "But which part of our lunacy did you have in mind?"

"Ha!" Emily exclaimed, and AJ laughed.

Cass had no idea what the other two were so amused about.

"Their dive boat is called *Lunasea*," AJ explained.

"But it's spelt L-U-N-A-S-E-A," Em added proudly. "It was my idea."

"That's cute."

"Cute? Bloody brilliant in my humble opinion," Emily declared, holding her chin high.

"Anyway," AJ took over. "We're numbskulls for not bringing all the books and notes. We were so excited when we figured out the first one, but there's still more. That's my fault for setting off half-cocked."

A wicked grin crept across Em's face. "Nothing worse than getting half-cocked."

Cass tried not to laugh. "Don't worry, love, it worked out. It took you to the stone."

"Yeah, but what if the next line says, 'beware of booby trap'?" AJ responded, shaking her head. "Or maybe, 'another gemstone inside milling machine.' If we'd brought all that stuff along, we might have been able to figure the rest out."

"But then you'd be diving at night," Cass said, looking sceptical.

AJ shrugged her shoulders. "That's what I was trying to avoid when I dragged us here in a big old hurry. But it's always dark inside the wreck. Doesn't really matter what's going on up here."

"That's true," Emily added. "And besides, I think AJ could find her way around that wreck blindfolded."

"Well, we didn't bring them, so how about we toddle back in and take another look at the note?" Cass suggested, stepping to the helm.

AJ started towards the bow and Em called after her. "Based on the fact we're still here, I'm going to guess it doesn't say 'beware of booby trap.'"

Thirty minutes later, they tied the Glacier Bay to the cleats on the dock and zipped up the soft enclosure. AJ had taken several pictures of the gem with her phone and they'd stashed it in the stool seat where they'd found the note. If the thug had been watching them, they didn't want to walk to the house carrying the precious stone. They may well need to hand it over the next day, but right now, there was more to figure out.

Cass took a bottle of white wine from the fridge, but AJ declined and suggested coffee might be more useful. Cass and Emily looked a little disappointed, but refrained in support. Cass brewed a dark roast instead.

"What time does the conference start in the morning?" Cass asked as they sat around the dining table once more.

"Registration is at 9:00am." AJ replied. "But don't worry about the conference. This is more important."

"I'm not letting you miss out on the reason you came here in the first place," Cass countered. "Especially over this nonsense."

"This nonsense is about making sure you and Rosie are safe. That's more important than anything else I could be doing."

"Well, let's see what we find with the rest of this bullshit," Cass said, waving the note in the air. "Maybe the next ciphers will tell us there's a million quid 'in the teapot', or 'behind the toaster.'"

Cass stood, handing the note to Emily. "You two make a start, and I'll throw some pasta on the boil. I'd better feed my troops."

Em looked over the second line of numbers. "Ready, number one?"

"Ready, sir," AJ replied, poised over the books laid out before them.

"Book 11, letter 4."

"*Slade Cutter, Submarine Warrior* by Carl Lavo, so that's a 'D'."

"Roger. Book 3, letter 2."

When they reached the fifth letter at the end of the first set of codes, AJ gave her the letter 'A', and Emily looked confused.

"Isn't it the *Duane*?"

"The *US Coast Guard Cutter Duane*, that's right," AJ confirmed.

"We must have screwed up somewhere then." Em held up her notepad, which had D-U-A-N-A.

"Let me check the last one again. Maybe I counted wrong."

"Book 20, letter 11."

AJ counted along the books and double checked the authors' names to make sure she didn't have one out of order.

"*The Codebreakers of Bletchley Park, The Secret Intelligence Station that Helped Defeat the Nazis* by Sir John Dermot Turing and Professor Christopher Andrew. It's book 20."

"How did they fit that title on the cover?" Em quipped.

"Maybe Rosie used 'Dermot' or even the second author, 'Andrew'?" AJ wondered aloud.

"We've had other books with multiple authors. They've all been the first author listed."

"I thought it was Alan Turing? Cumberbatch played him in a movie. Sad life the bloke had."

"Odd-looking fellow," Em added thoughtfully.

"Turing?"

"No, Cumberbatch. He's sort of dishy, but not quite... know what I mean? Besides, who names their kid Benedict these days?"

"Well, it's not really these days, is it? The geezer was born in the 70s."

"But not the 1870s, yeah?"

"True," AJ relented. "I bet he got his arse kicked in school."

"He would have in my school, I know that."

AJ flicked open the book and scanned through the introduction. "The author is John Dermot Turing, who's the nephew of Alan Turing. Alan was the codebreaker chap played by our mate Benedict."

"*The Imitation Game,*" Em blurted with a satisfied look.

AJ put the book down and made a sound like a game show buzzer. "Bonus points go to the trivia queen, Miss Durand."

Emily wiggled her hand in a royal wave. "I graciously accept the award."

"Ahhh…" AJ continued. "Here's the problem." She pointed to the second sequence of codes. "This one is book 22, letter 21. We don't have twenty-two books."

"Bollocks," Emily muttered. "That's right, we're missing one."

"Cass!" AJ yelled.

"What's up?" echoed a voice from the kitchen.

"We're a bit stuck without the missing book."

Cass walked in wearing a Union Jack apron with '*Herb – cos it has a f***ing H in it!*' emblazoned across the chest.

"Ooh, I love Eddie Izzard," Emily grinned.

"What are we missing?" Cass asked.

"Good question," AJ replied. "It's a book, but we have no idea what book. There's a reference to twenty-two books, but we only have twenty-one."

"That's right. We were going to search the boat again. Though I really don't think it's there." Cass replied. "We would have seen it before."

"SB could have taken it," Emily suggested.

"Good acronym," AJ acknowledged.

Emily looked over Rosie's note. "The first one worked fine, and it goes up to book 15, so we know the missing book is higher than fifteen in the order. We should be able to get most of these."

"What was the last one we just did?"

"Book 20, letter 11," Em replied.

"So our AWOL book is 16 or above in the order. Any more that work out okay above 15 will move that number up."

"Here we go then, 'cos the next word starts with book 21, letter 23."

AJ picked out the book and found the letter 'C'.

"Finish that sequence and we'll eat," Cass announced. "Dinner is nearly ready."

By the time they'd completed the cypher for the second line of numbers, it spelled out 'Duana cao? stern', and they'd narrowed the missing book down to 19 or above. The question mark was for book 22, as they didn't have one.

"Let me try the last book we do have," AJ suggested as Cass slid bowls of steaming pasta in front of them.

"Letter 21," Emily told her.

"That's a 'T.'"

"C-A-O-T."

"Ahh, it all makes sense now," AJ said, rolling her eyes.

Cass pulled the cork on a bottle of Chardonnay and poured out three glasses. "We can't have pasta without wine. The Italians will revolt, and we wouldn't want that."

AJ picked up one of the glasses and held it aloft. "Fair enough, so let's toast Rosie, and hope he's safe and sound somewhere, riding out the storm."

The other two joined her and clinked glasses.

"I hope he's safe now, 'cos I can tell you he won't be when I get hold of him," Cass grumbled, but her look was more of concern than anger.

"Maybe the ruby's for you," Emily suggested. "Wouldn't be a bad prezzie!"

Cass took a sip of her wine before replying. "That would be lovely... if a bunch of mobsters weren't after it too."

Emily curled her lip. "Oh yeah, there is that."

13

FRIDAY

AJ stirred to the sound of Metallica, blasting from her mobile phone.

"Shut that off," Emily groaned from the other bed in Cass's guest room.

AJ reached out from under the covers and snoozed the sandman from entering. It had been a long night trying to decipher Rosie's codes, with little sleep. They'd turned in at 4:00am and set an alarm for four hours later.

The next thing AJ knew, the band returned with a vengeance, picking up where they'd left off nine minutes before, and this time Em launched a pillow in the general direction of the noise. The bedside lamp tumbled to the floor, but the music played on until AJ fumbled around and turned it off.

They both trudged downstairs and were happy to find Cass had either got up earlier, or set the timer on the coffeemaker.

"You should still go to the conference," AJ said as she poured the aromatic dark liquid into two cups.

"No way," Emily protested. "I can't leave you two until we figure this out."

"We're supposed to be there representing the Cayman Islands dive industry. One of us has to go."

Emily sipped her hot coffee and thought it over. "But you can't dive alone."

AJ shrugged her shoulders. "I'll gear up for solo dives with redundant everything. I'll be fine. The dives will be in and out, anyway. Besides, right now I can only do one dive, as we have no idea about the other two."

They walked over to the dining table where the books were still laid out and Rosie's note remained tucked under the pad they'd used to figure out the ciphers. Well, tried to figure them out. Through a process of elimination, they'd confirmed book 19 in the sequence was missing. Any reference to book 19 or above returned a letter that didn't seem to make sense. A search of *Reel-Lee Hooked* yielded no more books.

AJ picked up the notepad and studied their results.

SPIEGEL LATHE
DUANA CAOT STERN
FIBC WHNELHCUSE
SPDEGEL NORT HNBICE

Too many words made perfect sense for them to be wrong about the cipher. They'd determined the second line had to be the *Duane* wreck, and 'stern' was correct, but the middle word had them baffled. Searching the stern of a 327-foot wreck in the hopes of finding a hidden three-inch-long cylinder would be futile.

AJ was sure the third line was '*Bibb* wheelhouse'. The *US Coast Guard Cutter Bibb* was a sister ship to the *Duane*, and the two had been sunk as artificial reefs in 1987, half a mile apart. Three of the four letters were in the title of books 19 or above, so only the 'B' was correct, but there were no other wrecks it could be.

"The last one has to be '*Spiegel* port' something," AJ mumbled, echoing their final thoughts from the night before. "All we can dive this morning is the *Bibb*, unless we find the missing book." She turned to Emily. "That'll be quick. The *Bibb* is deep, and it's on its side. Currents tend to run across the lower profile of the wreck, but I can nip into the wheelhouse where it's sheltered and look around. Not many people go in there as it's deep for recreational divers and not enough penetration for the techies."

"I still don't like the idea of letting you dive alone," Em complained with less vigour than earlier.

"We can't go home and tell the diving community we represented the islands by not going to the conference we came here for."

Emily wrinkled her nose, but gave up protesting. Cass walked in, dressed in shorts and a long-sleeved sun-shirt, ready for the water. "Take the Love Bug if you're going to Baker's Cay."

"Morning, thanks for the coffee," AJ said, holding up her mug.

"Figured we'd need as much of that as we could brew today," Cass replied, turning to Emily. "I overheard you talking about the conference. Do you know how to get there?"

"I think so. You pointed it out to me yesterday when we were driving around, and I can look it up on my mobile. You need to call me if you need help, though. Maybe I should come back at lunchtime?"

Cass looked at AJ. "I doubt we'll be here."

"I don't see why we'd make it easy for SB, right?" AJ agreed.

"I was thinking about this while I wasn't sleeping much," Cass continued. "What's the point in giving him some of what he's looking for? Presuming each location has more of these rubies, he'll want the lot. If we show up with some of them, he'll be after knowing how and where we found them. He'll probably want to come out on the boat with us if we dive again, too."

"I don't fancy being out on the open ocean with that plonker," AJ said, shaking her head. "Too easy to use that gun of his with no one around to see."

"My thoughts exactly," Cass said, tapping a finger on one of the books. "First things first. We need to find the missing book. Until we piece together all four sites, I say we avoid coming back here."

"We'd better load up on supplies, then," Emily suggested.

"We will, missy," AJ intervened. "You need to get your bum on the road."

Emily pouted, but took the car keys from Cass, who produced them from her purse.

"Fine. Text or call with updates," Emily demanded, and stomped her way towards the front door.

"Watch out for tourists," Cass warned her.

"How do I know they're tourists?"

"In Cayman we have different coloured registration plates for hire cars so you can tell," AJ inserted with a grin.

"It's easy here too," Cass explained. "They'll be driving Mustang convertibles with the top down and their luggage piled on the back seat, as it won't fit in the boot. Usually their airline luggage tags are flapping in the wind like a warning flag."

Em laughed. "I'll give all Mustangs a wide berth!"

AJ strapped the last of the nitrox tanks to the holder along the cockpit gunwale of the Glacier Bay. She had six tanks, which were all that were full in the storage under the house. She'd also borrowed a regulator and a spare reel. To dive solo, she needed independent back-ups for all the vital systems, starting with air supply.

All she'd brought on the trip was her recreational BCD, which carried a single tank on her back, and her regulator. Using a few clips she'd found amongst Rosie's kit, she could hang a second tank complete with its own reg from her chest. Without a partner to share air with if one of their breathing systems failed, it was imperative to have a spare.

AJ also had a back-up mask from her bag, which she'd stuff into a BCD pocket along with the extra reel. It was uncommon, but not unheard of, for a mask to lose a lens or break the strap, leaving the diver blind. The reel was important in case she was swept clear of the wreck by the current, losing the ability to ascend the mooring line. Inflating her safety marker buoy, or SMB, attached to the reel, she would be able to serve her safety stops underwater while signalling Cass at the surface.

The last piece of redundant equipment was a back-up pressure gauge, which was part of her standard gear attached to the regulator first stage. Her trusty Teric read the tank pressure, but in case the computer failed or was lost somehow, she would rely on the analogue gauge.

"I can't find the bloody thing," Cass complained, coming up from searching the berths once again for the book.

AJ looked at her watch. 9:05am. "We'd better get going. I'll have a butcher's on the ride out. I think I have everything ready back here."

Cass looked around the wheelhouse. She'd thrown all kinds of snacks and emergency rations, such as wine, in a shopping bag which rested on the couch. The freshwater tank was full and the fuel tank read half full. Fortunately, the boat had come with extra-large dual tanks in the back of the twin hulls, where the boat was designed to house inboard engines as an option. They could trundle around for a while without the need to come back to shore. Providing they didn't run wide open like they had the night before.

She started the twin outboards and let them warm up while AJ freed the dock lines, letting the catamaran bob gently in the notched-out dock, nudging its fenders against the concrete.

"That stone has to be worth a bob or two," AJ said thoughtfully, standing next to Cass at the helm. Her friend nodded as she dropped the boat in gear and idled into the canal.

AJ realised she hadn't given it much thought since they'd

opened the cylinder. They were all surprised by the impressive ruby, but their focus had been on the ciphers. She unlocked her mobile and searched for ruby values, cringing at the knowledge she'd now be inundated with ads for gemstones. The guideline for prices showed a massive variance, all based on the stone's '4Cs'. Colour, clarity, cut, and carat weight.

She clicked on a link to a ruby that looked about the same size as the one they'd found. It was 5 carats, an emerald cut, and selling for $300,000.

"Bugger me," AJ blurted. "That thing could be worth hundreds of thousands."

She clicked on another link as they neared the open ocean.

"Or, it could be a few hundred quid," she added. "All depends on quality."

"I wouldn't know a good one from a fake one," Cass admitted. "Never had much want or need for fancy jewellery."

AJ stowed her mobile. "Me neither, but I'm guessing this one is on the high end. I doubt SB and his boss would be bothered if it wasn't."

"I think you're right," Cass replied, and eased into the throttles.

14

FRIDAY

Baker's Cay was a sprawling resort nestled in the woods and mangroves on the bay side of Key Largo. Rooms, restaurants and bars all overlooked the calm, pale blue waters, and next to a small sandy beach extended a long L-shaped pier and boat dock.

REEF – the Reef Environmental Education Foundation – who were based just up the road, were hosting the conference and had invited representatives of the dive community from around the world to attend. The meeting room had capacity for 160 people, and Emily was sure they'd hit that mark based on the number of folks queuing to register.

When she finally reached the table, Em perched her bright green sunglasses on her head and introduced herself. The young woman found her packet, complete with T-shirt, schedule, and obligatory event lanyard, which doubled as a name badge. She slipped the lanyard over her head and read the front. Emily Durand, Babble Chasers, Little Cayman. She giggled, and the woman looked up.

"Everything correct?"

Em grinned. "Yeah. Oddly perfect actually."

She didn't have the heart to ask them to fix the 'a' for a 'u'.

"Do you have a car?" the woman asked.

"I do, and it's a classic," Emily replied proudly.

"Okay," the woman said hesitantly. "Well, here's a parking pass you'll need to display in the front window."

"Oh. It might blow away," Em thought aloud. "It's a convertible, you see," she explained, seeing the look of confusion.

The young woman grinned. "Get yourself a Mustang convertible?"

Emily grimaced and pulled her sunnies back down. "I wouldn't be caught dead in one of those common things," she announced, took the pass, and left the poor woman even more baffled.

The day was already roasting hot and the trees surrounding the car park blocked the breeze from the east. With the sun bouncing off the tarmac, Emily had droplets of sweat running down her back as she returned to where she'd parked the Beetle. She leaned in and hooked the cardboard pass over the rear-view mirror, wondering if it would stay in place.

"You a friend of Lee's?" a deep voice asked, making her jump.

Turning around, she saw a large, broad-shouldered man leaning against the back of a white SUV parked in the opposite row. Her instincts immediately put her on high alert. This had to be the thug they'd nicknamed Sore Balls. Her eyes inadvertently glanced at his crotch and she wondered if he was leaning because he couldn't stand up straight.

"Who?" she said, unable to come up with anything better on the spot.

"You're driving his wife's car, or did you steal it?" The man grinned.

"Someone I met in line asked me to hang their parking pass for them," she lied, digging herself deeper. She looked around. "That's my cool ride over there," she added, pointing to a Mustang convertible.

The man didn't bother looking, but stood up straight, putting on his best intimidating glare, which Em decided was quite effective. She was missing Boone and his fancy capoeira dancing/fighting moves.

She had taken defence training after a scary incident on the island of Saba, but this guy was easily twice her size, and she guessed he knew how to fight. Running away was starting to feel like her best option.

"You must be confused, blondie," he said menacingly calmly. "I watched you drive in here about 30 minutes ago in that piece of shit."

Em was certain Cass would give him a right pasting if she heard him insulting her Love Bug, but more concerning was the fact the bloke was following her. Although, maybe that was a good thing. If he was busy chasing the Beetle around, perhaps he wasn't watching the house and had missed the *Reel-Lee Hooked* leaving the dock. Regardless, she needed to ditch the guy and warn Cass and AJ.

"You're the one who's confused, Mr..?" she responded, seeing if he'd offer up a name.

He sneered and made a step towards her. "Where's Lee?"

Emily pulled her mobile from her pocket and unlocked it, aiming the camera at the man, who halted for a second when he realised he was about to have his picture taken. She snapped the photo and quickly turned to run. After one step, she tripped over the kerb and went sprawling across the pavement. The mobile flew out of her hand, skittered across a short patch of grass and disappeared into the shrubs by the building.

With heavy footfalls approaching, Em tried getting to her feet, but a large hand grabbed her under one arm and dragged her onto the grass. She grunted as her already grazed knees hit the turf. The brute began rummaging about in the shrubs in search of the phone, so Emily got to her feet and was about to run when she spotted her mobile at about the same time SB did. It had bounced off of a branch and lay at the edge of the shrubs.

The man bent over to pick up the phone and, with more reaction than thought, Em used her Krav Maga skills to boot him between his legs from behind. With legs spread and doubled over at the waist, SB was in the perfect position for a direct and excruciatingly painful kick. His knees buckled, and he dropped like a stone into the shrubs.

Emily scooped up her mobile, clicked one more photo of the man clutching his groin amongst the crumpled foliage, and ran for the resort entrance, carefully watching where she stepped. Out of breath, she smiled at the young woman at registration, who stared at Emily's bloody knees.

"I'd better get the promotion after that," she said in passing, and quickly sent a text with two pictures to AJ's mobile.

15

FRIDAY

Usually, there were two mooring buoys on the wreck of the USCGC *Bibb*, but Cass double checked her GPS coordinates before easing the Glacier Bay up to the only one she could find. AJ tied them in and Cass cut the engines, letting the boat drift with the surface current until the line went taut.

"I don't know if we're on the stern ball, or midships," Cass explained, looking at the mooring buoy half submerged under the strain of the tethered boat. "And the surface current is kicking. If this is stern, you'll have a challenging swim to the wheelhouse."

They both stared at the mooring ball. Occasionally, a strong surface current didn't automatically mean the same at depth, but more often it would be even stronger on the wreck. With the ship being on its side, the current usually swept across the *Bibb*, and as the top of the hull was at 90 feet, hiding below the gunwale meant the majority of the dive would be below 100 feet. Even on nitrox AJ wouldn't have much time on the wreck. If this was a customer trip in these conditions, they both knew they'd be finding another dive site.

AJ geared up and double checked her redundant equipment,

turning on both tanks and defogging both masks. She took a few long breaths through both tank and regulator set-ups, before stowing the back-up reg neatly under a strap, keeping it easily accessible. She waddled the two steps to the stern of the cat, feeling like a pregnant walrus with 100 pounds of equipment hanging from her body.

With one hand against the reg in her mouth and mask, one hand on top of the back-up rig on her chest, she took a giant stride into the water. Her legs shielded some of the impact, but the spare tank still jolted upwards upon hitting the water, and her hand holding it down stopped the aluminium cylinder from hitting her chin.

Cass had strung a wreck line for this dive and AJ was glad to use it. The moment she turned the corner at the stern, the current tried sweeping her away. The extra gear made a larger presence in the water, causing more drag, and her arms were aching by the time she reached the mooring buoy. Holding the line to the boat, she could feel the quivering tension. Her hand quickly checked once again that her rolled-up SMB was still hanging from a D-ring on her BCD. The chances of her needing to use it seemed higher than she'd like.

After a minute of relaxing and letting her breathing settle down, AJ dropped the air from the BCD and grabbed the line below the mooring buoy. The thick rope to the wreck was rigid and stressed, disappearing into the deep greenish-blue depths below. Flying like a flag on a windy day, she pulled herself down hand over hand. The current did not appear to be easing.

In these conditions, with the mooring buoy tugging the line tight at the greatest angle the tide would allow, the pull of the current always felt like it was trying to wrench her towards the surface. Everything easily becomes disorientating underwater, so divers with less varied experience often panic and feel like they'll be shot to the surface – potentially risking 'the bends'. AJ remained calm by reminding herself of the physics in play, and soon she could see the wreck appearing out of the darkness below. And, of course, she was descending to the stern.

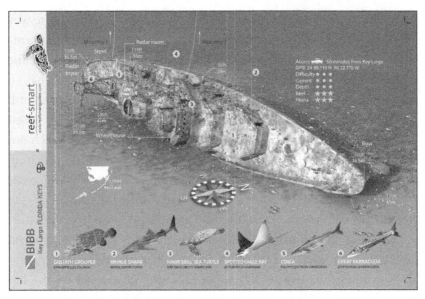

Dive map courtesy of Reef Smart Dive Guides

The massive hull loomed, but the superstructure was still beyond her view. AJ guessed the visibility was probably 60 feet or more, but filtered by the particulate being carried by the current. Tiny speckles were rushing past her mask, blurring her vision like stars whooshing by in a sci-fi movie. For a moment, she considered turning back. On any other day, she would in these conditions, or if someone else was with her. Endangering another diver would be too much for her to risk. But the dive could make the difference between Rosie coming home or not, and Cass being unharmed.

The first major hurdle, as AJ arrived at the base of the mooring line, was getting sheltered from the current. The line was anchored to a frame which protruded from the port side of the hull, level with the huge propellor. It was a good 10 to 15 feet of exposed swimming to reach the gunwale and slide over to the protection of the deck. Although the current was coming from the south-east, almost straight into the deck of the ship, the moving water redirected around the structure, offering shelter if she stayed close to the deck itself and below the gunwale. If she could get there.

Facing directly into the oncoming current, presenting the least frontal area possible, AJ finned with long strokes. It felt like she was working her arse off to remain stationary, so she wrapped her arms around the spare tank, pulling it into her body, making her profile even smaller. Thrashing her legs would only make things worse, so she kept her long, even strokes and tried to stay as close to the hull as possible without touching the surface. Slowly, she eased forward, steadily making headway until she could finally reach out and grab the edge of the gunwale. Normally, she'd avoid touching any exterior part of the wreck where organic life grew, but metal was already exposed where others had done the same, so she hauled herself into the lee of the *Bibb* and gasped into her regulator.

Nothing like starting the first five minutes of a deep diving sucking down gas, she thought, slowing her breathing and gently finning forward towards the superstructure. AJ passed by the tall metal-framed radar tower, which used to reach for the sky, but now extended south-east, parallel to the sea floor as the ship lay on its starboard side.

Several times as she finned over the side of the superstructure, the current grabbed her and tried to pull her from the wreck. The water found odd pathways and channels around the block-like shapes of the cabins, making the flow unpredictable. Fishing lines fluttered like thin monofilament streamers, long since snagged and snapped from rods at the surface.

Finally, she came level with the big funnel and, just ahead, the wheelhouse. Leaving the shelter of the gunwale once again exposed AJ to the ripping current. She could feel herself being tugged by the tank on her back as she carefully moved to the doorway, and was relieved to duck inside the cover of the bridge.

It was strange, being in a room on its side with a doorway above her and one opening to the dark shadows and sand below. AJ pulled out her torch and shone the beam around, noticing the pile of collected debris on what would have been the starboard wall. Everything was covered in thick coral growth, the series of front windows almost completely closed in by sponges.

She checked her Teric. 2100 psi tank pressure. 108 feet. Dive time 13 minutes. No-deco time nine minutes. That number was her current problem and the classic challenge of diving the *Bibb*. Nine minutes included the time she needed to get back to the line, and she couldn't angle up off the wreck to save time getting shallower or she'd be swept away.

AJ quickly turned her attention to finding what she assumed would be another small aluminium cylinder. They had stripped almost all the equipment from the wheelhouse before sinking the ship, so the room was quite bare. To the back of the bridge, old lines and conduits, thickly covered in growth, dangled like a barrier defending the next room. Looking for the cylinder in a room on its side was thoroughly confusing. Shelves or ledges were now vertical faces and few of the ship's features offered hiding places.

Sensing movement below, AJ looked down to see a nurse shark's tail disappearing out of the starboard door. She wasn't certain if it had entered that way and retreated after seeing her, or had come from deeper in the ship. She slowly rotated 360 degrees to search the wheelhouse, but also to convince her whirring mind that no other surprises lurked close by.

Facing the ceiling of the bridge, she noticed ridges running fore to aft. Covered in a variety of coral, especially sponges, the surface had lost all detail, but a distinct pattern told her beneath the growth were steel beams. AJ inverted and dropped to the starboard doorway, looking back up at the underside of the structure. Sure enough, hidden from any sunlight, the old metal of the closest few beams was visible, and attached to the one by the doorway was a cylinder. When her light fell upon the shiny body, it turned from dull brown to its true red. Zip tied to the aluminium body was a magnet, securely clinging to the steel.

AJ didn't pause for a moment. Snatching the cylinder, she stuffed it into a BCD pocket while finning to the port doorway. Emerging from the structure, the current immediately pulled her towards the deck, where it dumped her in the lee of the gunwale.

She started towards the stern and glanced at her dive computer. Two minutes of no-deco time left.

It wouldn't be disastrous if she went into deco. A few extra minutes on the line would meet the requirements, all calculated by her Teric. The bigger issue was her nitrogen loading for subsequent dives. If they could figure out the missing book, she had two more dives to do, possibly within a few hours.

Once the mooring line came into view, AJ made a risky call. With the surface and deep current running hard in the same direction, the line was angling up, but also towards the bow. If she could swim across the current while ascending, she should intersect the line at some point. Of course, if she didn't swim far enough, she'd miss the line and be swept away, relying on her SMB and Cass seeing it.

With her computer counting down seconds – now it was inside a minute of no-deco – AJ let the current pull her over the gunwale and kicked with all her might towards the stern. Her increased breathing was enough to start her rise in the water column and pretty quickly she needed to bleed air from BCD to slow her ascent to a safe rate.

Staying streamlined in the water meant keeping her head still and looking more down than forward. She could see the wreck below her slipping away, but the mooring line didn't appear to be getting any closer. She tugged on the dump valve at the base of her BCD, burping another slug of air, and pulled the back-up tank to her chest with her other hand. Risking a glance at her computer, she noted the no-deco time was climbing again as she passed through 60 feet.

Dumping the remaining air from her BCD, she kicked in long, tiring sweeps, using the power of the fins to propel her at an angle against the current. At 30 feet, she finally took a quick glance up and was relieved to see the mooring line above her. Thirty more seconds of hard work and AJ grabbed the line and finally rested, assessing her situation. She had plenty of gas left, had avoided deco, and was now at 22 feet. Hand over hand, she moved up to 15 feet, where her computer began counting down a three-minute safety stop.

AJ decided to make it five for good measure.

16

FRIDAY

AJ sat on the L-shaped couch in the pilothouse of the *Reel-Lee Hooked*, wrapped in a towel. The boat rocked as each swell rolled beneath her hull. Cass wrestled with the lid to the red cylinder, to no avail.

"Where's Emily when we need her?" she joked.

"Good point," AJ reacted, reaching for her rucksack and retrieving her mobile. "I haven't even looked at my phone since we left this morning." She unlocked the screen. "Bugger, I missed a text from her." AJ read the message aloud. "'Is this SB? If it is, he's XSB now, X meaning extra.' She attached some pictures." Scrolling down, she gasped and held up the screen for Cass to see.

"Bloody hell, that's him alright," Cass responded. "Is that him lying in the bushes too?"

"I think so. Looks like he's holding his meat and two veg. I think Em popped him in the goolies," AJ said and couldn't help but laugh. "That bloke's going to sound like the Bee Gees before we're done with him."

"Or shoot us on sight next time," Cass grumbled, handing the cylinder to AJ.

"We're probably wearing down his sense of humour," AJ

agreed, managing to loosen the lid and hand it back. "I wonder why he confronted Emily?"

Cass unwound the fine threads of the cylinder as AJ typed a message back to Emily.

'Sorry, diving. Have the second article. That's him. Good shot! Why was he there? Are you okay?'

Cass tipped the cylinder up and a similar soft pouch slid out with the transparent liquid. She slackened the drawstring and dropped another red stone into her hand. It was even bigger than the first one.

"Looks like Rosie was lining up your birthday prezzies for the next few years," AJ said, staring at the impressive stone. "I guess we know what to expect from the other two locations."

Cass nodded. "Wherever they are." She looked across the water towards the mooring buoys for the *Duane*, half a mile away. "Or where on the wrecks they are. Silly sod couldn't get a safe deposit box like a normal person, could he?"

AJ smiled. "Rosie's never been the regular, everyman type. That's why you love him."

"He's testing the last drop of love I have for him, I can tell you," Cass replied, her tone laced with anger, but her eyes were moist.

AJ rubbed her arm. "I'm sure he's fine. If XSB and his boss already had him, they wouldn't still be looking for him, would they?"

Cass just shrugged her shoulders and wiped her eyes. If she had more to say in that moment, the words wouldn't come. "Coffee?" she asked instead, and escaped to the galley.

AJ's mobile buzzed, and she read Emily's reply. 'I'm fine. I think he followed me, so watch for same. He asked about Rosie. People have been asking where you are. I told them you scored a gig at Woody's.'

AJ laughed. She'd pointed out the same sign along Overseas Highway, south of Key Largo, had been advertising the strip club in Islamorada since she'd lived there. Em wanted to take a picture outside the place and send it to Boone and Jackson, but they'd been too busy to venture farther down the Keys.

She texted back, 'I'm buying dinner tonight with dollar bills.'

After a brief pause with the three little dots on her mobile screen, Em's next message appeared. 'What's next?'

AJ sat back on the couch and pulled the towel around her shoulders. She shivered. Partly because she'd been submerged in warm water that was still a lot cooler than her body's core temperature, and partly at their situation. Cass was right to be upset. They were all ploughing on through the dilemma, trying to make light of it, but aggressive men brandishing guns were serious.

If she was home, her first call would be to her friend and police constable, Nora. They'd almost certainly then contact Detective Whittaker, who AJ often performed dive work for. But Cass was adamant about keeping the police out of it.

Everything came back to the missing book. With that information, they'd have the locations, which she presumed meant two more dives and two more stones. Then they'd hand them back to the thug and pray he'd be satisfied enough to go away. She looked at her Rolex Submariner on her wrist – a lavish gift from her family and friends on her 30th birthday. It was a few minutes after 11:00am.

Cass reappeared with their travel mugs refilled with hot coffee. She looked more composed and had obviously washed her face.

"What about his truck?" AJ asked, deciding a plan of some sort was needed.

"That old heap can wait until we've sorted all this out," Cass replied, taking a seat on the couch.

"I mean, could the book be in the truck?"

"Oh." Cass thought a moment. "I suppose it could. What I don't get is my stupid husband leaves an elaborate cipher, code, thingy, but only 21 of the 22 books needed to solve it. I would understand if it was next to his bed, or up here somewhere," she said, sweeping her hand around the pilothouse. "But we've turned the boat upside down. It's not on the *Reel-Lee Hooked*."

"Maybe XSB took it?"

"I guess that's possible, but why after tossing the rest of the books around the place did he choose to take one with him?"

AJ didn't have a great response to that. Maybe he liked the title and fancied a read? She didn't see the man as the studious type. Besides, they didn't notice a book on him when he came off the boat.

"Could it be Rosie's extra layer of security?" AJ pondered.

"You mean he hid the one book in case someone other than me knew his secret hiding place for the note and had two clever friends who'd help them decipher his magic bloody code? I think you give old Rosie Lee too much credit, my love."

AJ laughed. "Perhaps. Then let's go check the truck. I shouldn't get back in the water for a few hours if I'm going deep again, and we don't know where to search anyway. We can't go to your place, as Wobbly Bollocks will be there in an hour. Might as well see if the book's in the truck."

"Nothing better to do," Cass agreed.

She called the Monroe County Sheriff's office while she warmed the engines and AJ freed them from the mooring ball. After a few minutes on hold, she was informed the truck was in Tavernier at Buckley's Tow Service. Cass brought up Tavernier Creek Marina on her chart plotter and rolled into the throttles for the twin outboards, choosing a steady speed of 17-18mph, the efficiency sweet spot for the twin displacement hulls.

At the seven-mile mark, Cass chose to run on the ocean side of Tavernier Key. It was the longer route, but deeper water and low tide was only half an hour away. They wouldn't run aground on the coastal side, but she'd need to slow way down to avoid the risk of her props churning up the seagrass.

Well before they reached the channel into Tavernier Creek, Cass eased back on the throttles and grabbed the radio mic. AJ wondered what was going on and searched the sea ahead. She could see one other boat running slowly out of the channel. A pale blue centre console.

"*Hear No Evil*, this is *Reel-Lee Hooked*. Reply on 68. Over."

Cass waited, remaining on Channel 16. Finally, she heard a reply.

"Copy. 68."

She switched from the general hailing channel to 68 where they were free to talk.

"Hey Phil, it's Cass heading towards you. Over."

She waited again for what felt to AJ like a long time for a simple reply.

"Copy. Coming to you. Over."

The boats idled towards each other and AJ realised it was Phil Giles, the deaf fellow she'd met at Sharkey's. His delay must be some form of readout he used to display the transmissions. She threw fenders over the side and got a line ready to side-tie to the other boat. It was an older but clean-looking Mako 231.

Once they had lashed together, both cut their engines and stepped to their respective gunwales to talk.

"Where you heading, Phil?" Cass enunciated clearly.

"Fishing," Phil replied in his monotone. "Had to fill up. Heading out after grouper."

"Heard from Rosie?"

Phil shook his head. He lifted his salt-stained baseball cap and rubbed his forehead. "Not like him. You know, for this long."

"I know. I'm getting pretty worried. There's some other bloke looking for him, too."

"How do you mean? Who else?"

"I don't know who he is, but he's not friendly and he's pretty keen to find Rosie. You've got no idea what he's got himself into, Phil? This is no time for your he-man secret club bullshit, mate."

"I wish I knew something, Cass. I'm sorry," he replied, pulling the cap back down firmly.

"What about Wednesday night? You gonna tell me you weren't with him?"

Phil frowned and looked like he hadn't understood her at first, but then he slowly replied. "You talk to Poppers?"

"Yeah, I talked to Poppers," Cass replied, not letting on how little she knew.

"What he tell you?"

"He told me you three were at Dillons, then Mar Bar," she lied.

Phil nodded slowly. "That's true, Cass. I'm sorry I didn't tell you at Sharkey's, but Rosie made me swear. But that was the last I've seen of him."

"He didn't say anything about what's going on?" Cass persisted.

Phil shook his head.

"Alright, Phil, take care. I'll let you know if I find out anything, and please do the same."

"I'll do that, Cass."

AJ released the line, and the two boats drifted apart. Phil fired up his Mercury outboard and eased away, and AJ pulled the fenders back aboard and watched the Mako leave. She could see the tops of several dive tanks in the cockpit, along with fishing rods protruding into the sky from holders along the gunwales.

"I can't tell with him whether he's hiding something more from me or not," Cass said thoughtfully.

"He looked just as concerned as you," AJ responded. "You said he and Rosie are good mates."

Cass turned the engines on and put them in gear, aiming the Glacier Bay towards the channel. "They are. Which is more reason he'd hold out on me if Rosie told him to."

17

FRIDAY

AJ jumped to the dock with bow line in hand and tied the *Reel-Lee Hooked* into a cleat where Cass had pulled into a guest spot in the Tavernier Creek Marina. She threw a second line to AJ, then shut down the twin outboards. The marina was short on moorings but big on boat storage. Four towering, covered structures housed racks of boats, lifted in place by a beefy forklift.

An older gentleman approached. "Afternoon ladies, can I help you?"

"Good afternoon," Cass responded, as she gathered their things. "Am I okay here for an hour?"

The man looked her over as she hopped to the dock and handed AJ her rucksack. "You Rosie's missus?"

"Cass Lee," she confirmed.

The man nodded, his tanned skin weathered and wrinkled from a lifetime of sun and sea breeze. "You're good. Take your time."

"Thank you, sir."

"I ain't no sir, ma'am," the old man replied with a crooked grin. "Save that for officers and men who don't do much. People that know me call me Carl. People that don't, call me that 'cos that's what I tell 'em to call me."

Cass and AJ laughed, and AJ noticed the tattoos on the man's forearms, blurred and dark green with age. They were hard to make out, but she was sure one was the US Marine Corps emblem. The other arm had a dagger through a skull, the details of which were lost.

"Well, thank you, Carl," Cass said and began to walk away. She paused. "Have you seen Rosie this week? Maybe the past few days?"

Carl thought for a moment. "Don't recall seeing him this week. I noticed him fuelling up last week, but can't say we spoke any."

Cass nodded. "We'll be back in an hour, thanks."

They walked between the buildings, surrounded by boats of all shapes and sizes. Several dive and tour boats ran their operations from the marina, and with a marine shop, bait and tackle, plus Habanos On The Creek Cuban restaurant, the place was abuzz with people. Cass led AJ up the entrance road, running parallel to Overseas Highway, which was slightly elevated as it sloped down from the bridge crossing the channel.

Tavernier Creek bridge was fixed with 15 feet of clearance, so the channel linking the ocean and bay sides was used by pleasure boaters and smaller fishing boats. Anything taller had to travel six miles south to the Snake Creek Drawbridge, which had 27 feet of clearance when closed, and 76 feet to an overhead power line when open.

At the marina entrance, they jogged across the dual carriageway to Old Highway on the other side and turned left, back towards the channel. Buckley Tow Service was the last business at the end of the street, just beyond Captain Slate's Scuba Adventures. A tall fence surrounded a small lot with a shipping container converted into an office in the corner. Cass pointed to Rosie's truck, nestled amongst a row of other cars, mostly wrecked.

A slight man stepped from the office with a mobile phone pinned to his ear. He stared towards a convertible Mustang, which looked like it had been driven into something unforgiving. He noticed the two women and frowned.

"You're not understanding the 'not my problem' part of what I'm saying, lady. The longer it sits, the more you pay. I'll tow it anywhere you want in the 48 states, but you pay for that too." He paused impatiently. "Then have the rental company call me and they can pay." Another pause and he rolled his eyes. "That's between them and you. See how we came back to the 'not my problem' part?" He held the mobile away from his ear and AJ guessed the person on the other end was expressing her displeasure. "Your mother know you talk like that? Have a nice day, lady."

He ended the call and kept walking, turning to Cass and AJ. "I'm John Buckley. You picking up a vehicle, doll?"

AJ contemplated kicking a man in the delicates for the second day in a row.

"That truck," Cass replied, nodding towards the Ram 2500.

AJ recalled Rosie driving the very same truck when she'd lived in Key Largo. Its two-tone green and silver paint was now heavily sun faded, and the salt air had added a third tone of rusty brown along the door sill and rear wheel arches.

"Got keys?" the man asked.

"I do."

"Got money?"

"I do."

The man turned and walked towards the shipping container. "Step into my office, doll."

AJ looked at Cass and could see her blood was boiling.

"Not our biggest problem today," AJ reminded her friend.

They walked towards the office.

"True. But I could use some stress relief, and pummelling this wanker would help no end."

Cass gritted her teeth and managed to stay calm while Buckley ran her credit card and had her sign the paperwork. Relieved to be done, they left the office, just as a flatbed tow lorry pulled into the yard, followed by a cloud of dust from the crushed limestone gravel.

"What the hell are you doing here?" Buckley yelled from the office doorway.

A young man leaned across the front seat and shouted through the open passenger window. "Where else would I take it, Pa?"

"I texted you the address, Chris!" the father retorted, stomping towards the lorry.

"I don't got no text," his son replied, holding up his mobile.

"Check your damn phone!"

"I'm looking at my freakin' phone!"

John looked at his own mobile and furrowed his brow. He hit a button. "Look again!"

Chris looked at his device. "See, it only works if you send the freakin' text!"

"Well, I sent it! Now deliver that piece of shit and pick me up lunch on the way back."

The kid waved a hand in the air, dismissing his father, and started the process of turning the long lorry around in the small lot. Cass and AJ had stood mesmerised by the exchange, but now the show was over, Cass lay on the ground and slid under the back of Rosie's truck. When she came out, she dusted herself off and held a magnetic hide-a-key box in her hand.

AJ reached through the broken passenger window and lifted the lock knob. Tiny pieces of glass were scattered across the seat and on the floorboard. She looked around for the book, careful not to cut herself on the pebbles of glass. There were plenty of old papers, manuals, and junk in the glove box. Behind the seats, she found a pair of life vests, a small toolbox, a dinged prop, and other old marine parts. But no book.

They swept the glass out of the truck as best they could before Cass drove them out of the lot. She came to a stop in front of Mar Bar's building, where they'd stopped in the day before.

"Thinking of trying the barmaid again?" AJ asked.

"I'm thinking about what Phil said," Cass replied.

She pulled into an empty parking spot in front of the building and put the truck in park.

"That black eye look like Poppers hit himself with a cabinet to you?"

"Looked like he'd been smacked in the eye," AJ replied. "But I suppose it could have been a cabinet door."

Cass started typing on her mobile and clicking through a webpage. She began scrolling and AJ wondered what she was looking at. Cass slapped the steering wheel.

"I married a bloody idiot!"

"What did you find?"

Cass handed AJ her mobile. She was on the Monroe County Sheriff's Office website, looking at current arrests for the week. There was Rodney Lee. Arrested at 90775 Old Highway, Tavernier, on Wednesday evening. AJ looked up where they stood and saw the building number. 90775. She kept reading. Charges; 1 misdemeanour count of battery.

"Guess it wasn't a cabinet door."

"Why wouldn't Poppers tell me Rosie had clocked him? I don't get these bloody men."

"How long would they keep him?" AJ asked thoughtfully.

Cass shrugged her shoulders. "Just overnight, I think. He would have gone before a judge the next morning, then been released."

"Not a bad place to hide out," AJ suggested, and Cass looked over at her.

"That's the arse-backwards thinking Rosie might well come up with."

"Maybe Poppers took one on the chin for his mate. Well, in the eye, I suppose."

Cass shut off the truck and opened the door, and AJ hurried to keep up with her. Cass stomped through the passageway to Mar Bar and stood with her hands on her hips as she looked for Poppers. Every face in the place turned her way, but none of them were him.

"You alright, Cass?" June asked from behind the bar.

Cass went over and leaned on the bar top. June came closer.

"So Rosie was in here Wednesday night and concocted some

hare-brained scheme to clock Poppers and get himself arrested. Tell me I'm wrong."

June sighed. "You're not completely wrong."

Cass slapped the bar top. "What were they thinking?" she groaned.

"It was busy, so I don't know what started it. They seemed like their normal selves, sitting at the bar, chatting away. Next minute, Poppers is holding his face and one of the tourists calls the law," June whispered. "Rosie must have felt bad, 'cos before they hauled him off he gave me a fifty for Popper's bar tab for the week. I told them they should've taken their nonsense out front. We don't need word getting out that there are fights starting in the bar."

"Were they talking again? After their dust-up, but before he was arrested?"

"I didn't notice, to be honest. We were slammed busy, and the ruckus had people asking for their checks. Poppers just sat back down on his stool."

"What did he say?"

"He ordered a double."

A smile crept across June's face, and both women began laughing.

"Bloody men," Cass said, shaking her head.

"Was Phil with them?" AJ thought to ask.

"If I recall, he just sat at the bar the whole time," June replied. "I don't think he wanted any part of their shenanigans."

Cass leaned over, and June gave her a hug. "Let me know if you see him, love. No more secrets."

June gave her a wink as they separated. "I promise."

18

FRIDAY

Cass stopped at the intersection facing the entrance to the marina. She looked at AJ. "The courthouse is a few miles south. We could see if he left anything there."

AJ nodded. "We've got nothing else right now. All we've learned is that Rosie spent Wednesday night in the clink, and we're assuming it's because he knew people were looking for him. We still don't have any help for the other two locations."

Cass pulled across to the centre reservation, then turned left on Overseas Highway, heading south. The detention centre was behind the courthouse, set back from the highway on the south side of Tavernier. Cass made a right on High Point Road, then left into the car park. AJ was surprised to see a new construction along the front of the property facing the highway. High chain-link fences and an abundant use of orange traffic cones cordoned off certain sections of the car park.

"What's all that?"

"The new courthouse building."

AJ looked at the tatty-looking two-storey facility they were driving past and the even older looking detention centre office as they parked in front. The two-tone green building wore coils of barbed wire like a crown along the roof.

"I guess this one is a bit run down."

They entered the office, where an officer looked up from behind a counter fronted by a hefty metal cage.

"Can I help you?"

"My husband stayed in your hotel on Wednesday night, and he thought he left some personal items here," Cass said with a pleasant smile.

If the officer was amused, he refrained from showing it. "Doubtful."

"You don't have a lost and found?"

"We log all possessions when they enter, and check them off as they're released. No one leaves unless all the items are accounted for." The officer returned his attention to whatever he was pretending to do when they came in.

"Would you mind double checking for us, seeing as we've come all this way?"

The man's shoulders wilted as though she'd asked him to clean the bathrooms. Without a word, he turned to a computer monitor and tapped on the keyboard. AJ had imagined a big logbook of items but it made sense it was all on the computer these days.

"Name?"

"His name is Rodney Lee."

After a few more key strokes, the officer read aloud in a weary tone, "He had a wallet, set of keys, a cell phone, and a baseball cap. All signed back..." He paused.

"What? Did he leave something?" Cass asked.

"They must have forgotten to put the check mark for the cap," the officer grunted begrudgingly.

"Where would it be now?" AJ asked.

"On his head is my guess," the officer replied, maintaining a consistent level of disinterest.

"Let's just say for one moment that your fancy log system is actually correct, and he didn't leave with his cap," AJ soldiered on, trying to remain friendly. "Where within these walls could it be?"

The officer walked back into an office and they heard him rummaging around. "Miami Dolphins?" he called out.

"No," Cass replied. "It'll be a fishing hat of some sort."

"Jimmy Buffett for President?"

"Be better than the last few," Cass mumbled to AJ. "No, pretty sure it'll be something to do with fishing or diving."

"Mermaid Divers, Grand Cayman?"

"That's the one!" Cass shouted and AJ beamed.

"He wears one of my hats?"

"All the time, it's his favourite."

The officer returned and placed the hat on the counter, keeping it out of their reach. "ID?"

Cass handed over her driver's licence.

"Use the signature pad," he said, pointing to an electronic box bolted to the customer side of the counter. "You're signing for receipt of one baseball cap belonging to your husband, Rodney Lee."

Cass signed her name, and the officer slid the cap through the small cut-out in the steel cage. "Have a nice day."

"Thank you so much for your cheerful help," Cass responded, and they left the office. The policeman never looked up.

"Well?" AJ asked once they were outside.

Cass turned the cap over and looked inside. "I don't see anything."

AJ sighed. "Oh well, it was worth a try."

Cass tossed AJ the baseball cap and got in the truck. "Our day wouldn't have been complete without meeting Officer Smiles in there," she joked and started the engine.

AJ put her seat belt on and studied the cap. She'd sent them both a package of Mermaid Divers gear years ago when she'd first starting doing merchandise for her customers. The hat was black with her logo on the front: an anchor behind an old dive helmet with a shapely blonde mermaid wrapped around them. The hat was stained by salt water and plenty of use, with the edges beginning to fray. AJ flipped it over and looked at the underside as Cass had done. There was no cryptic notation penned on the inside, no obvious marking.

It had definitely been a long shot, but she'd become hopeful when it turned out he'd left something at the jail. It terrified her that she might be starting to think like Rosie, but there did always seem to be a method to his madness. She looked once more as Cass pulled back onto Overseas Highway, heading north.

The brand of cap was Flexfit, the kind with an elasticised band instead of an adjustment strap. The company logo was repeated five times around the band, barely visible after years of use. AJ looked again. The lettering was indeed hard to read, except for occasional letters, which she couldn't make out at all. Starting from the size label at the back, she worked her way clockwise around the band, reading out loud the letters she could still see.

"E-F-I-T-F-X-I-F-L-E-X-F-I-F-L-E-X-F-T-F-X-F-I-T."

"What the hells's that?" Cass asked.

"Probably nothing, but those letters are the ones left after the others are marked out."

"Which ones are marked out then?"

"F-L-X-L-E-F-T-T-I-L-E."

"That sounds like double Dutch too."

"Wait, the first 'L' is only half gone. What if that was an 'I'? F-I-X-L-E-F-T-T-I-L-E."

"That sounded like the last part spelt 'tile'?"

"I think it does. Fix-left-tile."

"Really?" Cass said in surprise. "That's what it says?"

"Looks like it. I mean, you could start at a different point, but I don't think it would make different words, it would just reorder them. Does this mean something to you?"

Cass laughed. "Yeah, it means something. But we need to go back to the house."

AJ looked at her watch. 12:55pm. "We don't need to go there

right now. This is when we're supposed to surrender ourselves to SB. I mean XSB."

Cass glanced in the rear-view mirror for the third time in half a mile.

"Something up?" AJ asked.

"Look in the side mirror," Cass replied. "Three cars back."

"The white SUV?"

"Yup. It's been back there since we left the courthouse."

"If he's heading north, this is the only road, Cass. SUVs are common as muck around here."

Cass checked the mirror again as they neared the turn for the marina. The road switched from one lane each way back to dual carriageway. She slowed, prompting the cars behind to move into the left lane and come past. AJ peeked again. The SUV was now behind them. Even the front window was tinted enough that she couldn't make out the occupants.

Cass put her left blinker on and cut off a car in the left lane. The driver vented his displeasure via a long blast of his horn. Cass whipped into the turn lane for the marina and accelerated across the road in front of oncoming traffic, eliciting further honks and shouts.

AJ looked over her shoulder and watched the white SUV, a Cadillac Escalade, drive on by as though they hadn't even noticed them. "Blimey, Cass, you're getting paranoid. It wasn't them."

Cass slowed down, her fingers tightly clenched around the wheel. "Sorry, love. You're right, all this madness is getting to me." She pulled over and parked near the restaurant.

"What do we do now?" AJ asked. "What we need is at the house, but we can't go to the house."

Cass leant her head back and let out a long breath. "Hell if I know."

"How did Rosie know we'd go to the jail?" AJ wondered aloud. "That was a long shot of all long shots."

"I think you'd go mental trying to figure out what goes on in that man's mind, my dear."

"I bet there are more clues, and we just missed them," AJ surmised. "Probably on the boat, in the truck, all over the place. He scattered them around and hoped we'd find one of them."

"You're giving him a lot of credit, love, I'm not sure he'd think this through to the extent you are. Besides, that loose tile at the house I've been nagging him to fix for months is four inches by four inches and behind it is backer board. One thing we won't find underneath is the missing book."

"It'll be another clue, I suppose then," AJ said brightly.

Cass chuckled. "You always were an optimist."

"We'll get it figured out, Cass. Maybe we should approach the house by boat. Moor in the marina and sneak around. That way, we could check for anyone watching."

"Be a bit bloody risky," Cass replied. "But better than driving up and finding that wanker pointing his gun at us."

"I hate guns," AJ replied. "Especially the kind pointed at me."

"They're the worst," Cass agreed, and the two managed a chuckle.

They both jumped at a knock on the roof of the truck.

"Hello ladies," came a deep voice, and a familiar face stared menacingly through the missing passenger window.

19

FRIDAY

AJ instinctively pulled away from the window and XSB slid his jacket back to reveal the gun once again.

"Looks like you weren't planning on meeting me as arranged," he growled. "My boss is tired of you playing games, and I must say, I'm starting to lose my patience."

"Who is your boss?" AJ asked.

"Someone you don't want to meet."

"Can't say I wanted to meet you," AJ responded.

The man scowled. "Do you have our merchandise?"

"No," Cass shouted back.

He reached inside his jacket, resting his right hand on his holstered gun, his left on the roof of the truck. "Then you're coming with me."

"How does that help us get the stones?" Cass retorted.

He paused, and both women realised Cass had let on that she knew they were in fact gemstones.

"Where's your husband?"

"We don't know," AJ replied honestly.

"Then how the hell do you know about... the merchandise?"

AJ looked at Cass. This was her decision to make.

"Because we have some of them."

He took his hand away from the gun and held it out towards them. "Hand them over then."

"They're not here," Cass replied, and AJ winced at how contrived that sounded.

A car drove by slowly and he waited for it to pass. AJ was glad there were witnesses around. She was sure he would be far more aggressive if there weren't.

He dipped his chin and talked through clenched teeth. "Enough of this bullshit. Where are they? And how come you've only got some of them?"

"If you want the rest, you'll have to trust us and leave us alone to get them," AJ interjected.

"I don't have to do shit," he barked back. "Right now I'm thinking I'll strip search the pair of you and then we'll see where you've hidden our stuff."

"What you have to do is get all the rubies back to your boss," AJ countered. "And we're the only people who can help you do that."

He sneered. "You don't even know what it is you have. Hand over what you've found so far, and I'll give you the rest of the day to get the others, but I'm coming with you."

AJ unlocked her mobile and opened the photos app. She held up the screen so he could see. The man slid his sunglasses down his nose and peered over them.

"Alright, hand them over, then we'll go get the others."

"That's not how this is going to work," Cass said firmly. "The hell we're going to hand these stones over to you without some way of guaranteeing our safety. And my husband's."

"All we want is our merchandise back. You return it, we move on and you'll never see us again."

"And you think we're stupid enough to believe what you say?" AJ retorted.

He glared at her. "You're acting like you have a choice."

Two men walked by talking, and XSB glanced over his shoulder, waiting until they were out of earshot. AJ watched them in the side mirror and wondered who else was around. They needed a distraction.

"Fine, come with us then," she said and turned to Cass. "Let's go."

Cass looked stunned. "Why would…"

"Let's go, Cass. Remember, you told Carl we wouldn't be more than an hour?"

Cass still looked confused, but she opened the door and got out.

"No bullshit, you two," he growled at them and stepped back so AJ could get out. "I take it we're going to your boat?"

AJ put the Mermaid Divers cap on her head, sweeping her hair behind her ears. "It's in the guest mooring."

The man took out his mobile and sent a quick text. AJ presumed it was to the driver of the SUV which she now saw parked towards the entrance.

"What are we doing?" Cass whispered as they walked between the buildings to the marina.

"Yeah, what are we doing?" the man hissed from closer behind than either of them had thought.

"What do we call you?" AJ asked, avoiding the question.

"My name isn't important."

"I'm sure it's not, but do we spend the afternoon saying 'Oi you'?"

"Call me Johnny."

"Johnny? Like Johnny Depp?"

"Like Johnny Cash," he said irritably.

AJ spotted Carl talking to the forklift driver by the boat ramp, and he waved. She waved back.

"I had you pegged for a George," AJ said with a tinge of amusement. "You know, like Boy George."

Johnny shoved her in the back. "Shut the hell up and just walk. Enough of this chatter."

AJ threw her hands in the air and pantomimed stumbling forward. "Hey!" she yelped, and glanced up to see Carl starting towards them.

"Cass? Are you two okay?"

AJ stopped, and Cass followed suit.

"Keep walking!" Johnny hissed.

"Hi, Carl," Cass greeted him, trying to look distressed, which wasn't difficult under the circumstances.

Carl looked Johnny over. The thug forced a smile.

"Who's your friend?" Carl asked, never taking his eyes off the man.

AJ knew she was taking an enormous risk and possibly endangering Carl, who was being nothing but a stand-up guy. It was take a chance, or end up on the boat with Johnny Sore Balls and his gun.

"Hopefully he's leaving," AJ said. "We've no idea who he is, but he's followed us through the car park. He has a mate sitting in a tinted-out white SUV back there."

"We asked him to leave us alone," Cass added.

"Wait, wait, wait," Johnny said with his anger brewing as he lost any form of pleasant expression. "They just invited me for a boat ride."

"Oh yeah? Who's we?" Cass retorted. "You don't even know our names."

"Lee," he mumbled, clearly realising he didn't know their first names.

"You need to leave, sir," Carl said firmly, stepping between Johnny and the two women.

The thug stood still and weighed his options, all trace of his fake smile having vanished. He was faced with an altercation in the middle of the car park of a busy marina, or retreat and regroup. AJ guessed his natural instinct was to fight, but she hoped somewhere in that thick head was enough common sense not to create a scene in public.

"Okay," he said, taking a few steps backwards. "Sorry if there was some kind of misunderstanding." He glared at AJ, sending her a message loud and clear. She'd got away with a strike yesterday, but she was sure her move today meant all bets were off. Running into him again would be detrimental to her health.

"Sir, be aware, we have cameras all around the property," Carl stated calmly. "You, your vehicle, and your actions following these two ladies have been recorded."

Johnny looked like he was about to protest, but he turned and walked away.

"Thank you Carl," Cass said. "He was being a wanker."

Carl nodded, looking rather proud of himself for coming to their aid. "I'll keep an eye out for him in case he comes back. Now, let me walk you to your boat."

Cass and AJ took an arm each and allowed Carl to escort them to the Glacier Bay.

"How do you think Johnny Sore Balls knew we'd be at the detention centre?" AJ asked as Cass idled them through Tavernier Creek and back out to the Atlantic.

"He said he'd know if we went anywhere near the police."

"But Officer Smiles was the only one we saw," AJ countered. "What are the chances of him being the one on the mobster's payroll?"

"Slim, I'll grant you."

As they cleared the bridge for US1 above them, AJ looked over to her right. Beyond a stand of trees was Buckley's tow yard where they'd retrieved Rosie's truck. Movement on the bridge made her look over her shoulder, and above them, on the footpath alongside the road, stood a man watching them idle by below.

AJ turned to her friend. "Cass, there's someone watching us from up on the bridge."

"Is it Johnny Sore Balls?" Cass asked as she turned to look.

AJ followed her gaze. "Shit. He's gone."

They both stared up at the bridge, seeing nothing but the roofs of passing cars.

"Maybe it was his driver?" Cass wondered. "We haven't seen him yet."

"Or maybe it was a tourist enjoying the view," AJ conceded.

"Did he look like a tourist?"

AJ tried to recall the brief glance she'd had of the man. She wasn't sure she could come up with an accurate description if her life depended on it. But he gave her a chill, she was sure of that. "Maybe. I don't know, Cass. I'm probably just being paranoid." She turned Rosie's baseball cap backwards on her head before Cass picked up speed once clear of the no-wake zone. "Back to the point I was getting to," AJ said, moving on. "JSB knew where Em was this morning and knew where we were this afternoon."

"He's JSB now?"

"Johnny Sore Balls. Johnny Extra Sore Balls seems over the top, don't you think?"

"Right. Just making sure I'm keeping up. We heading north to the house?" Cass asked, aiming the Glacier Bay for the open water outside Tavernier Key.

"I think we have to if we stand a chance of finding the other stones."

Cass nodded and brought up home on the chart plotter. Following Rosie's well-worn track from Tavernier to the house would require less attention than sighting it herself.

"I think they put a tracker on the vehicles," AJ said, and Cass frowned.

"Not likely. That seems a bit far fetched."

"Why? You can buy a tracker online for a hundred dollars and watch it on your mobile. The driver in the SUV could have stuck one on your Beetle while we were having our chinwag with JSB."

"What about the truck? It was in the lock-up at Buckley's."

"It was parked at Harry Harris Park for a few days before that, right?"

Cass pondered for a moment, constantly making a visual sweep of the water as they cruised along.

"I didn't actually see Rosie on Tuesday, but we know he took the boat out. That evening the boat was back but his truck was gone when I got home from work around 11:30pm. I worked a double shift."

"We don't know where he was Tuesday or Wednesday during the day," AJ contributed. "But Officer Reid said the truck had been at Harry Harris for a couple of days, so that means from Wednesday, yeah?"

"Wednesday evening he was at Dillon's, then Mar Bar, and then jail."

"And he didn't leave his truck at the bar, so I'm guessing it was already at the park, and he rode with someone else to the bars. Beyond that, we have no idea where he went." AJ finished and tucked a few stray blonde and purple hairs behind her ear.

"I suppose there was plenty of opportunity for someone to stick tracker thingies on the vehicles," Cass conceded. "But he must have hidden the gems on Tuesday, or during the day Wednesday."

"Had to be Tuesday," AJ said. "If the last he was on the boat was Tuesday, that's when he hid the note with the ciphers."

"Unless he snuck back on *Reel-Lee Hooked* later. Or used another boat."

"True, I suppose," AJ thought for a moment. "But before Wednesday night, otherwise he wouldn't have left the message in the cap."

Cass rolled her eyes. "This is all too much. My dimwit husband is leaving coded messages all over town, mobsters are putting trackers on our cars, what's next?"

"A tracker on *Reel-Lee Hooked*?" AJ suggested, looking around the helm station. "Wait, I don't think so. XSB…"

"JSB," Cass interrupted.

"Sorry, JSB, clearly didn't know we'd been to the wrecks."

"That might be our first piece of good news," Cass sighed.

AJ shrugged her shoulders. "Hopefully. Guess we'll see if we have a welcoming party at the house."

20

FRIDAY

Cass idled into Pilot House canal leading to Lake Largo and the marina. Without the wind rushing over the helm, AJ turned the baseball cap around the right way to shield her eyes from the sun reflecting off the white fibreglass. She glanced down at the chart plotter.

"Cass? Look at what we've been staring at all this bloody time."

"Huh?" her friend said, looking beyond the bow of the boat. "What do you mean?"

"Look at the GPS."

"What about it?" she said, staring at the screen. "Oh, bollocks!"

The GPS waypoint marking her house was labelled 'Home'. On a second line underneath it read 'Fix Tile.'

"That would have saved us a trip all over the houses," Cass said, shaking her head. "Couldn't just text me this shit, could he?"

AJ laughed. "We both missed it. I wonder how many more clues we've overlooked in plain sight?"

"Who the hell knows?" Cass muttered. "And seeing as the book isn't gonna be behind the damn tile, he's gonna send us on another wild goose chase."

They reached the side canal leading to the house, but Cass idled by, both women looking for signs of the mobsters. Trees blocked the end of the roadways, and houses lined both sides of the little dead-end canal, making it impossible to see much at all.

Reaching Lake Largo, Cass found the guest dock outside The Fisheries and aimed for an open spot. The lunch crowd had begun to leave, otherwise they'd have struggled to find anywhere to tie up. A young man ambled down the wooden pier and AJ threw him a line from the bow.

"Welcome to The Fisheries," he said with well-practised cheer.

Once the line was secure, Cass cut the engines. "We live just around the corner. Okay if we tie up for half an hour?"

The young man gave the boat a second look. "Oh yeah, sure. I didn't realise it was Rosie's cat. Take your time."

They thanked him and made their way around the restaurant, the pungent smell of fish, both fresh and cooked, wafting across their path. With little choice, they had to walk the road. It was that or hop fences and run across people's backyards. Justifiably, some-one, or someone's dog, would take offence to the intrusion.

AJ carefully peeked down Ocean Way from the cover of a pickup truck. She couldn't see the white SUV. They planned to jog the 300 yards to Mahogany but realised their flip-flops would hamper any running. Shoeless was out of the question. The tarmac was roasting hot, and the edges were limestone gravel. Walking quickly, they covered the ground and looked down Mahogany from behind a tree on the corner.

"Looks clear," Cass said. "I recognise all the cars I see. They're all neighbours."

AJ moved down the cul-de-sac, slowing before Cass and Rosie's lot, making sure no one unexpected was parked under the house. It looked clear.

"Cass!" came a man's loud voice from across the street.

It made them both jump.

"Bloody hell, Gene, you scared the shit out of me."

A dark-haired man stood behind his waist-high fence across the road. By his side, the head of what must have been a huge Alsatian looked over as well.

"Sorry. I guess your hearing's okay, then?"

AJ realised Gene was the neighbour who owned Admiral, the dog who'd inadvertently given Cass a pinhole in her eardrum.

"Feels fine now, no more ringing," she replied, giving him a thumbs-up.

"Glad to hear it," he called back. "We're barbecuing Sunday evening if you and Rosie want to come by? You're welcome to bring your friend."

Cass gave him another thumbs-up. "I'll check with Rosie. Thanks, Gene."

They quickly moved towards the house, ending the conversation across the street.

"So much for our stealth approach," AJ said as they reached the steps.

"Yeah, sorry. There's no going quietly in a small town you've lived in for donkey's years. At least Admiral knows me so he didn't bark. It's incredible: that dog knows every person and car in the neighbourhood. He'll only bark at strangers. If you buy a new car, he takes about a week to adjust. Not that we've ever challenged him on that front."

They ran up the steps, and Cass unlocked the door, stepping cautiously inside. All was quiet beyond the hum of cooled air blowing through the floor vents. She went straight to the kitchen, reaching for a backsplash tile at the left end of the counter. To AJ's surprise, the tile made a tearing sound as Cass plucked it from the wall.

"Is that Velcro?" AJ asked.

"That's Rosie's idea of a temporary fix. He scraped the mortar off so there was room for the Velcro and in his mind he'd fixed the bloody thing. I've been on at him for ages to mortar it back on properly and grout the gaps." She turned the four-inch-square tile over in her hand. "Home run," she read aloud, and showed AJ the writing. The words were in marker pen, all caps, on opposite sides of the tile, outside the Velcro.

"I hope you know what that means," AJ said, staring at the tile.

Cass looked at the exposed backer board where she'd removed the tile. A square piece of Velcro in the middle was all she could see. "I'm going to wring his bloody neck when I see him," she complained.

AJ avoided adding the obvious statement. The elephant in the room. If. As they sank deeper into Rosie's mess, they both knew the mobsters had as good a chance of finding him as they did. It didn't need to be said.

Cass turned the tile over several times to make sure she hadn't missed anything, then AJ snapped a picture with her mobile before Cass reset the tile in place. Once she knew the tile was reset in its location, AJ could easily spot it, but she hadn't noticed it before, and had been in the kitchen plenty of times since they'd arrived in Key Largo. Of course, she decided, anyone else finding it would almost certainly have even less idea what the message meant.

Cass opened a cabinet and took out two tumblers, holding them one at a time under the ice dispenser in the fridge. From another cabinet, she took down a bottle of Seven Fathoms Cayman Rum and began pouring.

"I'd better not," AJ said, holding up a hand. "I may have to dive again."

Cass poured two fingers in one glass, and a lesser amount in the other. "You're not leaving me to drink alone on a weekday afternoon."

AJ laughed and took the tumbler. "You're in the bloody Keys, Cass. The five o'clock drinking rule doesn't apply here."

Cass held up her glass. "Bottoms up."

"Here's to finding Rosie," AJ added.

"Sod him. He's the reason we're drinking on a Friday afternoon," Cass responded. "Here's to the girls who make this rockin' world go round."

They clinked glasses and took a swig.

"My favourite rum," AJ said, savouring her self-induced restriction of the amber liquid.

"You got us hooked on this stuff when we visited the island. Now they ship it in the US," Cass said, taking a longer slug.

"Home run," AJ murmured thoughtfully. "Rosie's not a baseball fan, is he?"

"Not really, and he knows I don't know baseball from lawn bowls."

"If it's not baseball, what else could it be?" AJ pondered. "Run home? The words are opposite, so they could read either way round."

"Home run, run home, either way it doesn't make any sense to me," Cass said, finishing her rum with a final tip of the glass.

"Could it be something about coming home, or something you do when you first get home?" AJ brainstormed. "But none of that incorporates run or running. Neither of you are runners, are you?"

"Not unless I'm being bloody chased," Cass quipped.

"Did Rosie ever tell you a story about running home as a kid or something whacky like that?"

Cass poured a little more rum in her own glass and swilled it around in the ice. "You're good at this sleuth business. You should be a private detective or something."

"I'm quite happy being a dive boat operator," AJ assured her. "But I have friends in the police back home and I've helped them out with diving from time to time. And some other stuff," she added with a roll of the eyes, recalling some of the drama that had found her over the past few years.

"We tried the running thing once, years ago," Cass said, sipping her second round of rum. "That didn't last bloody long, I can tell you."

"You'd run around the neighbourhood?" AJ asked, picturing Rosie making it as far as the Pilot House bar.

"He traded an old Honda outboard he'd had kicking around for years for this fancy treadmill. We had it under the house for a few months. Nice view of the canal."

"What made you stop after a few months?" AJ asked absent-mindedly as she racked her brain for what the message could mean.

"I didn't say we stopped after a few months. I said the treadmill was down there a few. After almost going arse over tea kettle my first time on it, I decided I'd rather be out of shape than in traction."

AJ chuckled at her friend. "Well, you've managed to stay in amazing shape. You don't look a day older than when I lived here."

Cass waved her off. "Nothing's as firm as it used to be, love, but nothing a push-up bra and sturdy spandex can't hold in place."

"Wait," AJ said, as a thought crossed her mind. "Did you sell the treadmill?"

"No, it's in the storage room with the rest of the junk we hoard down there."

AJ looked at Cass with raised eyebrows and waited. Cass's expression remained bewildered for several moments, then finally the ball dropped.

"Bugger, you think he meant the treadmill?"

"One way to find out," AJ grinned, starting for the door.

The storage room beneath the house stretched full length from front to back, and half the width. The moment Cass opened the door, she knew they'd solved Rosie's latest clue. A path had been cleared through the piles of boxes, marine parts, and other discarded items, all the way to the treadmill near the back. Sitting on the console was a copy of *Blind Man's Bluff – The Untold Story of American Submarine Espionage* by Sherry Sontag, Christopher Drew, and Annette Lawrence Drew.

21

FRIDAY

Memories of hunting for Easter eggs in the garden as a child flashed through AJ's mind. Finding the book gave her the same burst of euphoria she recalled from finding one of the craftily placed painted eggs many years ago. Except this time, the elation was short lived.

The two women, chatting excitedly, exited the storage room and stopped dead in their tracks.

"Sorry if I startled you," the man calling himself Officer Reid greeted them.

"Rosie?" Cass gasped.

"I'm sorry, ma'am?"

"Is it my husband? Rodney Lee? Have you found him?" Cass elaborated, her voice cracking, expecting the worst.

"No, ma'am, we have not. Which is actually why I stopped by," he replied. "You seemed concerned yesterday, so I was checking back to see if he's shown up."

Cass went quiet and AJ sensed her suspicions of the man returning now she knew he wasn't reporting a body which needed identifying.

"We think he's off having a bit too much fun with the lads," AJ said, trying to sound casual and holding the book out of sight.

The officer looked back and forth between the two women, glancing down at AJ's arm behind her back. "I did see he spent a night in our detention centre earlier in the week. Were you aware of that?"

AJ wasn't sure how Cass wanted to handle that question, so she stayed silent. It wouldn't be hard for him to find out they were there that morning if he called the detention centre and spoke with Officer Smiles. Of course, if this guy was in bed with the mobsters, he would already know she and Cass had been there.

"I'm aware," was all Cass replied.

"When was the last time you saw your husband, ma'am?"

Cass hesitated. "Earlier in the week."

It was hard for AJ to judge the man's expression behind his dark sunglasses, but her best guess was somewhere between confusion and annoyance. The two responses would indicate a very different perspective, leaving her none the wiser.

"Can you be more specific?" he asked, his tone even.

"Why is this important to you?" Cass responded, sounding more accusatory than AJ thought was prudent.

Officer Reid appeared taken aback. "Well, I was simply following up out of concern, ma'am. If someone close to me spent a night in jail, had their truck broken into then towed, and was missing all week, I think I'd be a little worried."

Cass held up her hands. "Sorry. Officer Reid, correct?"

The man nodded.

"I am worried, and I appreciate you following up, but my husband has done this before. I don't want to waste anyone's time. If he hasn't resurfaced by Monday, then I'll be really worried and I'll come by the sheriff's office and file a missing person report."

Reid nodded slowly. "Monday would be a week since you last saw him?"

"It would," Cass confirmed.

"Then I hope you're right and he'll find his way home this

weekend," the officer replied and began turning to leave, but stopped. "Do you have your cell phone with you, Mrs Lee?"

Cass pulled her mobile from her back pocket, but held it close to her chest.

"Take down my number," he continued and, surprised, she unlocked her mobile and entered the number he gave her.

"If he shows up, send me a text, please," he said with a pleasant smile. "I'll check your husband off my list of concerns."

"Okay," Cass replied. "I will."

"Ladies," he said, nodding to them both before walking to his car parked on Mahogany.

Cass led AJ to the steps up to the house and they took their time going up. Once the police car had turned around at the end of the cul-de-sac and driven back past them, they ran down and headed for the street.

"I honestly can't tell what's going on with that bloke," AJ said as they moved briskly down the road.

"Me neither, but I'm not trusting anyone at the moment."

"I think he might just fancy you," AJ added.

Cass scoffed. "Not likely. I'm probably old enough to be his mother."

"Once he heard you were separated, he became very concerned about your wellbeing," AJ teased.

"Oh stop it," Cass replied, but couldn't hide her grin. "More likely he's in those bastards' pocket and wants a text as soon as I set eyes on Rosie."

AJ was about to defend Officer Reid when she spotted a white SUV about to turn left onto Ocean Way. She grabbed Cass's arm and pulled her behind a small stand of gumbo-limbo trees at the end of one of the short canals.

"What the heck?" Cass spluttered before seeing the reason. "I told you! That bugger just called Johnny Sore Balls and told him we were home."

AJ still wasn't convinced. The thug would need to have been close by to get there that quickly, but the coincidence was certainly suspicious. The Escalade rolled by, and this time AJ made a mental note of the licence plate, wishing she had done so before. Sure enough, the vehicle turned on Mahogany, and once it was out of sight, the two women ran the opposite way to The Fisheries.

Stepping aboard *Reel-Lee Hooked*, Cass was completely out of breath. AJ stayed on the dock and freed the stern line, then jogged along the pier while Cass started the engines, ready with the bow line. AJ looked up at Cass, who was leaning on the helm station, red faced.

"If you say anything about using that bloody treadmill, I swear I'll leave you on the dock, young lady."

AJ grinned. She'd hardly broken a sweat, but she ran on Seven Mile Beach three or four times a week when she was home. Cass nodded and AJ freed the line before nimbly hopping aboard.

"Let's top off with petrol before we head out," Cass said as she backed the Glacier Bay away from the dock before turning her around, using the throttles on the widespread twin outboards to steer.

The fuel dock was on the far bank where the channel left Lake Largo, and once again, AJ hopped to the concrete dock and tied them in. An older man came out of the small building behind the pumps and waved to Cass. He wore faded, stained denim overalls over a once white T-shirt. On his head perched a Mercury Marine hat that may have been as old as he was.

"What's the good word, Cass?" he said, going straight to one of the three pumps.

"Afternoon, Stubby. Haven't seen Rosie around the past few days, have you?" Cass asked, opening the port-side fuel fill as the old man stepped aboard with the nozzle in hand. AJ noticed he moved with surprising ease for a man his age.

"Can't say I have," he replied thoughtfully. "Figured it was him coming over when I saw *Reel-Lee Hooked*. Ain't seen him in best part of a week or so. Everything alright?"

"I'm sure it is," Cass replied, forcing a smile. "You know Rosie.

He's probably crewing in Bimini for a few days and forgot to tell me."

"Poppers was by yesterday just after lunch. He got himself a real shiner," Stubby said with a wry grin. "Said he walked into a cabinet."

"That's what he told us, too."

"I thought he was talking to Rosie on the phone, but then he started arguing with whoever it was," Stubby added thoughtfully as he pumped petrol into the port-side tank. "Don't recall them two ever disagreeing about anything, so s'pose it weren't Rosie."

AJ looked at Cass and could see her interest was piqued.

"What made you think it was Rosie in the first place?" Cass asked.

The old man shrugged his shoulders. "Thought I heard his name said, but my hearing ain't what it used to be."

"This could be important, Stubby," Cass persisted. "Did Poppers mention Rosie by name?"

The old man looked at her quizzically. "You sure everything's alright? You seem awful worried about him."

"There's something going on, Stubby, but Poppers and Phil are being all tight lipped about it. So yes, I'm worried."

Stubby nodded. "Best I recall, he called him Rosie, but I'm wrong more than I'm right according to the missus. Anyway, 'spect he'll shout when he gets back," Stubby chuckled. "Seein' as you're takin' his house for a ride."

Cass managed a laugh. "Yup, I expect he will. This is our friend AJ, by the way. She's in town for a few days. We're heading out diving."

Stubby touched the tip of his ball cap. "Nice to meet you, young lady."

AJ heard the man, but her attention was on the road across from the marina. A white SUV was moving slowly along Ocean Bay Drive. She watched it speed up.

"Cass, we'd better go!"

Cass and Stubby looked up at her.

"Hurry, they're coming!" AJ yelled, and Stubby let go of the trigger on the nozzle.

"Thanks, Stubby, stick it on my account, love. We've gotta scoot," Cass urged, herding the confused man off the boat.

Behind them, they heard tyres squealing as the SUV made a right on Seagate Boulevard behind the CRF building and Pilot House Restaurant. AJ untied the bow line, then dodged around a stunned Stubby to do the same at the stern. Cass started the engines as more tyre squealing echoed around the neighbourhood.

AJ pushed the Glacier Bay away from the dock with her foot, then jumped to the gunwale and clung to the hardtop frame behind the helm. Dropping the motors in reverse gear, Cass steered them away from the dock, stern first, getting them clear enough as JSB ran around the building and came to a stop. The thug stood next to a bewildered Stubby, still holding the fuel nozzle in his hand.

"You didn't sign for the gas," the old fellow said, looking from the boat to the strange man at his side, wearing trousers and a sport coat in the marina.

Johnny Sore Balls glared at the two women and AJ felt like giving him two fingers, but decided she'd poked the bear enough already. Cass didn't hold back and showed him the middle finger.

"You've been over here too long, Cass. You're becoming quite American with your sign language."

"That's for him, not you, Stubby," Cass yelled out as they idled away. "Bye, love."

Stubby waved back with his free hand.

Once they were heading down the channel, AJ ducked down into the starboard cabin with the latest book in hand. Sitting at the little desk, she set out the last four books in the sequence, placing *Blind Man's Bluff* first. Checking her notebook, AJ searched for all the number codes for book 19 or above, and solved the cipher using the books in the new order. After twenty minutes, having double checked everything, she went back up top.

They were clear of Pilot House canal, but Cass was still idling along, waiting for a destination. "Did it make sense?" she asked eagerly.

"Spiegel-lathe we already had," AJ began. "The next one is Duane-hall-stern. We guessed Bibb-wheelhouse, and the last one is Spiegel-port-engine."

"Bloody hell," Cass muttered. "The hallway in the middle of the *Duane* is a bugger to get to, and there's only one way in and out." She turned to AJ. "And no way are we set up to reach the engines on the *Spiegel*. That's a full-blown decompression tech dive. It's dangerous at the best of times."

AJ nodded her agreement, but her mind was whirring. What would her friend Nora do? She quickly decided the young Norwegian's actions were a poor gauge and asked herself what Reg would do. Her mentor, island father, and trusted friend.

"Head to the *Duane*," she told Cass. "Let's get that done first, then we'll worry about the *Spiegel*."

"You're not going back in the *Spiegel*," Cass retorted, as she brought up the USCGC *Duane* on the chart plotter.

"Let's worry about one thing at a time," AJ replied. "That's good news if Rosie was on the blower with Poppers, right?" she added, changing the subject.

Cass frowned. "But Stubby's right. Those two joke and mess with each other all the time, but I've never known them have a row. If it was Rosie on the phone, at least we know he was still around yesterday. But, for the life of me, I can't figure out how my husband, as dopey as he is, could end up pinching gemstones from local mobsters. None of this makes sense."

AJ put her hand on her friend's shoulder and gave her a gentle squeeze. "After the *Duane*, maybe we should speak with Poppers again."

Cass nodded and eased into the throttles, aiming the bow for the wreck of the *Duane*.

22

FRIDAY

The wind had steadily picked up throughout the afternoon, kicking up a chop and three-to-four-foot waves. A sport fishing boat was moving off the bow mooring ball when they arrived, leaving them alone at the wreck.

Cass carefully eased up to the second mooring ball while AJ used a boathook to grab the line. The wave action caused the bow to dramatically rise and fall, and it took a few attempts before she snagged the hefty rope and tied them in.

Cass cut the engines and the Glacier Bay quickly drifted backwards until the mooring line went taut. The mooring ball had been half-submerged when they arrived. Now, with the mass of the boat trying to wrench the line from the wreck below, the top of the ball was barely above water.

"Current's still kicking," AJ commented as she carefully made her way along the starboard side to the cockpit.

"I don't know about this, AJ. Maybe we should try again tomorrow. These conditions are pretty bad."

AJ was already sitting on the small jump seat behind the pilot-house, pulling her wetsuit over her legs. The rocking and rolling of the boat making her wish she'd done this before they'd hit the deeper and rougher water. At least the catamaran was more stable in the conditions than a V-hull would be.

"I can hide from the current on the *Duane*, but let's run a tag and wreck line again."

Cass held on to the hardtop frame for balance and looked at the ocean, then back at her friend. "What about the bulls?"

AJ stood, and with the balance gained from years on the constantly moving decks of boats, pulled her wetsuit over her shoulders and zipped the back.

"We'll see. Who knows how long they fished. Maybe they didn't chum."

The deep wrecks were open to fishing, and the artificial reefs attracted abundant life from microorganisms up to the large predators. Bull sharks were common on the *Duane*, along with Goliath groupers. The fishermen weren't trying to catch either, but were competing for the same victims, such as jacks, king mackerel, cobia, and bonito.

It was common to chum the water, attracting the fish they were hunting, but the sharks would soon show up and steal the catch from the line. That was the fishermen's cue to move on, leaving a bunch of amped-up sharks behind.

Cass set up the wreck line from bow to stern and threw a buoy off the back as a tag line. "If it's too busy down there, come straight back up and we'll wait awhile until things calm down."

AJ staggered to her feet under the weight of the double tank setup, and Cass let her lean on her shoulder as they made their way to the stern. "Will do," AJ said, to appease her friend, but coming back without the third cylinder wasn't her dive plan. She took a stride off the swim step and held the front tank down with a hand, quickly grabbing the tag line before the waves and current pulled her away.

Dive map courtesy of Reef Smart Dive Guides

On both the *Duane* and the *Spiegel Grove*, the stars and stripes flew proudly from poles, the *Duane's* just forward of the midship descent line. As AJ arrived at the wreck, clinging gamely to the line, she noticed two things. Firstly, the flag was pulled dead straight with barely a flutter, supporting what she already knew about the current. The second was how clean the flag appeared, which meant Lew Bellows had changed it recently. A long-time diver and local resident, Lew worked in the office at Rainbow Reef Dive Center, and many years ago had taken it upon himself to purchase and maintain the flags on both wrecks.

Visibility wasn't bad, but once again the amount of particulate being stirred up made everything hazy. AJ pushed herself from the line, heading for cover on the starboard side of the wreck. Although the *Duane* was exactly the same as the *Bibb*, the two wrecks were night and day different to dive. Being upright, the *Duane's* main deck was at 90 feet and had doors removed along the structure, creating easy swim-throughs with plenty of light. Advanced divers could make safe penetration, and weaving back and forth through the cabins was a common dive plan. The lower deck was entirely different, and not intended to be accessed.

AJ followed the main deck along in the lee of the wreck, looking for a particular doorway. From the deep green haze to her left, she sensed movement and turned to look. Below her, nestled against the hull, were several large schools of jacks and schoolmasters, saving their energy from the current. But it wasn't the presence of the smaller fish she'd felt. She made a slow roll, checking all around. Silhouetted against the sunlit surface far above, the familiar profile of a bull shark swam away into the murky darkness beyond her view.

Bulls were fine; until they weren't. One of the top three shark species in terms of aggression and unprovoked attacks, the bulls had a reputation for being dangerous. They rarely attacked divers as sharks disregard the noisy, bubble-making creatures as a food source. But chum in the water and multiple sharks becoming competitive over a potential meal can lead to unprovoked 'taste tests'. The shark would usually leave after finding a mouthful of neoprene and nylon isn't what they'd hoped for, but that didn't help the stricken diver with a chunk of flesh missing.

Falling coconuts killed more people than shark attacks, but that provided little comfort when facing a handful of ten-foot-long toothy predators. However, AJ did make a point of avoiding walking under palm trees whenever possible.

She found her doorway, with another on the opposite side of the structure, allowing light in from both sides. She turned on her torch and played the light around the darkened rearward end of the room, scattering a school of grunts. Portions of the floor had rotted away, and small openings allowed access to the lower deck between the metal joists.

She eased inside and dropped carefully through the opening, squeezing past a frame in the lower room to a doorway on her right. AJ shone her light along the hallway which ran down the centre of the ship. Without her torch, the bowels of the wreck would be pitch black.

Unclipping her reel from a D-clip on her BCD, she sat her torch on the L-shaped bracket and wrapped two silicone bands around it. She'd now be holding her reel and torch together in one hand. Releasing the lock, she pulled a length of line from the reel and relocked the spool so she couldn't inadvertently unravel a mess of twine.

Reaching behind, AJ secured the line to the frame, then wrapped it several times around another piece of metal for extra security.

Slipping into the hallway, she turned towards the stern, unlocked the spool, and finned gently along, paying out the reel with one finger maintaining tension on the line. Covered in a bed of fine silt and small pieces of debris, the floor was waiting to be kicked into a blinding cloud, masking her exit, and flecks of rust rained down in slow motion as her bubbles dislodged them from the ceiling.

Rosie's note had read 'Duane hall stern', which seemed incredibly vague now she was in the hallway itself. AJ had made this dive before, but it was many years ago and she couldn't remember exactly what lay ahead.

She poked her head into the first door on her left, and shone the torch beam inside. The moment her light hit the entry, she saw the reflection of an eye, just before a deep guttural sound reached her.

AJ froze and stayed still, moving the light back to the hallway. She began to rise and realised she'd gulped in a big breath, which she was now holding. That was okay, she decided; the Goliath grouper could leave below her if it cared to. The sound had been the grouper's 'bark', letting the intruder know it was displeased with her presence. AJ hadn't got a look, but it was likely the fish weighed well over 400 lbs and, while it was unlikely to attack her, it could very well cause some damage if it decided to barge her out of the way.

Staying close to the ceiling of the passageway, she moved forward, and had almost cleared the doorway when water movement bowled her into the wall. Looking back between her legs, her torch beam illuminated a cloud of silt with a tail disappearing through the haze. Her reel line wrenched for a moment, pulling her backwards before going slack again. AJ quickly wound the spool and breathed a sigh of relief when it went tight.

The grouper had dragged the line, but hadn't broken it. It would take a while for the cloud to settle inside the narrow passageway, so she'd be relying on her reel to find the exit. Returning her attention towards the stern, AJ continued down the passageway to a doorway in a bulkhead where the hall came to an end.

Peering through the opening, AJ's torch lit up a large sheet metal box filling the right side of the room. She had no idea exactly what it was, but it looked like a duct of some description. Moving to her left she crossed the room to the next bulkhead door, looking around as she went. Nothing struck her as a great place to hide a cylinder.

Checking her Teric, she was at 115 feet, and for the first time wondered if Rosie had meant another hallway. There were passage-ways above her and below, but the one she was in was the first that come to mind from the clue. It was accessible, albeit tricky, and ran down the centre of the ship. She tried to dispel the doubt, and poked her head through the doorway.

To her left was what looked to be a square table, in an alcove-like room, and ahead another bulkhead door with steps to the side leading to the deck above. A faint hint of light leaked through the opening in the ceiling. AJ shone the beam to her right where a larger, rectangular table extended towards the port-side hull.

Locking the reel, she dropped it over the rim of the doorway, confident she could feel her way back if the room became silted out. She was sure this had to be where Rosie meant. The tabletop was covered in a layer of crud which appeared undisturbed, so she tilted herself head down to peer underneath. Careful not to kick the ceiling with her fins, AJ played her torch beam around the beefy pedestal legs securing the table to the floor.

Beside the farthest leg, the thick layer of silt and debris had a slight furrow in the otherwise smooth, carpet-like surface. She moved around the table and using breath control, she lowered herself down to look. Behind the leg, something amongst the muted brown and grey tones lit up red. Her torch returned the full light spectrum to anything it illuminated, picking out the little cylinder, tucked out of sight of anyone passing through the room.

Slipping the cylinder into her BCD pocket, AJ carefully made her way back to the entrance and picked up her reel. Leaving through the doorway, she crossed the next room, winding her reel in as she went. As she peeked through the next bulkhead, the path ahead seemed like she was staring into a thick broth. The silt cloud had partially settled, but her torch beam still only penetrated a few feet once she'd reached the Goliath's room. It was akin to head-lights in thick fog. She continued winding her reel, blindly moving down the passageway, hoping Mr Grouper wasn't blocking the way.

Her line began pulling her to the right, and pretty soon she bumped into the edge of a door opening. Looking up, she could see a faint light from her exit, a deck above. The dive had gone quickly, but she still had the toughest, deepest, and most dangerous dive left on the *Spiegel Grove*. Three deep dives on the same day was a bad idea, especially leaving the deepest one until last. The faster she reached the boat, the longer she could spend on the surface, letting her body get rid of the excess nitrogen in her system.

AJ unhooked the reel from her two anchor points and clipped it back to her BCD. Using her fingertips on the surrounding metal, she pulled herself up through the opening and headed for the door-way. Outside, the water was still a deep murky green with particulate ripping past in the current. She finned forward in the lee of the structure until the wheelhouse and CIC room towered above her. Taking shelter behind them, she hid from the current, and with two strong fin kicks, she made the mooring line.

AJ felt like the flag which whipped in the water column before her, her body pulled out straight from the line. Hand over hand, once again she carefully ascended, her mask jittering on her face. At

40 feet, she sensed movement and caught a ghostly image at the far reaches of visibility towards the bow. Too quickly to be the same shark, she saw one coming closer from the stern.

Bull sharks were large creatures with broad, thick bodies and a menacing mouthful of sharp teeth. They look every bit like the apex predator they are. AJ moved up the line until her Teric began counting down her safety stop when she passed 20 feet. Her computer was suggesting a five-minute stop.

She counted three bulls now, all staying below her, but making eccentric circles and clearly interested in the creature on the line. Time seemed to find the slowest gear in its arsenal and crept along, while the sharks continued to show interest. One swept in closer, a fishing hook in the corner of its mouth and line trailing the length of its sleek body. The shark's pectoral fins were pointing more down than outwards, and its mouth opened and closed; two clear signs of aggression. When it came closer than AJ cared to estimate, the shark quickly turned away, another threatening gesture and warning sign for her to back off.

AJ looked at her computer. She was halfway through the suggested five-minute safety stop. That was enough, she decided. Having not gone into deco, the safety stop was precautionary and, in this case, the least dangerous of the threats. Releasing the line, AJ let the current take her towards the boat she couldn't see.

Relying on the current pulling the Glacier Bay on the mooring line in the same direction it would drag her, AJ willed the twin hulls to appear. Steadily rising, her safety stop continued counting down as AJ drifted and watched all around for sharks.

The one with the hook appeared from below, and was moving quickly towards her. She was now in open water, silhouetted by the surface light and praying she didn't look like food. It kept coming so AJ unclipped her spare tank from the cummerbund of her BCD, letting the aluminium 80 cu ft cylinder swing down below her. With both hands on the tank, she readied to jab the tank at the bull shark if it lunged.

Everything was a blur as the shark moved far more rapidly than she could react to. It diverted and curved around her, bumping her with the side of its bulbous head before disappearing into the depths. AJ looked up and saw the hulls above her and the steps hung down at the stern. She couldn't get aboard *Reel-Lee Hooked* fast enough. Lying on the deck, with her spare tank laid awkwardly to one side, she took a few deep breaths.

"What the bloody hell happened, love? Are you alright?" Cass asked, urgently checking her for injuries.

AJ held up an okay sign. "I'm going to rest up for a bit, but here," she said, unzipping her BCD pocket, "have another ruby."

23

FRIDAY

AJ took her time wriggling out of her gear and wetsuit as the Glacier Bay rolled and bucked in the waves. Wrapped in a towel, she joined Cass in the pilothouse, where this time Cass had managed to open the cylinder herself. The two women sat quietly for several minutes, admiring the third deep-red stone they'd brought up from the deep.

"What do you think Johnny Sore Balls and his boss will do if we hand them back their rubies?" Cass wondered aloud.

"Well, first of all, I doubt they really belong to them," AJ replied. "But it's a good point. Would they be happy to move on and forget about us, or are we loose ends that need taking care of?"

Cass tipped her head back and groaned. "We don't even know how to get hold of them."

AJ laughed. "Show up in Key Largo and I think they'll find us. They seem good at doing that."

"True," Cass agreed and tapped the table with her finger. "You know, of all the things that puzzle me about this mess, and believe me, it all does, but if Rosie has his phone and was talking to Poppers, why the bloody hell can't he call his wife?"

AJ thought about the question for a moment. It was a good

point, and obviously they had no way of knowing the real answer, but her friend was looking for a theory. Well, to be more accurate, she was looking for comfort from a theory. Anything that would make her feel better about her husband's involvement in the strange situation. A sign that he had her wellbeing in mind.

"To protect you is my guess."

Cass scoffed. "I don't feel very protected."

"I didn't say it was working, but I think that's his motivation."

Cass's mobile buzzed before she could reply, and she looked at the text.

"I called June at Mar Bar while you were down there and I was up here, fretting about you being down there. Asked her to let me know if Poppers showed up. She says he just walked in and ordered food to go."

AJ jumped up and started towards the bow, glancing at her watch as she went. "I have to be up a while before I can dive the *Spiegel*, so let's go ask Poppers if he spoke to Rosie."

Cass moved to the helm. "Bloody good plan. Except for the *Spiegel* part. You're not going in the engine room, AJ. I can't let you do that."

AJ yelled back from the bow as she waited to untie them. "I can tell you how JSB will react if we hand him three of his four gems, Cass. Don't worry, I have a plan."

Cass started the engines, and let them idle for a few moments. "I hope your plan includes mixed gas and a deco profile."

"Put some slack in the line and stop fussing," AJ shouted back with a grin.

Cass shook her head, but dropped the boat in gear and moved forward, taking the strain from the mooring line.

The twin hulls of the Glacier Bay rode the waves smoothly, and the following seas allowed Cass to run harder than the trip out. But AJ noted their run back out to the *Spiegel Grove* would be a long and bumpy ride.

They were quiet for a while, and AJ was lost in her thoughts of Rosie and the other players in the drama she hadn't envisioned when she'd left Grand Cayman. It seemed like his mates were hiding something, and she couldn't decide if Officer Reid was a conscientious copper, or on the mobster's payroll. Johnny Sore Balls was someone she'd rather avoid entirely, of that she was certain. If they gathered all four of the cylinders, they needed to figure out a way to leave them somewhere and let him know. But the letting him know part might be tricky without also letting him find them.

Realising she hadn't checked her mobile since they left the fuel dock, AJ fished it out of the pocket of her rucksack.

"Oh bugger!"

"What's the matter?" Cass asked.

"We forgot about Em!"

"Oh shit, we did."

AJ quickly dialled her number. "She left a text a bit ago, said she was heading to the house."

The call rang twice, then went to voicemail. "Hi Em, sorry I missed your text. We're on our way to Tavernier. If you haven't already, don't go by the house. Meet us at Mar Bar. But call me back."

"That's good. She shouldn't go by the house," Cass said, drumming her fingers on the wheel. "I'd hate for her to run into that Neanderthal again."

AJ looked at the aluminium cylinder on the dash, rolling back and forth as the boat surfed the waves towards shore. "Think about what we're doing here, Cass. It's all getting a bit mental, isn't it? These are dangerous blokes we're messing with. What if Emily did go to the house? What if she's not answering because he grabbed her?"

Cass looked at AJ, her face full of concern, in stark contrast to her auburn hair blowing freely in the wind. "Try her phone again."

"That's not the point."

Cass turned back to the ocean ahead, avoiding AJ's stare. "What choice do we have?"

"The bloody police, Cass. Let them do their job."

"Do you trust that Reid bloke?" Cass snapped back.

"I wasn't planning on calling him. We call the sheriff's office and ask for a detective."

Cass finally looked AJ's way once more, with tears running down her cheeks. "And say what? My stupid husband happened across a bunch of giant rubies that are most probably stolen, then hid them in shipwrecks from these mobsters who've threatened us? First thing they'll tell us is to come by the station with the gems and as soon as our call is put in the system, Officer bloody Reid, or whoever else is on the take, tells Johnny Sore Balls. We'll never make it to the sheriff's office."

"So let's not call. We'll go straight there."

"Like they're not watching the truck?" Cass replied, wiping her face. "Or if your theory is right, they have a tracker on the damned thing."

AJ was about to respond, but stopped as a thought occurred to her. "Bugger. If I'm right, and that's how they followed Em this morning, then we just invited her to meet us, with that bastard tracking right behind her."

AJ dialled Emily's mobile again. This time it rang six or seven times before Em's cheery greeting proceeded the beep. "Really important you call me as soon as you get this, Em."

Cass reached over and pulled AJ into an embrace. "I'm sorry, love. For all of this. We've managed to ruin your trip, but you're still going above and beyond to help, and here's me raising my voice."

AJ hugged her back. "We're in this together, and we'll see it through together."

Cass nodded. "We'll go to the police if Poppers can't help us, alright?"

"Or if we can't find Em when we get there," AJ added.

"Agreed," Cass confirmed, staying to the outside of Tavernier Key.

AJ took the cylinder and went below, unscrewing the desk stool and adding the third stone to their collection. When she came back up, Cass had reduced speed to just above idle in the no-wake zone of Tavernier Creek.

"How are we going to do this?" AJ asked. "Bit risky going back to the truck."

"I planned to pull right up to Mar Bar. With a bit of luck, there'll be a mooring spot out front. If JSB shows up, we can make a quick getaway and it'll be tough for him to make a scene with customers around."

"I can keep an eye out for Em while you talk to Poppers," AJ suggested.

Cass turned to port into the last side canal before the bridge. On their right was the tow yard, Captain Slate's, and a handful more businesses before they came to the little outdoor restaurant. AJ checked the bridge for any strangers paying them too much attention, but a lone cyclist, focused on the path, was all she saw. There was indeed an open spot available to side-tie to in front of Mar Bar, so AJ handled the lines while Cass turned *Reel-Lee Hooked* around, ready to leave, and nestled her fenders against the concrete sea wall.

"Stern secure," AJ called out once she'd lashed the second line to a cleat on the dock, and Cass shut the engines down.

They quickly stepped from the gunwale to the opening in the railing along the dock and stood in the patio area of the restaurant. June waved from behind the bar and Cass went over, looking around for Poppers.

"He just went to use the little boys' room," June said, and nodded to a seat at the end of the bar. It was early for the evening crowd, but a couple of tables were taken and half the bar stools were occupied by local fishermen types. Several recognised Cass and took a break from their conversations to acknowledge her.

AJ walked through the passageway to the front of the shops and looked for Cass's Volkswagen. Walking back and forth, she couldn't see it parked anywhere. Returning to the covered walkthrough, she saw a man up ahead, ambling away from her, fixing the zipper on his trousers. He stopped short of the restaurant and quickly turned, picking up his pace for a hasty retreat. AJ stepped to one side and looked in the window of a small shop selling beachwear, sandals and all the accessories you'd expect in the Keys.

Two steps from AJ, Poppers looked back over his shoulder to see if Cass was following. She wasn't, but when he turned to the front, he met AJ's swinging arm as she clothes-lined him, sending the portly man sprawling to the floor.

"Cass!" AJ yelled as she dropped a knee to his chest, knocking the wind out of him.

Cass came running as Poppers gasped for breath and writhed around on the floor, one hand on his throat, one on his chest.

"Hello, mate," Cass greeted him. "You remember meeting AJ, don't you?"

24

FRIDAY

A woman stepped from one of the shops into the walkway, her mobile in hand.

"What's going on out here?" she asked, thumb poised over the dial icon.

Cass and AJ helped Poppers to his feet and walked him slowly towards a bench.

"Silly sod tripped over, but he's fine," Cass answered with a smile. "He's a friend of ours. He'll be fine, we'll make sure."

The woman didn't appear completely convinced, but Poppers didn't say anything, so she went back inside her shop. He didn't speak, because he couldn't. An intense diet of beer and fried food had steadily taken its toll on the fisherman, and as he was nearing 60 years old, his recovery time was not what it used to be. Being assaulted twice in the same week was also a contributing factor.

"Shit," he finally spluttered. "Could have... just said... you wanted... to talk."

Cass patted him on the shoulder. "You were running away from me, you old goat. Don't give me that load of bollocks. It's time you told me what the hell's going on."

"You don't want any part of this, Cass, believe me," he said, still wheezing, but managing to string sentences together. "I sure don't."

Cass sat down, but AJ remained standing, keeping an eye on the parking area outside the walkway.

"I'd love to stay out of it, but I can't, can I? My stupid husband is neck deep, and now we've got some mob blokes chasing us. So start talking, Poppers. I need to know where Rosie is and who these men are."

The man shook his head, looking forlorn with his black eye, unshaven face and ruffled hair. "They're not fooling around, Cass. This is Orn Danitess we're talking about."

"Who's that when he's at home?"

"You haven't heard of Danitess?" Poppers asked incredulously.

Cass looked at AJ and they both shrugged their shoulders.

"When you hear about drugs, guns, prostitution, or anything else illegal involving big money in Miami, he's it."

"No shit?"

"No shit, Cass. DEA seizes ten million dollars' worth of coke, and the guy laughs at them. Probably set it up himself to give the Governor something to crow about."

"They can't catch this guy?" AJ asked. "If everyone knows who he is, surely they could get him for something, even if it's tax evasion."

Poppers laughed, which caused him to cough and splutter again. "You're kidding, right? He's got all kinds of legit businesses, from resorts to nightclubs, office towers, golf clubs, you name it. Plus, he's the biggest contributor to the Governor. No way does a politician want to see his cash cow in jail. That's why Danitess throws the Governor a bone now and then. Coke bust here, rival gang arrest there."

"Okay, so this bloke is a nasty fella, but what does any of this have to do with my husband? He doesn't mix with that crowd."

"He has something of theirs," Poppers whispered.

"I know that. But why does he have something of theirs?" Cass snapped back, not in a whisper.

A couple entered the wide passageway and took their time looking in the shop windows as they headed for Mar Bar. Poppers waited until they were gone before replying.

"You know Rosie. If someone's gonna leave something valuable lying around, he doesn't mind picking it up."

"We know they're after the gemstones, Poppers, so stop buggering about and tell us how Rosie got hold of them, and where the bloody hell he is."

"I don't know where he is, Cass, I swear." He looked around again to make sure no one could hear him. "Do you know what those gems are?"

"They're rubies."

Poppers shook his head. "No, they're not."

Cass growled in frustration. "I don't really give a toss what they are. I want to find Rosie, and I know you spoke with him yesterday."

Poppers' eyes got wider. "I don't know where he is."

"Why were the two of you arguing?"

"We didn't. I haven't spoken to him."

Cass grabbed the man's tatty shirt. "We know he punched you on Wednesday night just so he could get nicked and hide in jail. We also know you were arguing with him over the phone yesterday, 'cos Stubby overheard you."

AJ tried not to grin. It was all speculation and hearsay, but Cass was selling it well. She was a dog with a bone now.

"He didn't hear right! That old man has had his head in too many bilges. He wouldn't know Cindy Crawford from Marge Simpson."

It seemed like a strange set of references to AJ, but the look on his face told her he was still lying. He'd stay a poor man if he played poker.

Cass shook him by the shirt. "You're so full of it, your eyes turned brown."

"My eyes are brown," Poppers replied feebly.

"One of them's black and blue, and I'm about to make them

match," Cass spat back, raising her hand as though she'd slap him.

"Maybe Phil's seen him," Poppers blurted, holding up a hand to defend himself.

AJ spun around at the sound of a vehicle's tyres crunching on the crushed limestone parking out front. It was a white SUV with a Cadillac emblem on the grill.

"Cass! We gotta go!"

"Come on," Cass shouted at Poppers, dragging his shirt to pull him up.

The man knocked her arm away. "You two go. I'll just slow you up."

Cass paused. "That's Danitess's thug! You don't want to stay here."

"I'll be fine," Poppers said, and waved her away.

The driver's door to the SUV swung open and Cass took off after AJ, sprinting for the boat. AJ daren't look back as she dodged between tables and leapt from the dock to the gunwale, never touching a step.

"What's going on?" June called out, as she looked up from wiping a table.

"Stop them!" AJ yelled back, freeing the stern line.

Cass was already at the helm and starting the twin outboards as AJ pushed the stern away from the dock before running nimbly down the side to the bow. She glanced up and saw Johnny Sore Balls jamming into the table as June dragged it in front of the opening in the wooden rail. Unhooking the line from the cleat, AJ tossed it aboard and pushed her foot against the dock with all her might. The bow moved away from the concrete agonisingly slowly and a shadow fell over her. Looking up, she saw the large form of JSB with a foot on the railing, getting ready to leap aboard.

Grabbing the boathook, AJ pointed the aluminium rod in his direction. The man barely halted his forward momentum, but managed to keep his balance and dropped back to the patio side, glaring at AJ.

Cass piloted them away from the dock and made sure she

stayed well clear of the shoreline, pushing a little harder than the no-wake rule.

"Poppers wouldn't come with you?" AJ asked, after re-stowing the boathook and joining Cass at the helm.

"I don't think he would have made it in time," Cass replied, turning right on Tavernier Creek.

"Probably true, but he didn't seem keen to help much."

Cass thought for a moment. "If this lot are so dangerous, why would he choose to stay?"

"And why would he lie through his teeth?"

Cass looked over and frowned. "He was more interested in scaring us off. I noticed that."

"It worked. I'm scared to death."

"Me too," Cass agreed. She bit her lip and looked back over her shoulder. "Still, I hope your mate doesn't hurt old Poppers."

"Not my bloody mate," AJ huffed, taking a few deep breaths to calm her nerves.

"Hey," Cass blurted. "Is that the bloke you saw on the bridge earlier?"

AJ swung around. "Where?"

"On the corner, by Buckley's. He just started walking away."

AJ saw the back of a man with buzzed hair, wearing casual trousers and a lightweight jacket. "Could be," she said. "I didn't get a good look either time."

"Who wears a jacket on a day like this?" Cass muttered.

They both turned back to face the channel and Cass slowed down to the proper speed. "Do you think this Danitess guy has a boat down here in the Keys?" she wondered aloud.

AJ stared ahead at the vast ocean before them. If there wasn't a tracking device on the boat, then the Atlantic was a great place to hide. There were far too many vessels along the coastline to pick them out on radar. On the flip side, if they were found, the *Reel-Lee Hooked* and all who sailed upon her could vanish and never be seen again.

She joined Cass in checking behind them once more as they left the channel. The mangrove and concrete world of the Florida Keys wasn't a bad place to hide, either. She hoped that's exactly what Rosie was successfully doing. Maybe they should slip into a small marina or find a pier, take an Uber and stay in Marathon for a few days. Go to the police station there. Or just take the *Reel-Lee Hooked* south.

They had options. The problem was they were all lousy, and when the prey doesn't know where the hunter could be, every shadow is a threat.

"If he doesn't own a boat here, he could certainly hire one," she finally said in reply.

They rode in silence for a few moments, Cass easing into the throttles and pointing the Glacier Bay towards the outside of Tavernier Key once more.

"We still haven't heard back from Em," AJ said, checking her mobile.

"She wasn't at Mar Bar, so I guess that's good. Maybe's she is at the house?"

"If she's got any sense, she's on her way to Miami International and boarding the next plane home," AJ joked.

Cass managed a smile. "She's friends with us, so I'm not sure how much good sense she has."

AJ laughed, but her mind had wandered elsewhere. "Didn't JSB say something earlier today about the rubies?"

"What do you mean?" Cass replied, looking at the chart plotter.

"He told us we didn't know what we had, and Poppers just did the same thing. He said they're not rubies."

Cass looked up. "They're fakes?"

AJ shrugged her shoulders. "Can't imagine this Miami mob bloke would be running around trying to recover fake rubies."

"Well, I'm not big on jewellery, but best I know, rubies are red," Cass said, turning her attention back to the GPS. "Now, where are we going?"

They looked at each other. They both felt tired, worn down, and terrified for themselves, as well as for Rosie.

Cass finally spoke. "Maybe we should go to the coppers and get them involved."

AJ nodded. "That's my vote, but I don't know how we're going to walk into the station now. We have no choice but to call."

"Yeah, I hate to do it, but I think it's time to call the law. Maybe we contact the Marine Police unit? Meet them on the water."

AJ thought for another moment before typing in the internet search bar on her mobile. 'Ruby, theft, news.' Scrolling through the results, the main hits were about Dorothy's ruby red slippers being discovered. Several articles referred to a hoax regarding a massive uncut ruby supposedly worth $29 million. She typed in 'gemstones like ruby' and clicked on the first result, which claimed to contain a 'List of All Red Coloured Gemstones'. Everything appeared to be of lesser value than an actual ruby, and many of them were cheap.

"Are you getting the number for the sheriff's office?" Cass asked.

"I will in just a minute."

AJ typed 'more valuable than ruby'. All the hits were comparing the 'big three', emeralds, diamonds, and rubies. She tried a few more searches, switching the wording and found articles on red beryls and varieties of garnets and rubies. The values were all over the scale, with flawless rubies being the most expensive.

She was about to give up and find a number for the sheriff's station when on a whim she searched for 'the rarest gemstones in the world'. The list was full of precious stones she'd never heard of, interspersed with rare colours of diamonds and sapphires. Most had odd names, all ending in '-ite'. Near the bottom of the list, which escalated in value as she scrolled down, AJ paused on a deep-red gemstone called painite.

"According to this article, painite is a very rare borate mineral first discovered in Myanmar by British mineralogist and gem dealer Arthur C.D. Pain, who misidentified it as a ruby. It was eventually proclaimed a new gemstone in the 1950s, and named after the man. Until the early 2000s, just a handful of stones had been found, and only two had been cut into faceted gemstones.

Over a thousand are now in circulation, but it is still one of the world's rarest and most sought-after gems. The stones are worth between $50,000 and $60,000 per carat."

"Bloody hell," Cass said and let out a whistle. "You think these are painite stones?"

AJ laughed. "I've no idea, but two people have tried to tell us they're not rubies, and I don't think they were suggesting the gems are worthless."

She typed 'painite theft' into the search bar.

"Bingo!"

"What?" Cass asked, leaning over to see the screen.

"Russian billionaire offers a $1 million reward for the return of the three painite gemstones known as the Three Eyes of Shiva. The stones were stolen from the workshop of a world-renowned cutter in South Africa, who wishes to keep his identity hidden."

"I bet he does," Cass quipped.

"The painite crystals had recently been faceted into emerald cut finished stones, ready to be set into a necklace. Sixty-one-year-old Valery Barinov, who resides in New York, was planning to give the necklace to his fiancée, twenty-nine-year-old former model Ivanka Mukhin, as a wedding gift."

"When did this happen?" Cass asked, having forgotten about plotting their course.

"Three weeks ago."

Cass looked at AJ thoughtfully. "But hang on a minute, we've already found three of these things. If they are these painite eyes of who's your father, then what's in the fourth location?"

AJ shrugged her shoulders. "Must be something good as it's in the hardest place to get to."

They both jumped when AJ's phone rang, playing 'Girls Just Want To Have Fun', her ringtone she'd assigned to Emily Durand.

"Em, we've been worried sick. Where are you?" AJ said, answering the call.

"This must be the blondie with the tattoos," an unexpected yet familiar voice responded.

25

FRIDAY

AJ waved at Cass, signalling her to stop the boat. A thousand thoughts rushed through her head, but none of them returned a circumstance in which Johnny Sore Balls would have Emily's mobile without also having their friend.

"Let me speak to Emily," she demanded, and heard laughter on the other end of the line.

"You watch too much TV. That's not how this works."

"What do you want?"

"You know what I want, and now you'll either bring it to me, or say goodbye to your cute little limey friend."

AJ tried to think clearly, but everything that had happened since they'd arrived was crashing down around her. Sensing this man was dangerous was one thing, but hearing him threaten Emily's life was completely different. As the *Reel-Lee Hooked* slowed to idle, Cass was staring at her with a deeply furrowed brow.

"We have three gems, and we'll get the fourth in about an hour," AJ said, unable to come up with any other path than to play it his way. "Where should we meet you?"

"Why an hour to get it?" he asked.

"Because all four were hidden in different places."

What was the point of lying anymore? Their only choice was to trade Em for the stones, but talking aloud about four gems made her realise the article had mentioned only three. What was in the final cylinder? Maybe it was the necklace itself. Or was it even a cylinder?

"Why did you hide them?" he asked, pointedly.

"We didn't. We were able to figure out where they were."

"'Cos Lee told you, right?"

Technically, Rosie had told them, but not verbally. AJ had already said enough, and they were wasting time.

"No, he didn't. But we're burning daylight and this is going to be difficult enough, so unless you want to chitchat all evening, I need to get on with it. Where are we meeting?"

"Keep your phone close. If I call, you'd better answer. You have an hour."

The line went dead, and right away, AJ wished she had told him more time. It would take them thirty minutes or more to get to the *Spiegel* and the same again or more for the dive. If she could find whatever was hidden there. The engine room of the old ship was full of machinery and places to squirrel a hundred little packages away without being seen.

"Cass, head for the *Spiegel* as fast as you can. I'll explain on the way."

"You're not making that dive, AJ. I can't let you."

"If we want to see Emily again, I have to make that dive, Cass. Now, are you driving your boat there, or am I?"

Cass reluctantly pushed the throttles forward, aiming south while she brought up the *Spiegel Grove* on her chart plotter. "You'd better tell me what he said."

The journey out to the wreck was rough going. Cass stayed over shallower water while they headed north, but the waves were still a choppy three feet and hitting them on the starboard bow. AJ went over the phone conversation several times, unable to answer most of Cass's questions. Once they turned for deeper water and took the building seas head on, AJ went aft to prepare her gear.

She would use the same set-up as the previous two dives, but also take a third tank with her, and have Cass hang a fourth from the boat in case she required an extended decompression stop. The third tank would be cumbersome to haul down, but she'd stage it at her entry point into the wreck, similar to how climbers on Everest place bottles for the descent, except in reverse.

Breathing even the nitrox gas at depth for too long saturated the body with nitrogen. Once a diver reached that point, the only solution was to ascend to a shallower depth until their body could dissipate enough of the molecules from its tissues through the bloodstream. A saturated diver could not return to the surface and atmospheric pressure without risking decompression sickness, or DCS, a condition that varied from uncomfortable to fatal.

One of the most dangerous situations a diver could put themselves in was going into deco, and not having enough breathing gas to stay down. Their choice was drowning, or DCS. That's why planned decompression dives were technical and advanced, requiring exotic gas mixes and long decompression stops using multiple tanks. The engine rooms of the *Spiegel*, buried deep in the recesses of the ship's hull, were usually only attempted as decompression dives. AJ would be attempting a rapid touch-and-go approach, which relied on speed. The staged tanks could save her life if she became delayed at any point.

"Hey!" Cass shouted back from the helm. "Look at this!"

AJ secured her gear and carefully made her way forward as the bow rose and fell over what now appeared to be four to five-foot swells. Cass pointed towards the open ocean ahead in the now dimming light, only an hour from sunset. As they rolled up a wave, AJ saw what Cass was indicating. A boat they both recognised.

"Is that *Hear No Evil*, your friend Phil's boat?"

"Looks like it to me," Cass replied. "And it's tied on the wreck."

AJ was getting tired of feeling puzzled and confused at every turn. Maybe the guy was out here fishing, but they hadn't seen any other boats in a while, with the seas and failing light driving them home. His 23-foot centre console was a hardy little boat, but no fun in these swells. Cass tried hailing Phil on the VHF, with no response.

"Might have a fish on," AJ suggested.

"Maybe," Cass replied, but she didn't sound convinced.

As they neared, it was clear no one was in the cockpit of the Mako.

"Is he a diver?" AJ asked.

Cass nodded. "He is, but not much these days. I can't remember the last time I heard he'd splashed in. He fishes seven days a week."

"You think he brought Rosie out here?" AJ blurted as the thought occurred to her.

"I'd say that's more likely," Cass agreed, and the lack of surprise in her voice suggested it had been her guess all along. "We'll wait for them to come up."

AJ looked at her watch. It was 7:10pm. Behind them, the sun was low over the Keys, lighting the distant clouds on both horizons in yellow and orange hues. Inside the wreck, it didn't matter whether it was day or night outside, but it would make a big difference finding her access point and making her way back. The ship was 520 feet long, and she hadn't been to one of the engine rooms in over ten years. She'd only made the dive once back then.

There were plenty of videos online and printed maps and guides, like Reef Smart's detailed waterproof cards AJ used all the time, but they only covered the upper decks, accessible by recreational divers. The bowels of the ship were sacred ground, a warren of secret tunnels and caves not for the faint of heart. The tech divers held their hard-earned info close to their chests, so maps or directions were not easily discovered.

"We can give them a few minutes, Cass, but then I'm going in. I don't want to start the dive after dark."

Phil's Mako was moored on the port-side crane number 4 mooring buoy, sternward of the number 6 ball they'd tied to the day before. Cass took the starboard crane, number 5 ball. The two large towers and the framework of the old cranes stretched across the beam of the ship, spanning the open well deck below and offering some protection from the current. The engines were housed below and forward of the cranes, under the well deck itself.

AJ patiently timed hooking the line, waiting for the bow to drop into a trough while Cass skilfully held the boat in place, into the oncoming waves. AJ threaded the boat's line through the loop on the mooring and let out more play than normal to lessen the violent tugs on the cleats from the heavy seas.

If conditions had been better, she'd have dropped from the stern straight down on the port side of the wreck to save time, but with the expected current, she'd be swept away before she laid eyes on the *USS Spiegel Grove*.

"You don't suppose anyone's on the Mako, passed out or something?" AJ asked once she was back in the pilothouse.

Cass looked at the *Hear No Evil* riding the swells, 100 feet off their stern. "What, like drunk or..." she trailed off as the options became clear.

"Got a line that long?" AJ asked, already stepping to the cockpit and grabbing her wetsuit.

Cass didn't answer but began searching the various lockers, cabinets and storage areas while AJ suited up. Tying the two ropes together she'd used as tag and wreck lines, Cass added a third she'd found, and fixed one end to a stern cleat. With the buoy on the tag line as the end marker, she tossed the line into the water and watched the waves and current pull the bright orange ball 20 feet short of the bow of the Mako, and 30 feet off the port side. They both stared at the line.

"I can make that," AJ said with more confidence than she felt inside.

"I don't know, AJ, these conditions are shit, and the currents are really strong."

They were both hanging on to the hardtop frame to support themselves as the waves rolled under the Glacier Bay. The seas were certainly a far cry from the conditions they'd experienced the day before.

"It's all south to north, which is normal for the *Spiegel*. All I have to do is swim west and the current will take me the rest of the way."

"What about coming back?" Cass asked.

AJ staggered to the stern and sat down on the transom to pull her fins on. "That might be a bit of a bugger. I'll take some help if you don't mind hauling me back."

"You'll have to make the line first."

"Yeah, that'll be the bugger part."

Without waiting for further debate, AJ dived off the starboard stern corner of the boat, and dolphin-kicked north-west, staying underwater for as long as she could. Which wasn't long. The swell pulled her up and as the water sank and formed a trough, AJ found herself on the surface. She sighted the Mako on the next rise, and swam with all her might.

Cass had intended for her to use the extended tag line until the buoy, and then swim across the last part, but AJ decided to give herself all the distance available to make up the offset, sensing the power of the ocean. She was right. Kicking with all her strength in the long dive fins, she missed the mooring ball, but just made it to the starboard side of the V-hull. The swells slapped against the side of the Mako as she made her way to the stern, but that was better than being dragged through the gap between the tag line and the boat where she'd be set adrift in the open ocean.

AJ grabbed at the swim step but her hand slipped across the wet fibreglass and for a moment she almost lost her hold on the boat. Fortunately, her fingers found the flimsy ladder hung from the swim step, which she clung to and gasped a few breaths. Climbing the narrow ladder as the seas bucked and kicked the lighter Mako was more treacherous than the swim, and she bashed against the outboard a few times before flopping over the transom on to the deck.

The older fishing boat was a simple centre console built for fishing. No cabin, just the helm station, and under-bench storage upfront. Instantly, she could see no one was aboard. An empty dive gear bag was lying in the cockpit, and straps hung free from a dual tank rack against the port gunwale.

AJ took off her fins and walked to the helm. A wallet sat next to a mobile phone on the dash at the base of the windscreen. She flipped the wallet open to reveal a Florida driver's licence behind a clear cover. Phillip Giles. She put the wallet back and tried the mobile phone. It was locked, but the home screen was a picture of the deaf man she'd met with his arm around a woman.

Putting the phone down, AJ looked for any other evidence or signs that Rosie may have been aboard. In turn, she raised the tops of all the bench seats, finding mainly fishing tackle and life vests. In front of the helm station, she lifted the last padded bench seat and found a tattered dive gear bag. Pulling the sticky zipper back, AJ found a technical, back-plate-style BCD along with fins, mask and a well-used wetsuit. 'Rosie' was written in faded white paint pen in the collar.

She glanced towards the land where the sun was between the distant clouds and the horizon. It would set in the next thirty minutes. AJ quickly made her way to the bow where the mooring line ran taut like a piano wire to the mooring ball, which was mostly submerged. The tag line looked to be farther away than she'd envisaged from the Glacier Bay, but if she used the Mako's mooring line to the ball, she might have a chance at swimming across the current.

Slipping her fins back on, she sat on the bow to the starboard side of the line. A dive would get her farther, but there was no way to stand in her fins with the boat rocking and rolling. With a firm push, she dropped into the ocean and swam towards the mooring ball. The line was tantalisingly close above her, but still out of reach, until a swell lifted her up and she was able to grab hold. Violently wrenched and thrown around, AJ managed to pull herself hand over hand along the line until she reached the big number 4 mooring buoy.

The orange ball on the tag line was barely visible, lost in the chop and waves, but she caught a glimpse of it 30 feet to her left. Aiming herself for the stern of the *Reel-Lee Hooked*, AJ began her manic swim against the current. It felt like she was going nowhere, but she dare not pause to look behind her. Keeping the Glacier Bay and Cass's worried figure in her sights, she pressed on, hoping her forward progress, combined with the pull of the ocean, would drag her across to the precious line.

In a full sprint, her heart rate soared and AJ knew she was operating in the anaerobic range, akin to the fuse burning down on a bomb. She could only maintain this intensity for a short time before she blew up and would be reduced to gasping and heaving for breath, unable to swim any farther.

She'd lost any sight of the orange buoy, and couldn't tell if she was any closer to the *Reel-Lee Hooked*, but she'd definitely been carried to her left. Her lungs were screaming and her strength sapping away. It felt like she'd been swimming for ten minutes, although she knew it could only have been a few. Around two, she guessed, as that was generally the limit of full anaerobic exercise.

All her energy was gone. As she flung her arm in what would be her last stroke, she wondered how far she'd drift before Cass could free the boat and search for her. Single handed, Cass wouldn't be able to release the tension on the mooring line with the engines and also free them. All she could do was cut the line, race back to the helm and hope she could get the Glacier Bay clear before being dragged into the number 4 ball and Phil's boat.

AJ's arm fell into the water, exhausted and powerless... but struck a familiar rope. With her last ounce of strength, she hung to the tag line and let Cass have the workout of her life, hauling AJ's limp, gasping body to the stern of the catamaran.

26

FRIDAY

Cass and AJ sat on the deck, slumped against the gunwales on opposite sides of the cockpit.

"That was daft," Cass wheezed.

"Told you it would be a bugger," AJ grinned, finally getting her breath back.

"No one over there, then?"

AJ shook her head. "Nope, and no sign of anyone except your mate, Phil. Only one gear bag. Looked like he'd taken two tanks, and the ladder was down. I suppose there could be two divers using a tank each, but they'd better be going to the machine shop and not the port engine." She paused and considered how to say the next part as delicately as possible. There was no good way. "No wreck, or tag line."

Cass nodded. "Silly sod, he should know better."

"If he was on his own, he'd have struggled to get tied in single handed."

"Ol' Phil's done that a few times on his own. He fishes the wrecks a good bit."

AJ hoped he was alone. He seemed like a nice bloke, but Rosie was a good friend, and unless the divers had gone in the moment before she and Cass arrived, they would be out of gas by now with a single tank each. It was far more likely Phil had surfaced alone and failed to grab *Hear No Evil* in the rough seas. She had almost missed getting hold of the boat, and she hadn't been in cumbersome dive gear. AJ knew Cass would have figured out the scenarios herself, so saying anything more was pointless. They would both silently pray Phil was solo, and drifting towards land on the open sea.

With very little sunlight left, AJ got into her BCD, and clipped her back-up tank to the front of her body. Cass busied herself stringing the wreck and tag line in place, then began rigging a regulator on the fourth tank, hanging it over the bow using the extra line she'd found. To use it, AJ would have to make it from the mooring line to the hanging tank, but it should be downstream of the current, and it was better than adding the extra distance by dropping it off the stern.

AJ's third tank was going to be incredibly awkward, both to carry on a recreational BCD and get in the water with. She opted to step down the ladder to the bottom rung and have Cass clip the third tank to her. The swells had other ideas, picking the ladder up, despite her weight, and swinging it outwards each time the stern fell, then smacking it back down as the next wave drove the back of the boat up. Cass hung on gamely and finally managed to clip the top of the tank to a shoulder D-ring, but AJ had to come back up the ladder to the top rung for her to clip the bottom.

Finally, with everything secure, reg in place and mask down, AJ held the tag line loosely in one hand and allowed herself to fall backwards into the water. The two tanks clunked against each other, the boat rose and fell before her, and her mask instantly flooded after being knocked askew, but she hung on to the tag line. Pulling herself around, AJ clambered back towards the stern to the wreck line which Cass had set on the port side of the Glacier Bay where the current billowed it slightly away from the hull. Having eight-and-a-half tons of fibreglass, aluminium and steel come crushing down on her would end all AJ's worries, so she was keen to stay away from the bucking catamaran.

Wearing a tech BCD, as AJ had done many times in the past, she would have a side-mount tank streamlined along each flank, and the third slung in front. It would be bulky, but far more organised and manageable than the jury-rigged system she was making do with. Everything attached to her body seemed to be a sail for the current to wrench and pull as she hauled herself towards the number 5 mooring ball. Wisely, she'd chosen to breathe from the third tank until her descent, saving the nitrox in her main cylinder for the dive.

Once again, when she reached the buoy, AJ was out of breath and ill prepared to start the dive. Dusk was upon them and the *Reel-Lee Hooked* was silhouetted by the fading glow in the distance. Everything about the situation screamed in her ear to abort the dive. But she couldn't. Em was being held, and until she brought up whatever was in the fourth hiding place, they couldn't get her back.

Calming her breathing as best she could while being tossed around in the swells, AJ switched to her primary regulator and released the air from her BCD.

Dive map courtesy of Reef Smart Dive Guides

Descending past 30 feet, pulling herself down the line, the top of the crane tower began to appear in the murky depths below. AJ had charged her torch batteries on the boat, but she still preferred holding off from using them until completely necessary. With the sun setting and the final glow of daylight fading, that time was fast approaching.

She reached the crane tower at 65 feet and quickly dropped in the lee, hiding from the moving water as best she could. The truss frame of the crane arm extended across the beam of the ship, with heavy coral growth covering the steel. AJ couldn't see the port side of the ship, less than 50 feet away.

Staying just below any structure on the starboard side, she made her way aft, passing under the second crane arm which loomed out of the darkness. Below her, the eerie well deck seemed like a bottomless cavern. When the thick metal grating of the helicopter pad appeared, AJ raised up and let the current sweep her across the expanse to the port side.

With the helipad over her head like a steel awning, she found the hatch in the top of the broad gunwale, and took a moment to unclip the third tank, relieved to be rid of the extra bulk. Setting it down beside the raised hatch, a small cloud of sediment billowed up, which she fanned away; she twisted one end of the small pen light tied around the neck of the tank, letting it dangle in the opening. The hatch was instantly bathed in a red glow.

Taking her wreck reel, AJ secured the line to a hinge at the side of the hatch, turned on her torch, and dipped head first into the shipwreck. She was dropping below the main deck, entering the second deck. Everything above the main deck was designated by levels, 1 through 5, and below by deck number counting up, using the Main Deck as 1.

The strange configuration of the amphibious transport ship meant long passageways within the wide gunwales, with small rooms and berths along the way. Hatches or stairwells between decks were spaced far apart and remembering the correct one to go up or down was crucial.

AJ recalled the route having spent weeks planning her original trip to the port engine room, but it had been a while, and it was a shipwreck at the bottom of the ocean; things inside tended to move and change. Doors didn't always stay open and sheet metal and debris could be carried through the inside of the ship by storm surge. She looped her reel around a pipe just above the floor before playing out line as she moved forward down a narrow passageway, with the emergency generator behind the wall to her left. Ahead, she came to the first doorway, which opened into a larger room, strewn with debris, silt, and a large piece of broken pipe. She was passing through the port-side berths, reserved for troops when being transported.

It was a sobering thought to be more than 100 feet below the surface, with no workable alternative means of egress options from here on out. Her only way home was by backtracking. The surroundings had immediately changed. Not a drop of light penetrated this far into the wreck. No coral growth, no colour in her torch beam except the drab grey-brown covering of silt and filth.

As her own line trailed along the floor behind, AJ noticed an older line already strung through the wreck. Without knowing anything about who, when, or where it was going, she daren't trust it, and continued wrapping her reel around various objects along the way to keep the line tight and secure.

She peeled the cuff of her wetsuit back to reveal bare skin and let the edge of her torch beam illuminate the notes she'd written in permanent marker pen. '4 doors. Down 2.' She'd passed through two doorways already and crossed another long room to the third. They had removed all the bunks and furniture before sinking, so the sparse, dark rooms felt more like a flooded dungeon than where men once slept, now void of all signs of life. Not even a stray fish ventured this far down.

The fourth steel door was wedged open three quarters of the way, just enough for AJ to slip through. Immediately to her left was a hatch in the floor, exactly as she had recalled. Without wasting time, she dipped her head through the opening and finned her way down. Continuing to descend, she passed through the third deck, which appeared no bigger than a large cupboard, and down the final floor hatch into an alcove. Turning towards the centre of the ship and throwing light into the room, AJ stared at the boiler to her left, and the steam turbine on her right. Locking her reel, she let it sit at the base of the ladder.

As AJ had remembered, the engine room was a cluttered mess of industrial--sized machinery. She'd made quick work of getting down there, but now she was at 131 feet with one minute of no-deco time left, and endless nooks and crannies to search. Her only chance would be to spot an area of recent activity. Silt moved away to reveal what's below, a fresh scrape mark, or anything recently left behind.

Her torch beam illuminated one small section of the cluttered room at a time, casting oddly shaped shadows as she played the light across conduits, ducting and framework. Most of the floor was rusted away, revealing a criss-cross of steel girders. She was now level with the sand outside the steel hull of the ship, which was cleaved into the sea floor. It was eerie to think she was almost underground, while being underwater.

Something in the corner caught her eye, and she swept the torch back, landing on a faded blue and red object. The damned gnome, she realised with a few quickened heartbeats. A techie must have brought it down and left it for the next visitor to stumble upon. She certainly didn't have time to relocate the little 18-inch garden decoration, so he'd be staying down here a little longer. She just hoped she'd be able to tell Em about it.

How well had Rosie hidden the fourth cylinder? The others had been hard to find even with the clues, and the location for this one couldn't be more vague. At a guess, she figured he'd hidden them for himself, then come up with the cyphers and clues afterwards. Perhaps when people came looking for him. Regardless, he'd left her with a needle in a haystack, and AJ was mad at herself for thinking she could pull this off on nitrox.

Far more suitable would have been trimix, which replaced a portion of the nitrogen with helium, or heliox, which replaced all the nitrogen with helium, both allowing far more time at depth. The helium had essentially no adverse effect on the body beyond a cartoony voice. But neither had been options under the circumstances. If she'd stalled until tomorrow, maybe they could have begged or borrowed proper tech gear and gas, but what would they do to Em with an overnight delay? AJ flashed her torch around the cramped space full of pipes and machinery, desperate to find some indication Rosie had been there.

Checking her Teric, she was now five minutes into deco. Her dive plan included going into decompression, but she couldn't risk going too far in. She still had to get out of the wreck, fight the current and ascend before her body would begin to 'off-gas'. To use a mountaineering analogy she'd always remembered, summiting was optional, descending was mandatory. It was time to leave.

The thought of returning empty handed was a devastatingly hard pill to swallow. She pictured Emily excitedly greeting her at Owen

Roberts Airport. Her friend, who always had a smile and a joke to share with everyone. What would the thug do when they showed up with three instead of four gems? The thought was too much to bear.

AJ moved as quickly as she could without stirring up the sediment, frantically searching all around the room. She begged for her light to turn a small object from brown to bright red as the artificial light returned the true colour spectrum to the eerie darkness of the shipwreck. But it wasn't to be. AJ had failed to find the fourth stone, and if she wanted to live, she had to face up to the fact and leave. Carefully turning, trying her best not to disturb anything, AJ finned over to the hatch, ravaged by disappointment and a sense of failure.

As she picked up her reel, turned vertical in the water and began rising to the opening in the roof, she panned her light across the engine room one more time. Like a gambler sliding her last chip across the cloth, AJ played her final hand, and busted. No miraculous last moment sighting. No vital clue so easily overlooked. No red, gem-filled aluminium cylinder to save Emily's life.

Pulling herself through the hatch and winding in her reel, AJ moved over a few feet as she ascended through the Third Deck, then eased herself through the next hatch, turning as she went. As her mask cleared the hatch, she reached up and softly grabbed the edges, her torch clanking against the metal rim as the beam danced around the silty floor. Inhaling, and twisting slightly so her tanks came through without getting stuck, AJ lifted her light towards the door and screamed into her regulator.

Slumped against the wall, half behind the open door, was the body of a diver.

27

FRIDAY

Vacant eyes stared through the lens of the dive mask, but the regulator hanging by his side left no doubt. AJ's heart was in her throat as she fought back the urge to panic. It had to be Phil Giles, Rosie and Cass's friend, as it was his boat up top, but she'd only seen him twice and between his pallid complexion and the dive mask, she couldn't be certain. One thing she did know for sure; it wasn't Rosie.

AJ shot the torch beam around the passageway, paranoid another body could be nearby, lurking in the shadows. Heck, she'd swum right by poor Phil on her way in. All was clear, but every fleck of debris caught in the light now startled her. The dark red reel line she'd noticed from the entrance continued down the passageway, leading past the toilets and shower rooms, if she remembered correctly.

AJ urged herself into action. She didn't have time to succumb to fears or what-ifs. Her Teric told her she was well into deco and still over 100 feet down. The number would continue rapidly climbing until she ascended.

What should she do with the man before her? Swim by again

and leave him down here? It certainly wouldn't make any difference to Phil, if that's who it was, but it still felt inhumane to leave him behind. Her predicament dictated action, so without further contemplation, AJ moved closer to the body and pulled his fins off. He would have been neutrally buoyant when his lungs were full of air. Now they were full of water, which is why he'd sunk to the floor. Given time, the body would begin to decompose, emitting gases internally, and a recovery team might well find him pinned to the ceiling.

AJ bumped the inflation button a few times, but his BCD didn't seem to inflate. Of course, he'd almost certainly run out of gas, so his tanks were empty. She'd have to manually inflate the BCD. Blowing air into the inflator was an awkward process at the best of times underwater, but in the dark at 100 feet, having to get so close to a dead body took all her nerve. Taking a long inhalation from her regulator, AJ held her breath and put the inflator in her mouth. Pressing the valve open, she exhaled into the line and felt the body move as the BCD filled out a little. It took three more goes to get enough air in the BCD to lift the body from the deck.

Putting her reg back in, AJ slipped through the doorway and took out her dive knife, cutting her reel line. She tied the end around the door hinge, locked the reel, and clipped it to a D-ring. No way could she drag a body and work the reel, so her red pen light would be her marker, and her line was now fixed to the exit hatch.

Reaching back through the doorway, she took a firm hold of the man's BCD shoulder strap and pulled him through the opening. His torso floated in the water as though she were towing a human balloon, but his legs dragged lifelessly behind, stirring up a cloud of silt. Three more doorways, she told herself, and then she could ascend. In a ripping current. With a dead body in tow... one hurdle at a time, she reminded herself.

Shaking away the morbid thoughts, AJ finned, crawled and clawed her way forward, with her torch shining ahead and a billowing cloud of sediment in her wake. At the fourth doorway, she finally saw the red glow as she dragged the body through the opening, his dual tanks making dull thuds against the metal.

Breathing hard, she paused below the large hatch leading out of the ship. When they began to ascend, they would both become more buoyant as the water pressure decreased, requiring the simple adjustment of releasing air bit by bit from their BCDs. Simple for her own BCD, but performing the task on the corpse while fighting the current would be a challenge.

She checked her Teric. Only 150 psi left. Purging the valve on the second tank's regulator, she switched over and tucked the primary reg away. AJ was petite with a fit, lean build, and exceptionally good on her air consumption underwater, but the fright, stress, and effort had her using more gas than usual.

The silt cloud had caught them and a brown haze enveloped the room, prompting AJ to push off the floor and rise through the opening. As her shoulders cleared, the current was immediately apparent, pushing her against the side of the hatch. Tugged to a stop, she looked down and saw the man's head awkwardly wedged under the rim of the opening. A wave of nausea rose in her stomach. He was dead, but it still felt brutal and callous to bash his body around. With a long, deep breath, she wriggled his body free and dragged him through the hatch, quickly twisting them into the current and kicking hard.

AJ had no choice. She had to stay at the same depth to remain under the helicopter pad, which offered their only protection. Looking back, she remembered the tank sitting next to the hatch. She hated to leave it there, but she had no way of carrying it now. It would take too long struggling to clip it to her. Besides, if all went well, her second tank would be plenty for her decompression stops, and if not, she'd have to rely on Cass's hanging tank.

Kicking hard, the corpse now felt like an umbrella behind her, making progress slow until she neared the starboard side. Once in the gunwale's protection, her pace quickened, and she angled forward, making for the crane tower. Rising a little brought her to 91 feet as they passed below the port-side crane arm. The moment she came level with the starboard tower, AJ released air from her own BCD and angled upwards in the lee, holding the man's inflation hose and releasing gas as she went. Letting air out was a lot easier than putting it in.

At 70 feet she felt the weight of the diver pulling on her arm, giving her confidence the body wasn't about to drag them both towards the surface. She cleared the top of the tower and kicked with all her might towards the mooring line fastened to the wreck by a huge clevis. The current pulled and tugged, trying to wrench the stricken diver from her grasp, but she continued fighting until finally, releasing hold of her torch and letting it hang from its tether, she grabbed the line.

Now they were stretched out like a pair of flags flying in tandem, attached to a flagpole by one hand. She was stuck, and the strain on both arms would soon become unbearable. She had to do something quickly, or they'd both be swept away.

AJ pulled against the rope with all her strength. It felt like she was attempting a one-armed pull-up. With every muscle in her arm and shoulder twitching and screaming, she managed to bend her elbow and pull her chest closer to the line. She had one chance to make this work. If she missed, there'd be no choice. She'd release the body and aim herself for the other crane tower where a mooring line at least had a boat on the other end. The wrong boat, but any port will do in a storm.

With a final pull, she let go of the line and threw her arm around it, catching the rope in the crook of her elbow like an oversized hook. With both bodies being tugged by the current, the strain returned to both her limbs, but her left was now threatening to give way and open the hook. Pulling on the limp diver with her right hand, she dragged the body towards her until his shoulder strap neared her left hand. Screaming into her regulator, she put every ounce of strength she possessed into closing the gap until her fingers slipped behind the strap and she grabbed hold.

The stress was now equalised around the mooring line, but painful as hell, and relying on her grip on Phil's BCD holding, which she knew was unsustainable. Her only chance of getting the body to the surface with any kind of control was to secure him to the line, instead of to her. It was now pitch black underwater, but with one hand free, she could aim her torch and search the dead diver for any usable straps or clips. His pale face was uncomfortably close to her own, his mask now knocked askew, revealing one eye still blankly staring into the world he'd departed.

A reel line might not be strong enough and would be impossible to slide up the hefty mooring rope. Dangling from the diver's wrist was a torch, tethered by a half-inch-wide strap and a sturdier than normal wrist loop. She assumed the battery had died along with its owner, which further suggested he'd been down there for hours. The idea of the light slowly dimming over time felt sad and symbolic to AJ. Life ebbing away until its flame flickered one final time before dying.

With her left arm throbbing, she struggled to loosen the wrist loop and slide it over the man's limp hand. She hated to do it, but without another option, AJ opened the clip from the strap to the torch and watched the expensive light disappear below them into the blackness. Using her fingers holding on to his BCD strap to hold the loop, she threaded the strap through a D-ring and then the loop, cinching it tight. Next, she had to get the strap around the rope and the body close enough to clip the strap somewhere.

Her left arm was going numb and could do nothing to help, and her right hand had to hold the clip. The only choice was to use her other two limbs. Hoping she never had to explain this to anybody, or repeat the process, AJ wrapped her legs around the body, and with her heels on the bottom of the two tanks and her fins angled away, she pulled her feet up. The man's face glanced off the mooring line, sending his mask off into the night, but just as his shoulder caught on the line, she was able to snap the clip to the D-ring.

AJ's feelingless fingers instantly let go of the man's BCD and he fell back until the strap went tight. Switching to her right hand on the line, she checked her Teric. Eighteen minutes into deco and they were still at 61 feet. Quickly moving above the prone body grotesquely hanging above the crane tower, held by the buoyancy in his BCD and AJ's makeshift tether, she tugged on his first-stage valve and began moving upwards. Awkwardly holding her torch in the hand she was using to pull the diver with her, she noticed 'PG' handwritten on the upper part of both tanks. If this wasn't Phil Giles, it was a bad day to steal the man's boat and dive gear.

It was slow going with the ever-present clock ticking, but as she passed above 50 feet, AJ figured she was no longer accumulating decompression time. Her Teric was directing her to 30 feet, and when she finally reached it, she was instructed to spend 21 minutes at that depth. The second tank would have enough gas.

Twenty-one minutes was less than she'd imagined, but now they were this close to the surface, the wave action above was adding to the current, throwing AJ and her human balloon all over the place. Phil began to rise above her, so she quickly dumped a little gas from both their BCDs. Riding out the safety stop in the dark, being tossed around like a washing machine, was no fun at all. Having a dead body along for the trip made it far worse.

With too much time to think, AJ began wondering why Phil was down there, and what went wrong. She found his pressure gauge, or SPG, and shined her torch on the face. It confirmed his tanks were empty. She reached over and checked both valves, and verified they were on. He was using an open manifold with one regulator, which gave him both tanks of gas, but no independent back-up. Unless his regulator had free-flowed and emptied the tanks, it appeared he'd simply run out of air. Next to the SPG was a console computer, but she dare not try to recall the dive in case she accidentally deleted vital information. The Coast Guard would want to see everything. They may tell her she should have left him down there until they organised a recovery dive, but sod it; she couldn't leave the poor bloke.

AJ reached over and unzipped the side pocket on Phil's tatty-looking BCD, and let her light dangle from her wrist. Slipping a hand inside the pocket, her fingers found what felt like a back-up torch. She didn't intend on taking it out, but a rolling swell jolted them both, so she grabbed for the line with both hands, still clutching the torch. Except it wasn't a torch. It was an anodised red aluminium cylinder.

28

FRIDAY

With her decompression obligation complete, AJ began moving up the line towards the mooring ball, dragging the body behind her. The rope was bucking and kicking in the heavy seas, and as she ascended, the air in Phil's BCD made him more buoyant as the water pressure decreased. She grabbed the line below him and let him float to the surface. Following, she could see the stricken diver in her torch beam being mercilessly beaten and banged against the underside of the 22-inch ball, and regretted letting him go.

How they would pull Phil from the water, she had no idea, but first AJ needed to surface herself. She could just see a faint green strobing glow in the darkness, which she guessed to be a light Cass had rigged on the emergency hanging tank. It was bizarre watching the green glimmer rising and falling with the swells, and she was glad of not needing to use that tank. Above her, a white light bathed the surface, so Cass was either up there with a big torch or had spotlights mounted on the boat.

Releasing the mooring line from four feet under, the current took AJ in the direction of where the boat should be, along with the line between the buoy and the bow cleat. Quickly ascending the final few feet, she swept her hand overhead, searching for the rope.

A wave lifted her up and, with a second attempt, her hand smacked against the strained line and she frantically grabbed hold.

"AJ, thank God!" Cass screamed, and AJ looked up to see her friend silhouetted by two powerful spotlights mounted above the hardtop. She waved back, keeping her regulator in her mouth.

"I thought that was you!" Cass shouted hysterically, and AJ realised the body appearing on the surface and being slapped around would have been a terrifying sight.

She risked taking her reg out. "I'm fine, but I need a line!"

Cass didn't move. "Is that..?" she asked.

"Yeah," AJ replied, having not looked forward to telling Cass about her and Rosie's friend.

Cass broke down, clinging to the railing and sobbing. AJ put her reg back in her mouth just in time before the next swell crashed over the mooring buoy and covered her with water. When she popped back up, she quickly took it back out.

"Oh, bugger. Cass, it's not Rosie!"

Cass's head immediately lifted up, and her legs visibly buckled. AJ thought her friend was going to collapse, but she managed to stay on her feet.

"It's not?"

"No, it's his mate, Phil."

Cass looked like she could breathe again, but scowled at AJ. "Why the bloody hell did you let me think it was Rosie?"

AJ looked beyond the *Reel-Lee Hooked* in the direction of Phil's boat, but all she could see was a faint outline under the light of the stars. She couldn't quite figure out why Cass had decided the missing diver from Phil's boat wouldn't be Phil, but she knew the mind could be a strange nemesis when it came to loved ones.

"Sorry!" she spluttered as another wall of water swept over. "That line would be good, Cass!"

"Shit, sorry," Cass called back and began hauling the extra tank up on the end of her extra rope. The aluminium tank banged against the hull as she dragged it aboard, and as a fellow boat owner, AJ winced.

"Make me a loop on the end, Cass," AJ shouted between waves and saw her friend efficiently tie a bow line before tossing it her way. AJ caught the rope and worked herself back to the mooring buoy. She had to switch Phil from the mooring line to the rope she carried, which wouldn't be easy in the conditions, and she considered her options.

One of his dual tanks was breaking the surface, his head and chest held under by the buoy, twisting his torso sideways. Each swell rolled everything up on the wave, then deposited them back in the trough, making any task near impossible.

AJ took her large stainless steel carabiner from her BCD, the one that she used for signalling against her tank, and hooked it to the loop at the end of the line. Fumbling underwater while being tossed around, she found the bottom edge of Phil's BCD and ran her hand around until she felt a D-ring. Waiting until the pause in the next trough, she clipped the carabiner to the D-ring, then blindly searched for the torch strap she'd used on his chest. In the next trough, the tension lessened for a moment, enough for her to release the clip, and the current pulled the body towards the boat.

"Tie the line to the stern cleat, Cass," she yelled as Phil's corpse unceremoniously bumped into the port-side hull and dragged along the side of the catamaran. Bloody lucky he didn't go between the hulls, she thought, realising what a disaster that would have been. Cass moved swiftly down the port gunwale, using the hardtop frame for support, and tied the line off to a cleat. Rising and falling in the rolling water, the body disappeared into the darkness. The only sign that his progress had been halted was when the line went tight.

AJ moved wearily along the wreck line, letting the current do the work. At the stern, she grabbed the tag line and pulled her fins off one by one, throwing them up to Cass. Although the ladder was much smaller and lighter than on her Newton custom dive boat, it was still dangerously flailing around as the stern made six-foot swings from trough to peak. With the timing borne from experience, AJ placed a foot on the bottom rung and both hands on the side of the ladder as it laid out behind the boat on the downswing. When the stern rose, she hung on tightly as the ladder swung back against the boat, then took two steps up and let Cass pull her across the narrow swim step and over the transom.

AJ was exhausted. Cass helped her out of her gear and wetsuit, then gave her a towel to dry off. The Florida night air was hot and humid but tempered by the strong winds which had brought the rough seas. After an hour underwater and her macabre task, AJ was chilled despite the wetsuit.

Cass looked at her from across the cockpit. "I'm sorry, love. I don't know why I thought it was my stupid husband. Because he's still missing, I suppose."

"I'm sorry for putting the frighteners on you."

"You were down so long, I thought it was you at first," Cass continued, shaking her head and wiping salt water from her face. "I was already a bloody mess." She looked off the stern into the darkness. "What are we going to do with poor Phil?"

AJ reached into her BCD pocket and retrieved the fourth cylinder, holding it up. "I don't know, but we need to hustle back to shore and get Em."

"Bugger, I forgot all about that damn thing. I guess we could pull him aboard and take him with us?"

"The Coast Guard will have a conniption if we do that," AJ replied. "They'll already be mad at me for bringing him up."

"That's bloody ridiculous. Do they expect you to just leave a body down there?"

"Helps them piece together what happened."

"Alright, then we'd better call them," Cass said, moving carefully towards the pilothouse.

"They'll keep us here forever, Cass. We'll have to give statements and probably go to the police station for an interview."

"Then we have to take him with us," Cass said firmly.

"We can't schlep the poor bloke around like it's *Weekend at Bernie's.*"

Cass threw her hands up, then quickly grabbed the table for support. "Then what do you suggest?"

AJ looked over again at the faint image of the Mako. "Put him on his boat, and we'll tell them he's there."

Cass followed AJ's gaze to the boat riding up and down no more than 100 feet off their stern. "And how the hell are we going to do that in six-foot seas?"

"I don't know, but I managed to drag the poor sod up from inside the *Spiegel*, so I'm sure we can plonk him back on his boat somehow."

Cass shook her head again, looking between the two boats and the turbulent seas. "Fine, you figure out how we're gonna do this and I'll drive the boat, but I think you're bonkers."

AJ managed a smile. "I'd say the last few days have proven we're both a little doolally, my dear."

"That's the truth," Cass replied and began working on pulling in the tag and wreck line. She paused a moment and looked over her shoulder. "So why the bloody hell was Phil down there?"

"Because Rosie sent him was my guess," AJ replied, sitting on the L-shaped couch and twisting the top off the red cylinder.

"Rosie's twice the diver Phil ever was. Besides, why would he send him out here alone?"

"Because Rosie couldn't come along for some reason?" AJ replied, letting the viscous liquid spill out of the tube.

"Then why did he leave all these stupid clues for us, if he was having Phil get them anyway?"

A cloth bag slid into AJ's hand and she wedged the cylinder under her leg while she opened the pouch. She paused before loosening the ties. "Maybe he doesn't know Phil was after them." She looked up. "Bugger! Phil was trying to nick them for himself. I bet he was thinking that reward money would set him up very nicely in Tahiti."

Cass stowed the lines in a locker and made her way to the pilothouse. "I think you might be right. I can't come up with any other reason, but it's hard to imagine he'd screw Rosie over. They're best mates." She sat down next to AJ. "Silly sod won't be going to Tahiti now, will he?"

Several times on the ascent, AJ had struggled with the idea she was bringing a dead human being up from the wreck. It was a sobering experience to get a first-hand look at how things could quickly and dramatically go wrong when diving deep. Especially inside wrecks.

Her best guess was Phil had spent too long hunting for the cylinder inside the engine room. Once he came up through the hatches to the passageway, he may have become disorientated and lost. It was easy to become completely turned around inside a massive wreck like the *Spiegel Grove*. Nothing looked the same going in the opposite direction, yet many areas look the same as others. A hundred and thirty feet was the recommended recreational maximum depth for a reason, and only for advanced divers.

Many people felt the effects of nitrogen narcosis at depth, also known as 'rapture of the deep'. It slowed thinking and hampered decision making, sometimes to the point of losing all sense of surroundings. Narc'ed divers were known to take their regs out of their mouths or keep swimming deeper and deeper into the abyss. The fix was to ascend where the effects would clear in the same manner they'd developed. In all likelihood, no one would ever know the exact details of what happened, but Phil's dive computer would at least provide clues with a record of time and depth.

"Well?" Cass asked, bringing AJ back from her thoughts.

"Oh, right." She loosened the top of the soggy, wet pouch and dumped out another large, sparkling gemstone. Except this one was a diamond. The biggest diamond either of them had ever seen.

29

FRIDAY

Cass turned the diamond over in her hand, shaking her head. "That news report didn't say anything about a diamond being stolen, did it?"

"Not that I saw," AJ replied, jumping up from the couch. "Where's my mobile? Did Sore Balls call while I was down there?"

Cass shoved the stone back in its bag. "Shit, yeah he did. I could see it was Emily calling you just as I got to the phone, but I missed the call. I couldn't unlock the bloody phone to call back."

AJ found her mobile on the dash. The screen read 'one missed call'. "Bugger," she groaned. "I didn't give you the code. That was so stupid of me. It's 1026, like the U-boat, U-1026."

"You'd better try calling him," Cass said, making her way down to the port-side hull and the guest stateroom, where she could add the stone to others under the stool.

AJ unlocked her phone and hit 'call' on Em's name from the recent call list. It rang twice before being answered, but no one spoke. "Hello? I missed your call a bit ago."

"Damn right you did," growled a now too-familiar voice. "You told me an hour, and it's been nearly two. You'd better have what I want."

AJ leaned against the dash, trying to keep her balance on the rocking boat, shielding the phone with her hand from the wind. "We do. Took a little longer to get the last one, but we have them all."

"There's a dirt road on the left-hand side, three quarters of a mile up 905 after the turn. Know where that is?"

"I don't know the dirt road, but I'm guessing it's a little past Dagney Johnson State Park, right?"

"If you say so. Be there in twenty minutes."

"We can't get there that fast, it'll take us forty minutes just to get back..." AJ looked off the stern where Phil's body was somewhere in the darkness. "A bit longer, probably. And then we'll have to drive there."

"Where the hell are you? You're still on the water?"

"Yeah," she replied, surprised he didn't realise that. He'd seen them leave on the boat. "So you'll need to give us over an hour, more like an hour and a half."

"You keep thinking I need to do things, tat girl," the man seethed. "It's you that needs to do things, and that starts with bringing me our merchandise."

"Not really yours, now is it?"

The line went quiet for a moment and then AJ heard Em's voice squeal in the background. "I'm over screwing around with you!" he practically yelled into the phone. "The longer you take, the more fun I'm going to have with this little bitch, so I'd hurry up if you give a shit about her!"

"Tell him to bugger off!" AJ heard Emily shout.

AJ took a deep breath, fighting desperation and panic at the prospect of her friend being hurt by this monster. She had to stay calm and think. Cass came up from below and looked at her, her face mirroring how AJ felt inside.

"We can be at Cass's house in forty-five minutes," AJ said firmly. "If you want your stolen gemstones, that's where they'll be."

The line went silent again, and AJ held her breath.

"Forty-five minutes. Every second after that, cutie here starts getting broken parts. And remember, if you call the law, I'll know, understand?"

Apparently it was a rhetorical question, as the line went dead.

"My house? Is that wise?" Cass asked with a worried frown.

"Better than the secluded dark trail in the middle of nowhere he wanted us to meet him. We'd have two chances of leaving there alive."

Cass nodded. "Fair enough. Mind you, his intention will still most likely be the same."

"I'm sure you're right, but it'll be a bit harder at the house, and much harder to get away without being seen."

"Still leaves us dead," Cass mumbled.

"That's the part we'll try our best to avoid," AJ replied, making her way to the cockpit and pulling the wreck line out of the locker.

"You got a plan on how to do this?" Cass asked.

"Yeah."

"Is it a good one? One that doesn't involve us killing ourselves before he has a chance, or sinking the boat?"

AJ reached over the stern and tied one end of the wreck line to the rope pulled tight off the back of the boat by Phil Giles's body. "Not sure it's a good one, but it's the best I could come up with on short notice."

"Alright, love, tell me what to do."

AJ dropped the rest of the coiled line in the cockpit and quickly made her way towards the bow, keeping a firm hold on the hardtop frame. "We'll start by getting off this mooring. Then you'll need to get me close enough to the Mako for me to swim over. Then the next part will be the difficult bit."

Cass started the outboards while AJ waited for Cass to drop the boat in gear and take the tension off the mooring line. As soon as there was slack, she freed their line from the cleat, and held up an okay sign. Cass took the boat out of gear and let the current drag the *Reel-Lee Hooked* backwards, while AJ stowed their rope. She made her way back to the cockpit.

"Any chance you can manoeuvre on just the starboard engine, Cass?"

Her friend turned around and looked at her from the helm as though she was mad. "In these seas?"

"It was worth asking," AJ responded, shrugging her shoulders. "In that case, you have to do this without cutting Phil loose with the port propeller."

They both looked off the stern. They were drifting backwards with the current, but would have to use the engines to keep the bow pointed into the waves or they'd be turned sideways.

"I'll make a circle to port and pull you as close to the Mako as I dare. That should keep poor Phil off the port side and the rope clear of the props."

"Perfect."

"Oh, what's the last part?"

AJ tried to force a smile. "You have to release Phil from the stern cleat once I'm on the Mako."

Cass's shoulders dropped. "I thought I said don't kill us?"

"Get her nice and square into the waves, then toddle back here, undo the line, and you'll be back at the helm before you know it," AJ said as cheerily as she could fake. "Bob's yer uncle."

Cass let out a long sigh, but dropped the outboards in gear and began a wide circle in the rolling seas with the spotlights alternating between illuminating the waves and getting lost in the night sky. AJ made a loop in the end of the coiled line, slipping it over her wrist, then donned her fins, ready to dive back in the water. She'd prefer to wear her wetsuit for the warmth and the extra buoyancy, but there was no time. Her Mermaid Divers leggings and sports bra would have to do.

Cass brought the catamaran within ten feet of the starboard side of the Mako, pulling slightly ahead. Doing her best to hold *Reel-Lee Hooked* steady, she waved to AJ, who vaulted over the port-side gunwale into the water. Diving would have given her a better start, but balancing on the gunwale in the roiling seas wasn't happening. She struck out for Phil's boat, aiming for the bow, knowing the current would carry her towards the stern. If she missed, poor Phil would be waiting at the end of his line and she'd join him on hers.

Without the cumbersome dive gear, the swim was easier than the last time she was in the water, and she managed to grab the swim step on her first try. AJ quickly pulled herself aboard and gathered up the slack in her rope, leaving enough for the rolling of the two boats so she wasn't plucked back into the ocean.

"Go, Cass!" she yelled across the water, waving at the same time, although she wasn't sure Cass could see her in the dark. The cat had cockpit spotlights, but the beam didn't reach far to the side. She heard the outboards being taken out of gear and watched Cass rushing to the stern where she heaved on the line, trying to pull the body closer to the boat to relieve the strain.

The Glacier Bay was quickly being pushed backwards by the waves and was already alongside the Mako. In a few moments, AJ's line would go tight and pull her overboard. She slipped the loop from her wrist in anticipation of tying it to a cleat, but if she did that and Cass couldn't free her end, the two boats would be tethered.

Normally, that wouldn't be a problem, but in these seas and with Phil's line off the port stern of the *Reel-Lee Hooked*, the catamaran would be spun around and the line cut by the port-side propeller whenever the boat was put back in gear. Which would have to happen at some point. If she simply let the line go, she'd be stuck on Phil's boat with no idea whether the key was in the ignition or tucked inside his wetsuit.

The bow of the Glacier Bay was beginning to turn to starboard. AJ had to decide. She was about to release her line into the water when Cass screamed.

"I've got it!"

AJ looked over, and Cass was throwing Phil's line into the water. Now AJ needed to get him tied in before he was swept away. She stuffed the loop under the cleat and got one side around the forward horn of the cleat just as the rope wrenched tight.

"Got him!" AJ yelled, but Cass couldn't hear. She was already back at the helm and pulling the catamaran clear.

AJ took a handful of line and pulled. The literal dead weight, plus the current, felt like she was trying to drag the Florida Keys aboard. As soon as she had enough slack in the line, she wrapped the rope around the back of the cleat, over the loop already in place, letting the rope on rope friction help her hold steady.

As the stern rose and fell, there were brief moments when the tension lessened on the line, and each time AJ was able to pull another few feet aboard. Once she felt there was enough on the boat to be secure, she waited for the next time the strain was relieved, unhooked the loop, and left the running line behind the cleat. Now it slid easily against the polished stainless steel, but also pulled harder when the swells tried to keep Phil in the water.

Bit by bit, AJ hauled the mass to the back of the boat, and once she saw the glint from the aluminium tanks within reach of the swim step, she secured the line to the cleat once more. How she was going to pull an adult male in hefty dive gear onto the back of the boat, she had no idea, but leaving him in the water felt unconscionable.

Kneeling on the step and hanging on to the transom with one hand, she reached out in the dark and felt for a shoulder strap. Her fingers quickly found where the rope was attached and AJ pulled with all her might. Cass had made another circle and now positioned herself off the stern with the spotlights illuminating the water behind the Mako. The sudden brightness made AJ blink a few times while in her hand, she was surprised when she was able to pull Phil to the swim step. It must be the lee of the *Hear No Evil*, sheltering the body from the worst of the current, she thought, and looked down.

She had hold of the man's BCD, but Phil Giles was gone.

30

FRIDAY

AJ sat on the L-shaped couch in the pilothouse, wrapped in a towel, with her face slumped into her arms on the table. Cass was running as hard as she dared in the rough swells, making good time with a following sea. She kept glancing back at AJ.

"There was nothing else you could have done, love," Cass called back over the sound of the wind and the engines.

AJ picked her head up, her eyes red and cheeks damp. She never cried. Well, almost never. She was an only child to a father who was the CEO of a large business, and a barrister for a mother. She had a loving family, but she'd been raised to sort it out rather than cry about it. Her parents weren't heartless, but practical. Don't raise a problem unless you're prepared to at least help find a solution. AJ was stuck for a solution regarding Phil Giles.

"I should have left him down there. We could have called the Coast Guard and been on our way. They would have brought him up tomorrow. Now the poor sod could be anywhere."

"Do you think a shark got him?" Cass said, and by the sudden change in expression, she clearly realised it wasn't the best thing to have said.

"If one didn't pull him out of his BCD, they're bound to have a go at him on the way to shore," AJ replied, wiping the tears and snot from her face. "Poor bastard."

"Remember, he may have screwed Rosie over," Cass responded, with less sympathy than AJ currently felt. But she had a point. What was he doing retrieving the stones?

"The body will make shore by morning, love. With these seas, it won't take much time at all," Cass added, and the catamaran rose high over a wave for emphasis. AJ was used to her V-hulled Newton, which would crash down off the swells much more than the Glacier Bay. The twin hulls made for a smoother ride in the choppy conditions.

For a moment she felt slightly relieved, knowing Cass was correct; Phil's body would wash ashore quickly. But then she considered what that might entail.

"What if some little kid paddling around in the morning finds him? It'll traumatise the lad forever. Poor nipper will never get in the water again."

"I can call the Coasties and they'll start searching tonight," Cass offered.

AJ picked herself up from the couch and used the hardtop frame for support as she moved to the helm alongside her friend.

"We can't call the Coast Guard now. There's far too much explaining to do, and if we do it anonymously, they'll figure we're on a boat and they'll start looking for anyone coming in off the water. We'll call when we're done getting Em back. If we live long enough."

"Well, the one bloke who's not worried about it is dear old Phil," Cass said in a softer tone. "Hopefully he's bellied up to a bar with endless beer and wings, the fishing boat of his dreams, and a cabin overlooking the water in whatever heaven has that looks like Tahiti."

AJ nodded but couldn't bring herself to smile. The process of bringing the body up from the wreck was disturbing, but at the time, she'd been focused on the task. Now, all she could see in her mind was his limp body bashing against the mooring ball, and visions of her running his head into the hatch.

"What if they never find him?" she blurted as the idea hit her. "If they don't find a body, they'll still have the boat and his dive gear. I bet I left traces of DNA, fingerprints, and all kinds of evidence at the scene. They'll think I bumped him off."

Cass turned to her. "Look, we have to get Em back, and then figure out where the bloody hell my idiot husband has disappeared to. The Coasties will only know we were out there when we tell them we were."

AJ was taken aback and couldn't think what to say. Which didn't matter, as Cass was on a roll and gave her no opportunity.

"No one's coming running after you except your old mate Sore Balls, and believe me, he'll be after all of us. So you better get your arse and your mind in gear, young lady, 'cos I'm not planning on any of us dying today, or being arrested. Got it?"

AJ stared at her. "That's a bit bloody harsh, Cass."

"It's 'go time', or whatever the Americans say in the movies, love. You may disagree, but if we don't have our shit together when we get there, Johnny Swollen Nuts'll have our guts for garters."

"I didn't say I disagreed. I just said it was a bit harsh," AJ mumbled.

Cass threw her arm around her. "Yeah, well, you know me. I get a tad forthright when I'm nervous, and right now I'm more in the terrified range."

"Okay," AJ said firmly, wiping her face. "You're right. So what's our plan when we get there?"

Cass looked at her again. "That's why I need you back in the game, love. I haven't a clue what to do."

When they reached Pilot House canal leading to the house, the *Reel-Lee Hooked* was finally riding smoothly. After hours in the open ocean on heavy seas, AJ would have felt relieved if her stomach wasn't full of butterflies. The working holiday and conference she'd been looking forward to had certainly not turned out as planned, culminating in a rendezvous with the heavy for a Miami crime boss. She felt woefully ill prepared, like they were bringing a plastic picnic knife to a gunfight.

It was gone ten o'clock and many of the homes along the canal were already dark, the residents in bed for the night. It was Friday, so a few were still up, and a couple had gatherings with people chattering and drinking on the patios overlooking the canal. The Glacier Bay idling by earned a few glances, but most people were busy having a good time. At this moment, AJ didn't see them as Cass's neighbours, but potential witnesses, and the more the merrier in her mind.

She was convinced their only defence would be an audience. For JSB to escape the neighbourhood, and then the Florida Keys, by either of the two available roads would be almost impossible if enough people saw him and the white Escalade. She also had the registration plate, which she'd noted on her mobile. As Cass turned into the small canal where her home sat on the left bank, AJ gave her a nod, and she leaned on the horn three times. They both waved towards her house, although they couldn't see anyone there. Various moans and complaints echoed around the quiet neighbourhood from backyards close by, no doubt wondering when the Lees became so inconsiderate.

Cass used the twin outboards to skilfully steer the boat into the notched-out berth, and AJ stood ready with bow line in hand. Two lights from both corners of the house cast a soft white glow across the backyard and dock, having automatically come on at dusk. AJ wondered when they were set to go off. She also wondered where the hell Johnny Sore Balls was hiding. She couldn't see any sign of him or the white SUV.

Stepping to the dock, AJ tied the starboard bow to a cleat, then moved to the port side and grabbed the line she'd left draped over the railing.

"I don't see anyone," she whispered, just loud enough for Cass to hear.

"Probably watching from somewhere, making sure we didn't bring anyone along," Cass replied, and shut down the engines.

With the Glacier Bay secured, they both stood on the dock and looked around. Between house lights and street lamps, most of the property was lit to some degree, but still no sign of JSB.

"What do we do now?" Cass asked.

"Wait, I suppose, or I could call Em's mobile." The adrenaline had been pumping all the way here, and now it seemed anticlimactic. AJ was hit with that drowsy feeling that followed when the chemicals dissipated if the body decides they're not needed. She disagreed with her body's decision; she was pretty sure they were still needed. Taking out her mobile, she called.

After a few beats, they both heard Pink singing 'Get the Party Started' from the shadows beneath the house. Em's ringtone for AJ. No one answered, but AJ ended the call and tucked her mobile away as JSB stepped from the darkness.

"Where's Emily?" she called out.

The man walked forward and stopped at the edge below the house. "Give me the merchandise."

"We have them, but this is going to be an exchange, here in the backyard, so you'd better bring her out where we can see her."

"There you go, making demands again," the man responded flatly. "I have your friend. I say how we do this, and I'm telling you to bring the merchandise over here."

Cass held up the four pouches, dangling them from the draw-strings.

"How about she starts tossing them in the canal one by one until you hand Emily back over?" AJ demanded.

JSB took a deep breath, considering his options. AJ was gambling on his main objective being to leave with the stones, and that he'd compromise the circumstances to do so. Her loosely strung-together plan was built around staying in the open where they hoped to be visible, and not getting close to the man or the SUV. She was sure if they walked under the house, he'd pull the gun and they'd all be heading north in the Escalade. A one-way trip for the women.

He looked livid, but didn't reply. Instead, he pulled another mobile from his pocket and made a call. AJ couldn't hear what he said as he spoke quietly into the phone, but it was short, and the white SUV pulled up a few moments after he hung up.

From across the road, Admiral, the neighbour's dog, barked in his deep, distinct tone, notifying the cul-de-sac that a stranger was arriving. The driver parked under the house where Cass's beloved Beetle usually sat. AJ wondered where it was now. Presumably wherever they'd snatched Emily from.

JSB opened the back door and from the faint glow of the interior light, AJ could see it was Em who he pulled from the back seat. She was grunting loudly and struggling against the man. He managed to dodge a knee intended once more for his crotch. Em had her hands tied behind her back and some kind of gag over her mouth. JSB held her at arm's length to avoid further efforts, easily overpowering the diminutive but determined young woman.

"Come and get her," he called to AJ. "I can't wait to be rid of her."

"Out here," AJ said, standing firm.

The big man dragged Emily along as he walked to where he stood before, just at the edge of the concrete slab below the house. "Come get her and make it quick."

Once he had the stones, and they had Emily back, what would be his next move? One phone call and the Escalade would be pulled over before it even made it out of Key Largo. He had to know that. Surely he'd need to either take them with him or kill them?

"Give me the stones," AJ said, turning to Cass. "No matter what he does or says, don't come to him, alright?"

Cass handed AJ the pouches. "What if he grabs you?"

"Then calling the police is our only hope, and you'll be the only one who can do it." AJ lowered her voice. "He'll threaten to kill me, or whatever, unless you come to him. He'll wave his gun around and sound real mean. But remember, if the three of us end up in that vehicle, we're all dead. Our only chance is you. Make a shit-load of noise and call right away. If he comes after you, jump in the canal and swim to a neighbour's and call."

"Enough bullshit and chatter," JSB growled. "Bring me the bags."

AJ faced him again. "Calm down, Johnny. You and your big boss, Danitess, will have what you want soon enough." She took a step towards him and noticed a confused look on his face.

"Danitess?" he said, as Admiral's booming bark echoed around the neighbourhood again, and a black SUV rolled into the drive-way, blocking the white one from leaving. The front doors flung open and two Hispanic-looking men got out. Both had guns. Aimed directly at Johnny Sore Balls. AJ instantly recognised one of the men from the bridge over Tavernier Creek.

31

FRIDAY

AJ stood motionless, her eyes on Emily as one of the new gunmen strode confidently towards JSB, who raised his hands in the air.

"Just leave the diamond," AJ heard Johnny say.

It was hard to see details in the shadows under the house, but she swore the man with the gun grinned. He moved into the light from the interior of the Escalade and she noticed he had tattoos on his neck and was wearing a lightweight tracksuit jacket. She figured these goons must sweat like crazy in the Florida heat, having to wear jackets all the time to hide their bloody firearms.

"Give me the stones," Neck Tattoo said in a heavy accent.

JSB nodded towards AJ. "She has them."

The Hispanic man pushed JSB and Emily forward, level with the front of the Escalade, and noticed the driver still sitting behind the wheel.

"Get out," he ordered, and the man complied.

He was an older, scruffy looking man, who AJ instantly recognised.

"Poppers?"

He looked scared. And embarrassed.

"You back-stabbing sod!" Cass shouted from the backyard.

"Shut up!" the Hispanic man growled. "You," he said, pointing the gun across the front of the SUV at Poppers for a moment. "Move to the back and give him your phone."

Poppers didn't argue and trotted over to the second gunman at the black SUV. The man took his phone from him and shoved him in the back seat, closing the door.

The first gunman beckoned AJ towards him. She stayed put. He moved his gun barrel slightly, aiming at Emily's head, then beckoned again. AJ knew her earlier hypothesis still rang true, despite the threat shifting to a different thug. But something told her Neck Tattoo wasn't going to ask twice. She noticed the barrel of his handgun was much longer than she'd seen before. AJ didn't know squat about firearms, but she'd seen enough movies to guess it was a suppressor. The man could shoot them without waking up the neighbours.

She walked forward, keeping the four pouches held clearly in sight. Neck Tattoo pointed the barrel back at JSB. Emily stood still, wide eyed. AJ paused when she reached the edge of the slab under the house, letting her eyes adjust to the darker surroundings.

The thug beckoned her closer. "Bring them to me."

AJ moved between Emily and the SUV, giving her friend a reassuring nod. What reassurance she was giving, AJ had no idea, as the frail plans she had were long out the window now the new players were involved. Standing within a few feet of the Hispanic man, she could see him more clearly. His scalp was also tattooed, slightly hidden below his shortly buzzed hair. He was smaller in frame than Johnny Sore Balls, but lean, with cold eyes that seemed to stare right through her. Uncaring and thirsty for violence.

"Open the bags," he grunted, and one by one, AJ did so, showing him each of the gemstones in turn. From where she stood, she had a better view of his cohort, who'd remained by the driver's side door of what she now noticed was another Escalade. She wondered if Cadillac knew their audience was split between wealthy soccer mums, golfers, and mobsters. Their marketing strategy had to be quite diverse.

The second man was not lean. He was short and fat, but the gun in his hand made him just as threatening. He gave her a lecherous look that made her skin crawl.

"Put them there," Neck Tattoo, said, nodding to the bonnet of the white SUV next to them. AJ set the pouches down. He waved the barrel of the gun, signalling for her to retreat, which she gladly did. Moving past Em, she took her by the arm, leading her away.

"Stop there," the gunmen said.

"You have what you want. Now let us go and be on your way," AJ said, unsuccessfully trying to hide the shakiness in her voice.

He ignored her. "Take the gun slowly from inside his jacket and hand it to me."

AJ's first thought was maybe she could turn the gun on Neck Tattoo. Her second thought was 'What are you thinking?' She hated guns and had reluctantly held one only a few times in the past. She'd managed to nearly miss a target only a few feet away. Admittedly, it was a human who was running and trying his best not to get shot, but that's generally what people did. Especially seasoned killers like the men before her.

She stepped over to JSB, who looked at her blankly. If he was scared, he didn't show it. "Inside my jacket," he said. "Be careful, the safety's off," he added in a whisper, and gave her a slight nod.

"Hey," Neck Tattoo grunted, and AJ looked up. The gun was back against Emily's head. "Don't even think about it, chica. I'll drop all three of you."

AJ had no doubt. She slid the front of JSB's jacket aside and took his gun from its holster, holding it by the grip between two fingers so it swung harmlessly from her hand.

JSB gave her a look of disappointment. "He's going to kill us all."

Neck Tattoo stared at AJ with calm indifference, and a lump formed in her throat. She prayed Cass had the good sense to dive into the canal behind them. If she tried anything else, all she'd accomplish would be to die alongside them. AJ's eyes met Em's.

Neither had an ounce of reassurance left to give. Emily's expression turned to a scowl, her gaze falling to the gun.

Often, it's only people who have faced the brink of death who truly understand the precise moment when all hope is lost and the inevitable is indeed taking place. Human nature leaves most victims believing this can't be happening to them, and somehow they'll still be saved. Recognising and accepting the fact that they're absolutely about to die is the only way to push the psyche into making a move, which will almost certainly have the same result. But they'll go down swinging. That one look from Em gave AJ permission to swing.

Her first problem was getting the gun moved in her hand so she could fire it. Her eyes flicked between JSB and Neck Tattoo. Their looks both seemed to be willing her to shoot. JSB, so he'd have a second to react while AJ was being shot, presuming the shooter would take out the biggest threat first. Neck Tattoo, because he simply enjoyed shooting people. He was going to do it anyway, but she guessed he got a bigger kick if his victims were fighting back.

AJ let her shoulders slump in defeat and lifted the gun a little higher to pass it to Neck Tattoo. She caught the disappointment on his face. AJ was about to sidestep in front of JSB to use him as a shield, while getting a proper grip on the handgun, when Admiral barked from across the street. Car tyres crunched over the limestone gravel and Neck Tattoo risked a glance back. AJ saw a sheriff's car come to a stop.

For a moment, everyone froze. To AJ, it felt like a match had just been tossed into a box of fireworks and they were all waiting for the first one to go off. But the flame fizzled out. Neck Tattoo took several steps back to stay clear of JSB and tucked his gun inside his jacket. Johnny eyed AJ, and she knew he was angling after getting his own gun back. Instead, she tucked the gun in the waistband of her leggings, under her T-shirt.

The door to the sheriff's car opened, and Officer Reid stepped out, looking around suspiciously. The passenger door opened next, but no one got out. Their radio crackled, and AJ saw the second officer inside the car talking into the mic. Was Cass right? The question hammered around her mind. If she was, and Reid was a bent copper on the payroll of the Miami mobster Danitess, then he was about to take sides. But whose side?

JSB seemed genuinely confused when AJ had mentioned the mobster's name. If he wasn't the heavy for Danitess, then maybe the other two were. Made more sense as they were Hispanic. He had to be with one or the other, as his timing couldn't be ignored.

"We received a 9-1-1 call from this location," Reid announced, staying shielded behind the driver's door. "What seems to be the problem?" AJ followed his gaze as his eyes finally found Cass, who was still standing in the backyard. "Mrs Lee?" Reid asked.

"They're trespassing, officer," Cass called back.

Reid turned his attention back to the two Hispanic men.

"We were just asking for directions, man," Neck Tattoo lied. "We got lost around all these little roads and shit. She's talking about this guy." He pointed towards JSB.

AJ watched the policeman carefully, trying to spot any covert signals between him and any of the thugs. If he made one, she missed it, but his face was shadowed by the street light behind. His partner said something from inside the patrol car, his face illuminated by the computer screen mounted to the dash.

"Let's start with some IDs, gentlemen," Reid announced, and AJ noticed his hand rested on his holstered sidearm.

Nothing made sense anymore. She had no idea what Johnny Sore Balls had to do with all this. It was only an assumption that the other two worked for Danitess, and that Reid might be a bent copper. Or not. In which case, he was in grave danger, facing off against the three armed goons. Well, two armed and one disarmed.

"You first, sir, nice and slow," Reid added, looking at Neck Tattoo.

AJ's heart was in her mouth as she watched Neck Tattoo reach for his back pocket, expecting all hell to break loose. Emily grunted next to her, behind the gag, and AJ realised she could untie her now. But Emily was nodding her head frantically towards Cass. AJ turned. Cass was pointing at the pouches on the bonnet of the white SUV, and then thumbed towards the boat. In the backyard spotlights, AJ noticed the port bow line had been untied on the *Reel-Lee Hooked* and wondered how that had happened.

"Do you have a firearm on your person, sir?" she heard Reid asking as Emily grunted again, right before she bolted across the yard, hands still tied behind her back. AJ grabbed the pouches and sprinted after her.

"Ma'am! Hold it, ma'am!" Reid yelled from behind.

In the few seconds it took AJ to reach the dock and free the last line, Cass was starting the outboards and Emily had somehow leapt into the cockpit without going arse over tea kettle. With the line freed, AJ jumped aboard as Cass was already backing out, the props thrashing at the water as she revved the engines.

Reid was running across the backyard with his firearm in hand, shouting at Cass. "Stop right there, Mrs Lee!"

AJ was sure he was going to shoot them, which would seem to answer their question about his allegiances, but with a glance towards the house, she was confused once more. The second officer held a shotgun, which he aimed at the ground. The SUVs blocked her view, but it had to be the two Miami thugs he had laid down on the concrete.

Looking back at Reid, she realised his gun was actually pointed at another man running ahead of him. Having backed into the narrow canal, Cass shoved the throttles forward and the Glacier Bay lurched just as JSB threw himself over the starboard bow railing, landing heavily on the raised foredeck. For a second, AJ thought his burly mass was taking him straight through the railing on the other side, but somehow he managed to hang on.

"Mrs Lee, please stop! We need to sort this out!" Reid yelled from the dock, having lowered his gun. Anything else he said was lost to the engine noise, as Cass blatantly ignored the no-wake rule in her haste.

Johnny Sore Balls got to his feet and grabbed one of the hardtop supports, a scrape blossoming red on his forehead. AJ pulled the gun from her waistband and pointed it at him.

"You're a pain in the arse, mister."

AJ heard frantic grunting from behind her and turned.

"Bugger. Sorry Em," she said and pulled the gag down from her mouth.

"Give me the bloody gun!" Emily yelped. "I wanna shoot the bastard!"

32

FRIDAY

AJ made Emily promise to calm down before she finally cut the zip ties binding her wrists. JSB sat on the raised foredeck and assured her he'd stay put, but AJ gave Cass the gun just in case. Emily swore she was fine, just pissed off. The men hadn't harmed her, and the driver had actually been a pleasant fellow who'd made sure she had water and snacks. After explaining to Em who he actually was, AJ went below and hid the pouches again. She then hunted for zip ties, which she found amongst a toolkit.

Cass was running faster down the canal than she should, but the catamaran was stable in the smooth, sheltered waters, so AJ went forward and told JSB to stand so she could secure him. He didn't protest and let her restrain his wrists behind his back.

"Let me explain what's going on," he said.

"I wish somebody bloody well would," AJ grumbled. "Are you going to behave? We'll be out in rough water, so I need to sit you down somewhere or you'll end up over the side."

"There's three of you, you have the gun, and I'm tied up. What the hell am I going to do?" he said, all of which was true. "I was never going to hurt any of you. I'm not like them," he added. "It was all hot air."

"You smacked me to the ground!"

"I'm sorry about that. I had to stop Mrs Lee from screaming."

"Well, all your hot air was quite convincing, so don't expect us to trust you for one second. And don't turn us into murderers by making us shoot you. Especially Em. She won't need much persuading."

"I think you've already paid me back," he responded, furrowing his brow. "I don't think I'll ever have children now."

AJ led him along the side of the boat to the cockpit. "Believe me, there's more where that came from if you mess us about," she said before sitting him down on the couch in the pilothouse, so everyone could hear what he had to say. "So, what's your real name?"

"Johnny," he replied.

"Seriously?" AJ and Emily both questioned.

"It is."

"Okay, Johnny, you've got about two minutes before we're in open ocean, so start talking," AJ demanded, and stood next to Cass at the helm. Em remained in the cockpit, giving Johnny threatening glances.

"Have you seen my mobile?" Cass said, frantically searching around the dash.

AJ helped her look. "You called the police, right? So you had it at the house."

"Bloody miracle I remembered which two buttons to press for an emergency call. I had to keep it in my pocket so no one saw. Of course, I didn't expect Reid to show up."

"Where did you put it when you got on the boat?" AJ asked.

"I thought I tossed it in the cubby there," she said, pointing to a recessed part of the dash. "But looks like I missed. Bollocks, I've only had that one a few months."

"We'll have to use mine," AJ said, and turned back to Johnny. "Let's hear it then, and don't waffle on, or I'll let Em shoot you."

To his credit, Johnny managed a grin. "Back at the house, you mentioned the name Danitess. That's who the other guys work for,

Orn Danitess. He's the one who stole the the Three Eyes of Shiva that belong to an expat Russian guy named Valery Barinov. Danitess hired some pros to break into the workshop of a lapidarist in South Africa and take them. The three stones are actually painite, which is ridiculously rare, and together those three gems are priceless."

"You'd better get to something we don't know, or you're in for a long swim, mate," Cass told him.

"I didn't know any of that," Emily complained. "What's a lap-who-daddy?"

"You've been out of the loop for a bit, Em. We've been busy while you were swanning about with this guy," AJ replied with a grin.

Emily made a face.

"A lapidarist is a gem-cutter," Johnny explained. "A guy who facets gemstones."

Emily made another face.

"So, who do you work for?" AJ asked the man. "You said he's no one we'd want to meet."

"Yeah, that was part of the hollow threat stuff. He's a tough businessman, but he's actually a decent guy. His name is Johan Botha, and he owns a diamond mine in South Africa. While the thieves were there, they helped themselves to a diamond, too."

"Which belongs to Botha?" AJ guessed.

"Exactly."

"It's a whopper," Cass added, letting out a whistle.

"So wait a sec," Emily interrupted. "You have all three of these painite, ruby-looking gems, and a bloody great big diamond?"

AJ nodded. "Yeah. I told you we've been busy."

"That diamond is the largest single stone ever pulled from Botha's mine, but more importantly, it was being set in his only daughter's wedding ring. She's getting married next month."

"So you were never after the rubies... I mean painites?" Cass asked.

Johnny shrugged his shoulders. "Botha told me if I recovered them as well, I could keep the reward money. All he cared about was getting his diamond back."

"So how come the story about the robbery didn't mention the diamond?" AJ asked suspiciously.

"Johan Botha is a very private man who doesn't like to advertise his problems. Bad business for a diamond miner to let the world know they can steal from him. He chose to take care of it himself, and that's why he contacted me. I do freelance problem-solving when discretion is required."

"You mean kidnapping," Em snapped back. "Not very discreet if you ask me."

"My apologies for that too, but you did make it easy."

"The hell I did!"

"You literally came around the corner and walked right into me," he said, and laughed.

AJ was surprised how pleasant he seemed now he wasn't attacking them or pointing his gun around.

"But I put up a good fight after that," Emily said defensively.

"If you call biting the crap out of me a defence."

"I got a good boot in first."

"Do you ladies go for the nuts every time?"

"Krav Maga move," Emily gloated.

"What about the biting?" Johnny asked, laughing. "That Krav Maga too?"

"Nah, that was just to make you squeal like a little girl."

"Well, while you were busy biting instead of screaming for help, it was easy to toss you in the back and leave."

"Oi!" Cass shouted, and they all fell quiet, looking her way. "This is all bloody fascinating, but we still have to find my idiot husband. So let's have some more answers."

"Of course, sorry," Johnny replied. "But I'm afraid I don't know where Mr Lee is."

"Poppers didn't tell you?"

"Poppers swore he didn't know where he is."

"How come Poppers was driving you around?" AJ asked.

"Yeah, some bloody friend he turned out to be," Cass chipped in.

"I was asking around on Wednesday evening, and someone told me to look for a guy named Poppers who hung out at Mar Bar. I found him and at first he said he didn't know anyone named Lee. When I offered him cash, he starting getting his memory back, and half an hour later I'd talked him into driving me around to all the places he might be. This afternoon, we hadn't eaten all day, so I dropped him off at the same bar to get food while I filled the Escalade up with gas. I was just pulling in to pick him up when I found you two there."

AJ slapped the framework. "That's why Poppers stayed put and didn't run with us."

"But he warned us about Danitess," Cass added. "Didn't he tell you Rosie gave him the black eye?"

"Told me he'd walked into a cabinet," Johnny said.

"We know Rosie spent the night in jail for popping Poppers on the noggin," AJ explained. "We figured they set it up so Rosie could hide for a night."

"Well, Poppers never told me that, or I would have picked your husband up when he was released the next morning." Johnny shifted uncomfortably on the couch, his brow knitted. "Come to think of it, the guy never really took me anywhere I couldn't find on my own."

"He's still coming off my Christmas list," Cass moaned.

"Then who did pick him up from jail?" Johnny asked. "His truck was at a park with a boat ramp on Wednesday, and then got towed. After that, it stayed in the tow yard until you two collected it. He either got an Uber or someone picked him up."

"We think it might have been Phil," Cass said sombrely.

"Who's Phil?" Johnny and Emily asked together.

"Another friend of Rosie's," Cass replied, looking at AJ.

"Was this guy deaf?" Johnny asked.

"That's him. How did you know?"

"He was at Mar Bar when I met Poppers. Never said a word.

Poppers explained later that he's lost his hearing. Any chance this guy, Phil, knows where your husband is? Where is he now?"

"Good question," AJ muttered.

Johnny looked at her. "Which one?"

"The where part," Cass clarified, taking the conversation away from AJ. "But wherever he is, he can't help us. AJ brought his body up off the *Spiegel Grove* earlier tonight."

"Blimey," Emily whispered, giving AJ a sympathetic look. "But why was he diving the wreck? Bit of a coincidence, yeah?"

Cass was about to reply, but AJ cut her off. "Hold up. Before we give up any more information, we need to know where he stands," she said, nodding towards Johnny. "All we know is he claims the diamond belongs to this Botha chap who hired him. The facts are he's broken into this boat, and I'm guessing it was you who broke into the truck?"

"It was," he admitted.

"Right. He's attacked and threatened us, kidnapped Emily, and now he's letting us fill him in on a bunch of details he didn't know. What's your angle here, Mister Johnny Extra Sore Balls?"

Emily snickered, and Johnny frowned. "I told you, my concern is the diamond."

Em stepped from the cockpit into the pilothouse. "Yeah, but how do we know you're not some wanker with a good story who's looking to steal the diamond?"

He thought for a moment. "You can look up Johan Botha. His name will light up Google. You can see what I said about him is true. I'm sure there'll be something on there about his daughter's wedding as well."

"Sure, but like you just said, anyone can look all that up on the net," Em responded, tapping a finger on the table. "You're not giving us proof."

"As of right now, I can't think of any reason not to hand you over to the police and let them sort you out," AJ added.

Johnny nodded a few times while he thought it over. "Fair

point. You're right, of course. But, if I'm not mistaken, you just ran away from the police?"

"That was different," AJ replied defensively. "Cass knows a detective who's on the up and up," she lied.

Johnny gave her a sly look, which seemed to imply he knew she was making it up. "Tell you what. It's about 5:00am in South Africa at the moment, so we can't call now, but in a few hours we'll video call Johan, and you can talk to him yourselves. How's that?"

The three women all looked at each other and no one complained, so AJ spoke up.

"That's better, but what do we do with you until then?"

"I'll help you."

"Help us do what?" Cass scoffed.

"Help you find your husband."

"You've spent all week trying to find him. What makes you think we need your help?"

"Because you haven't found him either. Besides, what if more of Danitess's men show up?"

"That's a good point," Cass agreed.

"Look, here's the deal I'm offering you," Johnny continued. "I'll help you find your husband and keep you three safe while we do it. We'll call Mr Botha so you can see I'm legit, and then you give me the diamond to return to him. After that, we split the reward money for the painite."

"I don't give a monkey's about any rewards. I just want Rosie back so I can throttle him myself."

"How much is the reward?" Em asked.

"A million," Johnny and AJ replied at the same time.

"Blimey! That'll buy lunch for a while."

Cass shrugged her shoulders. "Okay, I suppose I do give a monkey's about the money, but only after we find Rosie."

"Does that mean we have a deal?" Johnny asked hopefully.

Cass nodded. "I suppose so. But I'm not ready to cut you loose just yet, and you're certainly not having your bloody gun back."

"We still don't know about Reid, either," AJ pointed out.

"Who's Reid?" Johnny asked.

AJ eyed him suspiciously. "The copper who showed up at the house. You don't know him?"

"No clue, never seen him before. You think he might be on Danitess's payroll? Is that why you ran?"

AJ shrugged her shoulders. "He's either a really diligent copper, got the hots for Cass – which is what I think – or he's bent."

"It's number three," Cass said, waving her hand dismissively. "And if he's on the take, those two thugs will be back after us."

"Don't forget, they have Poppers," Johnny added.

Cass's shoulders dropped. "What do you think they'll do to him?"

Johnny raised one eyebrow. "Nothing pleasant, I'm afraid. They'll probably make him sing like a canary."

33

FRIDAY

Cass stayed close to the coastline, avoiding the swells of the deeper water. The Florida Keys barely poked above the ocean, and for a mile or two offshore, the depth didn't go below six to ten feet. The reefs at Molasses and French were in 30 feet at most, before sloping away over the next few miles to where the deep wrecks sat in the sand. Waves coming in lost much of their energy across the long shallows, tickling the mangroves of Pennekamp and the riprap sea walls protecting the condos and homes to the south. But the wind chop still made for a rocky ride.

As they headed south, AJ stared off the starboard side towards the coastline. Neighbourhood lights had dominated the first few miles, but now it was ink black for a stretch along an undeveloped section of state-owned land, opposite Rodriguez Key. They'd decided to check Phil Giles's home in Tavernier, and now AJ wondered if she was unknowingly looking at the man's battered body draped in the long roots of the mangroves.

"Are we picking up your truck, Cass?" AJ asked after a prolonged silence.

"Not unless someone wants to ride in the bed," she replied, glancing at Johnny.

He was fidgeting on the couch, trying to get comfortable. Or less uncomfortable. They'd left him tied at the wrists, still not completely convinced he wouldn't try something.

"Your Beetle is at Mar Bar," Em offered. "At least it was at the time of my abduction." She gave Johnny one more annoyed look to go with the several hundred she'd already dealt him.

"Get my phone from my pocket," he said, ignoring her venom.

"I'm not putting my hand in there," she scoffed. "Don't think you're getting any cheap thrills from me, mate."

AJ rolled her eyes. "Here, I'll get it. I have a feeling I know what he wants to show us." She rummaged around in the man's trouser pocket and found his mobile.

"I know what he wants to show us, alright," Emily continued. "He's after a little how's-your-father, but all he'll get from me is another kick in the cobblers."

"That's why I had to put the gag on her," Johnny moaned. "She never shuts up and I can't understand half of what she says."

AJ grinned. "What's your passcode?"

"9-1-3-5."

AJ unlocked the mobile. "Is it an app?"

"Yeah. How did you know?"

"Because you showed up everywhere we drove, but had no idea where we were on the boat."

"What are you talking about?" Em asked. "What app?"

"A tracker," AJ replied. "Is this Mrs Sore Balls?" she asked, looking at his home screen.

"She's my wife, if that's what you mean."

"Pretty fit," AJ commented, and showed Em the picture of a beautiful brunette smiling at the camera.

"What's she see in a wanker like you?" Em asked, hands on hips. "She know you go around attacking women and kidnapping?"

Johnny shook his head. "Look, I am really sorry. I've never done either of those things before. This gig is a lot more pressure than the usual assignments. And no, I'd certainly be embarrassed for her to know."

Em scoffed, but let it go for now.

AJ showed Johnny the screen and pointed to an icon.

"That's it," he confirmed.

AJ opened the application and waited while a map came up. One by one, three dots flashed at different locations. She zoomed in.

"That must be your Escalade. It's still at Cass's house."

"I'm surprised. I figured Danitess's guys would have grabbed it. Poppers had the key."

AJ found the next location. "Truck is at the marina where we left it." She scrolled across to the final dot. "This must be the Beetle."

"Should be at Mar Bar, I parked just down the road a bit," Em said, leaning in to see the screen. "Is that Mar Bar? I thought it was by a canal."

"It's not," AJ replied, still examining the map. "And, it is."

"What? Is it there or not?" Cass asked, looking over from the helm. "If anyone has pinched my love bug, you're buying me a bloody new one, mister diamond mine, fancy Escalade bloke!"

"I meant, no that's not Mar Bar, and yes, Mar Bar is on a canal," AJ clarified. "Someone's moved it."

"The Beetle, not the bar, yeah?" Em said and grinned when AJ gave her a sideways look.

"Correction. Someone is moving it. Cass's love bug is currently travelling north on Overseas Highway."

"Someone's half-inched my baby!" Cass groaned.

"Guess we won't be taking the V-Dub either, then," Em said, patting Cass on the back.

"We don't need a car," Cass responded. "There's a little marina at the trailer park where Phil lives..." she trailed off, realising her error. "Lived," she mumbled under her breath.

"You know what we haven't seen?" AJ asked thoughtfully, still watching the little dot moving on the screen.

"Tacos," Em blurted. "We haven't seen any tacos, and I'm starving."

"I'm bloody hungry too, come to think of it," AJ agreed. "But no, tacos were not what I had in mind." She looked up and scanned the darkness across the water. Pinpricks of white light showed where a handful of boats were at anchor for the night, but she couldn't see any red or green lights on moving vessels. "We haven't seen any sign of the Marine Police or the Coast Guard. You'd think they'd have had someone out on the water looking for us. We just ran from an officer of the law."

It was Cass's turn to scoff. "I'm telling you, that bloke is bent as a nine-bob note. Only person he called was Danitess. Probably his goons who just nicked my love bug."

Cass slowed and studied her chart plotter, turning starboard towards the shore where lights from the homes dotted the coastline. They passed a long, narrow wooden pier, which extended out into the shallow waters from a small peninsula, barely visible in the dark. Ahead, a pair of soft lights illuminated a small marina, cut into the limestone, guarded on one side by a large tree.

It was nearing midnight, and Driftwood Trailer Park was eerily quiet once Cass shut down the engines. AJ side-tied them to the main dock next to the boat ramp. The little man-made bay had capacity for about a dozen boats, but only four were present, all small centre consoles. Phil's Mako would normally be spending the night alongside them.

"How are we going about this, Cass?" AJ asked, and picked up Johnny's mobile from the table again.

Cass looked towards the rows of trailer homes, most illuminated by low-voltage lighting leading to their doors. "I guess we'll start by knocking on his door."

AJ frowned. "Cass, he's not going to answer, is he?"

"Of course not, love, but I'm hoping my Rosie will come to the door. He'll give us some ridiculous reason why he sent poor ol' Phil out there, and we'll have to tell him... you know... it didn't work out."

"Ladies," Johnny said, shifting on the seat. "This is the part where I may be of service. I can get you in the place without knocking or making any noise."

The sound of a car driving into the trailer home park from Overseas Highway echoed around the still night. AJ held up the mobile.

"Looks like your love bug has come to you, Cass."

They all heard the distinctive sound of the Volkswagen come to a stop and the engine switch off.

AJ and Cass looked at each other. "Poppers?" they both guessed.

"He knows where Phil lives," Cass added.

"Where is Phil's trailer?" AJ asked.

"On the far row, towards the road," Cass said, and they all glanced that way, but couldn't see beyond the first few homes. They hadn't even seen headlights when the car pulled in.

"Unless you're sure the car thief is friendly, I'd like the opportunity to hold up my end of this deal," Johnny offered again.

Cass and AJ looked at each other. "I'd rather he was cannon fodder than one of us," AJ said with a grin.

"Agreed, but we keep the gun," Cass responded.

"If he plays up, let me shoot him, please," Em added, and Johnny looked at her curiously.

"You sure know how to hold a grudge, young lady."

"Best you remember that, too. You know where I'll aim first."

AJ couldn't hide a smile. "Alright, turn a bit," she instructed the man, and he twisted his large frame in the narrow gap between the couch and the table. AJ cut the zip ties with a pair of side-cutters and Johnny rubbed his red-marked wrists in relief.

"Thank you," he said, standing and stretching his legs. AJ took a step back. His unbound presence still felt slightly menacing.

"My advice is to let me go up there alone, but I'm guessing I haven't earned that much trust yet," he said, moving out to the cockpit.

"Correct," Cass quickly responded.

"Fair enough. Then may I suggest one of you comes with me

and the other two stay here? Sneaking around a quiet neighbourhood at night is hard enough alone, but with four of us, someone's
going to get suspicious."

Cass stepped from the gunwale to the dock. "Fine, come on
then."

Johnny didn't move. "Hold up Mrs Lee, hear out the plan first."

Cass put her hands on her hips impatiently.

"Me and..." he turned to AJ, "I'm sorry, what's your name?"

"It's not tats, or sweet cheeks."

"Again, I am sorry for the way I acted, but I assure you it was
just that, an act."

"AJ."

"Okay, I'll walk up the road with AJ, as though we're just
coming home from an evening out. We'll chatter quietly, a couple of
laughs, nothing for anyone to be alarmed about. Then I'll assess the
situation at the house and weigh up our options based on who and
what we find."

Cass waved him to the dock, but he still didn't move. "Come
on, your plan's fine, except it's my fault we're in this mess, and my
husband we're looking for. So I'll be going with you."

"I understand you feeling that way, Mrs Lee, but here's why AJ
is going with me." He finally stepped over to the dock and nodded
for AJ to follow. "If your husband is hiding in the house and sees
you wandering up the road with another bloke, I'm guessing he'll
have something to say about it. We don't need him coming out all
fired up to win his pretty lady back. Someone is over there in your
car they stole. We have them to worry about, too." He turned to
Emily. "This one is going to have a hard time keeping quiet, and if
she does talk to me, it will not seem like we're having a nice
evening out. That leaves AJ."

"Sod it, Cass, I don't mind going, let's just get on with it," AJ
said firmly, joining them on the dock. "If he comes back without
me, shoot him." She strode off into the trailer park.

"Which trailer?" Johnny quickly asked Cass.

"It's on the far row, a few in from the end. I don't remember the number, but you can't miss it. Look for the ugly pale green single-wide with a boat trailer as old as the house." Johnny nodded and hurried to catch up.

"I'm a good actress," AJ heard Em complaining as they walked away. "I was in a movie once. Did you know that, Cass?"

Four paved lanes ran through the park between US1 and the water. Each row had around ten trailers on each side, many of them double-wides. Some, well-maintained, comfortable-looking homes, and others were not so much. At the ocean end, the only lighting was from the homes which had decorative lamps of some sort. One dwelling had their Christmas lights up well in advance.

"Do you like sushi?" Johnny asked, catching up to AJ.

"I do," she replied, then remembered she was supposed to be making happy banter with him. "But I don't eat meat, I'm pescatarian."

"I'm a Pisces," he said and laughed at his own joke.

AJ couldn't bring herself to do the same. "Generally, I only eat local fresh-caught fish, but I do cave in and have sushi as a special treat."

"I'm a steak guy myself," Johnny said, keeping the conversation going. He was speaking quietly, but in a happy tone, and as awkward as she felt sneaking around a trailer park with a guy she didn't trust, she realised his plan had merit.

"If I'd been forced to guess, that would have been my assumption," she responded, forcing a buoyant tone.

Ahead, the Beetle sat in front of a trailer, and Cass hadn't lied. It was one of the more run-down units, painted a shade of green that had to have come from a sale rack at the hardware store. They both fell quiet as they approached, and Johnny put a hand out, signalling AJ to stay behind him. She was happy to do so. She hadn't been kidding about him being the first one fed to the cannons.

He paused under a tree between Phil's house and the neighbour's. They were in full shadow, but could see the front door was closed, the old boat trailer between them and the house. Behind the boat trailer was a run-down shed with the door open. Sounds of careful movement came from inside.

"Wait here," Johnny whispered, then started down the fence line on their side of the boat trailer.

She noticed he moved incredibly quietly for a big man, and quickly, too. He only seemed to take a few steps, but he was already next to the shed. His timing was perfect. From beside the shed, he stepped forward just as a figure came out of the door. Johnny had a hand over his victim's mouth and an arm twisted behind his back before the unsuspecting fellow knew anyone was there. AJ heard the man grunt and swing his free hand around, trying to bat his assailant away.

She sprinted between the house and the trailer, rushing to help. "Let him go!" she hissed.

"Huh?" Johnny asked. "Who is this?"

"That's Rosie!"

Johnny released him and Rosie Lee stumbled forward. "What the hell do you think you're doing?" he gasped. "You nearly gave me a heart attack."

"I'm sorry, Rosie," AJ apologised. "It's so good to see you. You're alive!"

Rosie got his breath back and smiled at her. "It's good to see you too, AJ."

She looked her friend over. "What on earth happened to you?"

His clothes were damp and bedraggled, his hair matted to his head, and his face pale. He looked exhausted. "I had a bit of a swim. I could do with a shower and a bite to eat. How's your trip been?"

34

SATURDAY

Johnny walked back to the dock to fetch Cass and Emily, while Rosie let AJ into the trailer with the key he'd retrieved from Phil's hiding spot in the shed. The inside of the home was only slightly more appealing than the outside. It was relatively clean and tidy, but everything was old and worn out. Except for the TV. It was a sports-watching behemoth flatscreen dominating the wall opposite a well-worn couch.

"Who's the big guy?" Rosie asked, once Johnny had left.

"He works for the bloke whose diamond you managed to end up with," AJ said, preferring not to say too much until Cass arrived. "He's sort of helping us. His name's Johnny."

"He fits the description of the guy that was after me. How's he helping?" Rosie asked suspiciously. "Are you sure we can trust him? I'm pretty sure he's the guy who broke into my truck. I was on Phil's boat, so we were a way off, but it was a big guy like him."

AJ chewed her lip for a moment. "Can't say we trust him completely, but maybe things will make more sense when you tell us what's been going on."

Rosie shrugged his shoulders. "Hell if I know. I've been hiding on a derelict boat off Rodriguez Key since yesterday. Have you seen my mate, Phil? Deaf guy. I'm really worried about him."

AJ sighed. "Yeah, we've seen him. Why don't you wash up a bit and when Cass is here, we can tell you what we know."

Rosie's face lit up. "I can't wait to see her."

AJ wasn't so sure he would be once Cass let loose on him, but there again, AJ didn't understand the strange dynamic of their relationship. Except that they both clearly still loved each other.

Cass burst through the door like a steamroller, with Johnny and Emily in tow. Hearing the commotion, Rosie stepped from the bathroom to be assaulted by a hug from Cass. She buried her face in his shoulder and AJ could hear her sobbing.

"Sending me back alone wasn't the greatest idea," Johnny said quietly to AJ as they gave the reunited couple their moment.

"Huh?"

"If you remember, you told them to shoot me if I came back without you."

"Oh, bugger. That's right." She looked at Em, who was grinning.

"I thought Annie Oakley here was going to empty the magazine into me."

"I was trying to fire a warning shot in the air, you pillock, just to let you know I was serious."

"I would have taken you more seriously if you'd known where to find the safety."

He was grinning too, so AJ assumed he hadn't felt seriously endangered. "Apparently I need to be more careful with my off-hand comments."

"I follow orders, sir," Em declared with a salute. "Next time I'll know where that little switchy thing is."

A yelp from across the room made everyone turn. The 'relieved to see you' phase was over, and now Cass was whacking her husband with her hand as he tried to protect himself.

"Come on, hon, my phone died... ouch! I borrowed someone's phone and tried calling you as soon as I swam ashore... ouch! You didn't answer!"

Cass paused her corporal punishment. "I lost my phone earlier this evening," she said meekly. "Escaping from the bloody hoodlums trying to kill us because of you!" Her voice escalated as she spoke, and the beating resumed.

AJ did her best to coax Cass away from Rosie, steering her towards the couch where she finally sat down, out of breath and rubbing her now sore hand. Rosie dropped into a wooden chair by a small dining table.

"Okay, now that's all sorted, let's figure out what's happened, and what we do next," AJ said, positioning herself between the two of them. "Rosie, this is my good friend, Emily, and the fella is Johnny."

Everybody said hello, then AJ continued. "So, as best we know, there's a mobster from Miami who had all these gems stolen from a jeweller bloke in South Africa, which somehow you got your hands on. Well, hardly surprising, he wants them back."

Rosie looked at her with his brow furrowed, so she carried on. "Johnny here was hired by a diamond mine owner to get his stone back, and he chased us around, trying to find you. He says his job is to return the diamond."

Johnny nodded, and Rosie eyed him up and down.

"The mobster's thugs showed up at the house as we were about to exchange Emily for the gemstones, but Cass got us away in *Reel-Lee Hooked* with a bit of quick thinking."

Rosie looked at Emily, who smiled and batted her eyelashes.

"Exchange? You were being held by the mobster guys?"

"No. By him," she replied, back-handing Johnny on the arm.

Rosie frowned. "He kidnapped you and now he's standing here supposedly helping us?"

"We made a deal with him. He helps us find you, and he gets his diamond back and a split of the reward money for the painite gems," AJ explained, as though it all made sense.

"Easy result, as it turns out," Emily scoffed.

Rosie's eyes shot back to AJ. "So they are painite?"

She nodded. "Seems that way. The Eyes of Shiva, or something like that."

"'The Three Eyes of Shiva,'" Johnny corrected.

"With a million bucks reward?" Rosie asked.

"Yes," Cass snapped. "And how the bloody hell did you end up with them?"

Rosie grinned. "They fell off the back of a lorry, as you would say, my love."

"What a load of bollocks! Where did you nick them from?"

"I swear, they actually fell off a boat, not a lorry, but they fell off nonetheless."

"Four priceless gemstones just slipped over the side of a boat?" AJ asked, knowing there had to be more to the story.

"Well, a guy dropped them over the side while the Coasties were chasing him. But yeah, they fell over the side, and I just happened to be fishing nearby. I saw them go in, so I took a little swim and fished them out. It all happened near the *Benwood* back on Tuesday morning."

"And what did you think you were going to do with the bloody things?" Cass challenged.

"I didn't know what to think at first," Rosie replied, shaking his head. "But they were the biggest rubies I'd ever seen, and the diamond was huge. At the time, I didn't know what they really were. I figured something had to be a bit shady, so I searched the internet for recent robberies, and I stumbled across this report about priceless painite gems stolen from a Russian guy. I couldn't find anything about the diamond, but the three red stones fit the description. A million bucks reward for returning them, that's what the article said."

"So you always planned on handing them in?" Johnny asked.

Rosie looked at him warily. "Of course. I've been known to turn the other cheek for a TV of dubious heritage, but nothing like this. Once I knew what they might be, I was worried about the guys on the fancy Sea Ray who'd tossed them over the side. The Coasties escorted them away, but I didn't know if they were about to show up again. They probably saw my boat in the area, so I figured they'd want a word with me when they couldn't find their stuff on the sea floor. I decided the best thing was to hide them and wait a while until things calmed down. Then I'd go back out, pick them up and hand them in to the police for the reward."

"Then why did you leave all these stupid clues and ciphers for us?" Cass asked, getting to her feet and pacing around. "A bloody phone call would have been a lot easier."

"You found all the clues?"

"I don't know if we found them all, but we found enough," Cass snapped back.

"Wait, you mean you know where the gems are hidden?" Rosie seemed genuinely shocked.

"Yeah," Cass replied, hands on hips. "They're where I hid them now."

Now Rosie stood up. "Why did you do that?"

Cass and AJ both stared at each other, then back at Rosie.

"Because this guy threatened all kinds of things if we didn't get him the gemstones," AJ said indignantly, throwing a thumb towards Johnny.

They all turned towards the big man, who held his hands up in surrender.

"I was trying to find Mr Lee, hoping you'd lead me to the diamond," Johnny explained. "Honestly, I was clutching at straws. I'd been tracking the Sea Ray from Nassau, but when they were picked up by the Coast Guard, I reckoned I was dead in the water. Figured they'd search the boat and find the gemstones. Then I found a report on the Coast Guard Sector Key West social media page about the Sea Ray being detained under further investigation. There was a short comment on there about the *Reel-Lee Hooked* being in the vicinity. Probably in case they needed a witness at some point. I looked up who owned the boat and went by your house."

"That's when we found him searching the boat," Cass interrupted. "And he made it sound like you had his merchandise. Told us to bring him either the stuff, or you, and gave us a day. We had no clue what this merchandise was or where you were."

"Again, I'm sorry about all of that, but I really was under a lot of pressure to recover the diamond. I had no idea if your husband here had anything to do with it, but then you guys starting figuring things out. To me, it seemed like you'd lied and were finding out the details from your husband. I didn't care about Mr Lee as long as I recovered the diamond."

Rosie shook his head in disbelief. "All that clue business was in case anything happened to me. I thought, one day, if I was gone, you'd stumble across the note and maybe you'd figure it all out. I didn't think you'd do it in a day or two. My clues must have been superb."

Cass glared at him. "They were a pain in the bloody arse! If it wasn't for these two, I'd have never figured any of it out."

Rosie looked at AJ and Emily, a grin creeping across his face. "They were good, weren't they?"

AJ knew better than to say anything and put herself between them.

"I thought they were ace," Em replied, having no such worries.

"So, where are the stones now?" Rosie asked, turning his attention back to his wife.

She glanced over at Johnny before replying. "Never you mind, they're safe, and probably where you should have put them in the first place, you sodding idiot. Why you had to go all Bletchley bloody Park about it, I'll never know."

"Odd-looking bloke," Emily mumbled, and AJ nodded in agreement.

Rosie wasn't sure what they were talking about, so he moved on.

"Anyway, the gems seemed to make everybody act crazy, including me, so I was getting worried. I even gave ol' Poppers a shiner."

"We thought you did that to get a night in jail," AJ chimed in. "You know, to hide from all these blokes chasing you."

Rosie frowned. "Why would I do that? Anyone can look up the daily arrests."

"Yeah, that's actually how we found you'd been there," she admitted, realising her assumption had been horribly flawed. "The cap was brilliant, though."

"Did you get my cap back? I love that hat."

"We did," AJ said, regaining a small amount of pride after having her theory blown out of the water. "Got the clue in it, too."

Rosie laughed. "I was just bored, so I marked it up for something to do. I really did forget my hat when they let me out."

"Then why did you punch your best mate?" Cass asked, her tone softening.

Rosie sat back down and thought for a moment. "It was stupid, really. He was feeling all left out about this 'big score' 'cos I wouldn't tell him any details. He kept badgering me. I told him I'd make sure he was alright, but that wasn't good enough for him. We'd had a couple, you know, and next minute I was swinging at him. Felt awful about it later, but someone in the bar called the sheriff's office. They must have had a car close by as they were there right away and hauled me off."

"This was which night?" Johnny asked.

"Wednesday."

Johnny thought for a moment. "That's the night I met Poppers. It must have been after you'd been arrested."

"And you said Phil was there too, yeah?" AJ asked, recalling his earlier comment.

"That's right."

AJ looked over at Cass and their eyes met. "We saw Phil earlier in the evening at Sharkey's, and he swore he didn't know where you were," AJ said, turning back to Rosie.

He laughed. "Good ol' Phil. That man can keep a secret. He'd taken me out that morning to hide all the gems."

"He must have met with you and Poppers at Dillon's after that," AJ continued, stringing the timeline together.

"That's right. Then the three of us went to Mar Bar. Speaking of which, you know you left the keys in the Beetle?"

"Sorry," Emily said, raising her hand. "That was my fault. Well not really," she continued, back handing Johnny again. "It was his fault."

"How did you get to Mar Bar?" AJ asked. "You said you were hiding on a derelict boat?"

Rosie shook his head. "I couldn't stay on that relic any longer, so I swam to shore earlier tonight."

"Blimey, that had to be a mile or two." AJ said in surprise.

"Felt like ten," Rosie scoffed. "Then I borrowed a bike from that RV park at Mile Marker 96 and rode to Harry Harris Park, but my truck was gone. So I kept going to see if anyone was at Mar Bar. They'd already closed, and no one was there, but the Beetle was parked out front."

"Bloody hell, that's what? Five or six miles?"

"And that felt like twenty. Believe me, I was glad to get off that bicycle. Riding a bike in wet shorts does a number on your crotch."

Johnny winced.

"Anyway, I then drove here to see if Phil was home." The smile quickly left Rosie's face. "You were going to tell me where he is. I've been really worried. He's been gone since he dropped me at the derelict boat yesterday morning.

AJ knew her expression mirrored Cass's, and Rosie could tell something was wrong.

Cass moved to her husband's side and put an arm around him. "We found *Hear No Evil* at the *Spiegel* this evening, love. And AJ found Phil inside the wreck."

Rosie's head dropped, and Cass pulled him into her embrace. "I'm so sorry," she whispered.

35

SATURDAY

There were still a few questions left unanswered in AJ's mind, but everybody was dog tired, and they couldn't stay in the little trailer all night. Rosie had taken a while to compose himself after hearing about Phil. He and Cass leaned against the counter in the kitchen, talking in soft tones while the others sat quietly in the living area, not wanting to disturb them.

"Right," Rosie finally declared. "We can't sit here moping all night. Let's get a move on."

Everyone jumped to their feet, but AJ wondered what exactly the next move would be.

"If you're all set with the painite, I'll take the diamond and be on my way," Johnny said.

"That'll be a bit tough, seeing as you don't have a vehicle," Cass pointed out. "You're unlikely to get an Uber around here at this time of night."

"Where are we going?" AJ asked.

"Sheriff's office," Rosie said firmly. "Best thing to do now is hand these over to someone official, get them out of our hair."

Johnny frowned. "I thought you suspected that Reid guy of being on Danitess's payroll?"

"We do," Cass quickly replied. "But he won't be on the desk, and the whole station isn't on the take."

Johnny didn't look convinced. "If it's all the same to you, I'll hang on to Mr Botha's diamond, but I wouldn't mind a ride to your house. My Escalade is still there."

"This ought to be fun," Em chimed in, looking around the room. "Five of us in the love bug."

"Cass, why don't you take *Reel-Lee Hooked* home, and we'll meet you there?" Rosie suggested. "You could take this guy with you, and maybe AJ's friend."

"Not on your life, mate," Cass scoffed. "You're not leaving my sight. I think we should all stay together until this is over and done with."

Rosie nodded. "Probably best. Come on then, let's get the gems and we'll be on our way."

They turned off the lights and locked the door, returning the key to the shed. Em drove the bug to the dock while the others walked in silence. Occasionally, a car hummed by on US1, but other than that, the only sounds were cicadas and the ocean sloshing against the shore. Cass held tightly to Rosie's hand, which he didn't seem to mind in the least bit. AJ smiled. It was good to see them together, although she was sure they'd all prefer a different set of circumstances to rekindle their affection.

Cass went below and recovered the stones from under the stool. She checked each cylinder until she found the diamond and handed it to Johnny.

"We have a deal on the painite reward, correct?" he asked, watching Cass's reaction carefully.

"You mentioned something about a deal earlier," Rosie said. "What are we talking about here?"

"We agreed to split the reward with him if he helped," Cass admitted.

"Which was what?" Rosie questioned. "The helping part, I mean. He got a free boat ride and scared the shit out of me, and for that, he gets a few hundred grand?"

Johnny shrugged his shoulders. "That's the way it turned out, but it could have gone down differently. I was prepared to risk my life for your wife and friends."

Rosie raised an eyebrow. "We'll never know about that, will we?"

"Sod it, Rosie," Cass said impatiently. "I just want rid of these bloody gemstones. I made the deal, so we need to stick with it."

Rosie nodded to his wife. "You're right. A deal's a deal," he said dejectedly. "How did you agree to split it up?"

Cass looked at Johnny. "Actually, we didn't talk about that, did we?"

"I guess we didn't," Johnny admitted.

"Even. Three ways then," Cass declared, firmly.

Johnny frowned. "Three ways?"

Cass pointed to AJ and Emily. "Them, us, and you. Em was kidnapped and traumatised, and AJ risked more than anyone making the dives."

AJ was about to protest, but Cass gave her a glare that warned her to keep quiet.

"Agreed," Johnny replied.

Cass extended her hand, and they shook on the deal. "Good. Now that's set, let's get these bloody stones to the coppers."

Cass and Rosie stepped to the cockpit, but Johnny didn't move. "Just one more thing."

Cass looked back. "What's that?"

"I'd like my gun back. It's registered to me, and it wasn't cheap."

"Gun?!" Rosie barked. "You have his gun? He had a gun?"

"It's a legal, licensed firearm, Mr Lee. I often run into unsavoury characters in my line of work."

"It also works for…" Cass began, but stopped herself. "You can certainly have it back once we've handed the stones over to the police."

AJ guessed what her friend had been about to say, but Rosie

knowing how threatening Johnny had been wasn't going to help matters.

Johnny nodded his agreement, and they zipped up the Eisenglass on the Glacier Bay before walking towards the VW.

"I can't speak for Em, but I can tell you I don't need any reward money, Cass," AJ whispered as the two of them hung back from the others. "I've been helping a friend. There shouldn't be a reward for doing that."

Cass kept her voice even lower. "You deserve it more than we do, but the main thing is Johnny Sore Balls doesn't get half. We made a deal, so I'll stick to it, but half a bloody mil for doing bugger all is a bit steep."

AJ felt a sharp nudge in her side and looked down. Cass was handing her the gun.

AJ groaned. "I don't want the bloody thing."

"I've got to drive," Cass whispered back. "Just keep it out of his sight."

AJ reluctantly took the gun, and they joined the others by the little car. Everybody looked at each other for a moment.

"Well, I'm driving, so the rest of you can figure it out," Cass declared and tipped the driver's seat forward for whoever was getting in the back.

Em was first in. "I know, shorties in the back."

Rosie looked at Johnny. "Looks like you get shotgun seeing as you're nearly as big as the vehicle."

Rosie manoeuvred himself into the back and AJ squeezed in next to him on the bench seat. They all had to tilt their backsides to fit. Johnny tried opening the passenger door, which wouldn't budge.

"Hop over the top," Cass said, and he straddled the door with his long legs, which he then jammed against the dashboard as he slid into the seat.

"Don't suppose I could move the seat back a notch or two?"

Em had a few inches of room to her short legs, but Rosie was already twisted up like a pretzel.

"Not a chance," he muttered in reply.

"Right then," Cass said as she cranked over the engine. "If we're all sitting comfortably, we'll toodle-oo."

The air-cooled engine spun over, but refused to fire.

"Seriously? Now?" Rosie grumbled.

"Hey!" Cass scolded. "She'll never start if you talk to her like that."

Johnny gave Cass a sideways glance.

She turned the key again, and after several seconds, the old motor caught and sparked into life. Em and AJ gave a little cheer from the back seat.

Overseas Highway was dead quiet, not another vehicle in sight. Cass turned north, made a left at the first opportunity to cross the central reservation, then south towards Islamorada. Everyone was too worn out to make small talk, even Emily. They passed by the 24-hour McDonald's in front of the Winn-Dixie shopping centre. A couple of cars in the drive-through line were the first signs of life AJ had noticed, and her stomach rumbled, reminding her of how hungry she was.

They crossed over Tavernier Creek and she wondered if they'd stop and collect Rosie's pickup truck on the way back. AJ tried not to fidget as she knew no one was comfortable in the tiny, cramped car, but her bum was killing her. Well, she thought, Cass was probably okay, but now she was checking her rear-view mirror more than usual. Turned out her paranoia was spot on the last time she did that.

"What is it?" AJ asked, instantly back on high alert despite her fatigue.

Johnny started to turn around, but Cass put a hand out to stop him. "Don't, I think it's a copper."

"Do you think it's that Reid guy?" Johnny asked, mirroring AJ's first thought.

"Buggered if I know, but it's a car with lights on the roof."

Cass drove on, keeping to the 45 mph speed limit, passing Coral Shores High School on the left where the road narrowed to a single lane each way.

"What's he doing?" Rosie asked.

"He's just following us."

AJ desperately wanted to turn around and look, but she knew it wouldn't make any difference. And indeed, it didn't matter either way.

"Shit!" Cass blurted, and AJ noticed red and blue lights shining on the back of Johnny and Cass's heads in front.

"How far to the sheriff's office?" Johnny asked urgently.

"Another mile or so to the Tavernier substation near the courthouse."

"Keep going," Johnny responded.

"I can't keep going. I'm being pulled over. He'll ram us or something if we don't stop."

"Pull over! Turn into the church!" blared the demand from the police car's speakers, making AJ jump in her seat. She was sitting on the gun as she couldn't come up with anywhere better to hide it, and now she was not only physically uncomfortable, but unsure what she was supposed to do with it if they were getting nicked. She could hand it to the licensed owner, but she didn't want him shooting an innocent policeman. But if this was Reid, there was little chance the man was innocent in any way.

Cass slowed and turned into the car park for San Pedro Catholic Church.

"Pull up further," blasted the voice over the speakers.

"This is bad," Johnny hissed. "Give me back my gun, now. We're screwed."

Cass drove forward another 50 feet and AJ realised they were stopping where the trees blocked the street lights from US1. Only a faint illumination from accent lighting on the church allowed them to see the car park was empty besides them and the sheriff's car, which pulled closely behind them.

"I'm telling you, we need to take off as soon as he steps out of the car," Johnny continued. "Give me the damn gun, Cass."

"If it's not Reid, we can explain what we're doing to the officer and he can escort us to the station," Cass said, not sounding sure of herself.

"I hate to say this," Emily chimed in, "but I'm with the Neanderthal on this one. I think we might be a teeny bit screwed."

AJ was still sitting on the gun, but she reached underneath her backside and tried to wriggle it free.

"He's not getting out of the bloody car," Cass said, looking in the mirror, and AJ began to wonder if her friend might actually make a run for it. The idea had merit. They hadn't been doing anything illegal.

"Switch off the engine and hold both hands in the air with the keys where I can see them," the officer announced over the speaker.

"Do not shut off the engine, Cass!" Johnny told her.

"I think he's right, Cass," Rosie spoke up, looking strangely at AJ, who was squirming around next to him. "We only have to make it a mile."

"Can you see who it is through the windshield?" Johnny asked.

"I can't in the mirror," Cass replied, keeping the engine running.

In unison, everyone except Cass tried to turn and look at the car behind them, no one having enough room to actually see.

"Oh shit! We are screwed!" Cass yelped.

Hearing the sound of another vehicle, AJ whipped back around to see a large black SUV screech to a halt in front of them, blocking their escape.

36

SATURDAY

The front doors of the SUV opened and two burly men stepped out. They were better dressed than the two at the house, wearing sport coats and neatly pressed trousers. Both trained handguns at the Beetle, and AJ noticed they were fitted with suppressors as the others had been.

From behind, the police radio crackled, but AJ couldn't make out the message, and she guessed the cruiser's doors were still closed. The volume on the radio was quickly turned down.

The first man, with a military-style crew cut, started towards the driver's side, his barrel aimed at Johnny, who he must have perceived as the greater threat.

"Give me the gun, Cass," Johnny demanded under his breath.

"AJ has it!"

"Give it to me now, or none of us are leaving here alive," he said without taking his eyes from the gunman.

It was too late. The man had already reached Cass's door.

"Turn off the engine," he ordered in a calm but firm voice with an Hispanic accent.

Cass complied and held up the keys, which Crew Cut took from her.

The second man had a bald head with a dark shadow showing where his receding hair would be. He was overdue for a shave. Looking beyond the VW, he nodded, signalling the policeman to leave. AJ heard the car back up and turn around. She wondered what it paid to leave five citizens in the hands of the Miami mob.

Their fate was now sealed. Johnny had been right all along. AJ had managed to get the handgun out from underneath her backside and now had it under her leg with a hand on the grip, but in her mind, it may as well be back on the boat. She had no idea how to use it properly and gave herself a one in a hundred chance of hitting anything useful.

In their current predicament, useful meant one of the human beings aiming their guns at the Volkswagen. When she'd fired a gun once before, on Little Cayman, she'd fought her way free from a hateful young man who was intent on raping and murdering her and another woman. It was a mixture of rage and instinct that drove her to fire, and she'd almost missed from only a few yards away. It had taught her that pointing in the general direction and closing her eyes was not ideal for marksmanship. She'd winged the guy, but he'd been able to run away. Nothing about the experience gave her any confidence now she was holding a gun again. Their only chance was getting it into Johnny's hands, but that horse had bolted.

She and Cass had both fallen for the compliant route when they should have recognised that now was the time for decisive action. Johnny had tried to tell them, but they hadn't reacted in time. Now they faced the inevitable, and she cursed herself.

It was silent in the church car park, beyond the ticking of the VW engine as it cooled in the back of the car. AJ wondered if it would start next time. A problem for the tow truck driver, no doubt. She doubted the Buckleys would have the patience to coax the love bug into life. It would be easier to drag the old car up the ramp of the truck.

Baldy took a few steps back, opened the rear door of the SUV, and a man emerged. He looked short, especially next to his towering bodyguard. An older man in his sixties, if she had to guess, wearing a pale yellow golf shirt and chinos. Heavy gold chains hung from his neck and wrist, his chubby fingers decorated with chunky rings, and the diamonds encircling the face of his gold Rolex sparkled as he lifted his arm and pointed at the Beetle.

"You have caused me a lot of grief," he said in a gravelly voice which reminded AJ of mafia movies. This guy had to be Orn Danitess himself.

"You took some things that belong to me – now you're going to give them back."

"Don't say it, Em," AJ whispered across the back seat. Emily just groaned.

"And then what happens?" Cass asked.

"I'm sure we can come to an arrangement," Danitess replied.

"Can you tell us what that arrangement might be?"

Johnny scoffed from the passenger seat, but he didn't say anything.

"I can tell you if you don't hand over my gemstones, right now," the man replied, nodding towards Crew Cut. "He'll start shooting you one by one."

"Then we don't have a guarantee we'll leave here alive," Cass pointed out what was clearly obvious to everyone.

"Correct."

Danitess rose on the balls of his feet to see into the VW. He looked over the group as though he were choosing a sweet from a neighbour's bowl on Halloween.

"Shoot the blonde in the back," he ordered, and Crew Cut aimed at AJ's head.

AJ felt her body freeze and her breath stop as a lightning bolt of paralysing fear coursed through her body. Her eyes instinctively closed, and she heard Cass try to scream, but only a strangled gasp came out.

"Which one, boss?" Crew Cut asked, and AJ opened her eyes. "They're both blonde."

"Not the one with the purple shit," Danitess said, pointing to his own grey hair as though his thug wouldn't know where to look for purple. "The cuter one."

This time, Cass managed to scream. "No! We'll give them to you!"

But it was too late. Crew Cut's barrel shifted to Emily and the deafening gunshot rang out, echoing around the car park, and destroying the still of the night. An unsuppressed gunshot.

AJ watched aghast as the large figure of Crew Cut looked like he'd been punched in the chest as his body jerked. He took one step backwards, then fell heavily to the ground, cracking his head on the tarmac.

Facing her own death, AJ hadn't been able to respond, but the moment the threat had shifted to Emily, she'd immediately raised the weapon, aimed and fired. There had been no conscious decision, simply an impulse. A reaction. Now, staring at the man's unmoving body on the ground, she was overwhelmed with anger. He'd forced her into doing something she'd hoped to never face in life. Deliberately killing another human being. She felt no remorse, no regret, simply a rage at having been placed in the situation by other's actions.

AJ felt the VW rock as everyone but her ducked. An odd tinging sound was followed by a grunt from Rosie, and AJ realised Baldy was shooting at the car, the bullets passing through the windscreen.

"Gun!" Johnny yelled, and AJ reached forward between the seats and felt the weapon snatched from her hand.

Several dull thumps close by were followed by gunfire as the sound reached her after the bullets had hit. The shots sounded like they were coming from far away as Baldy fired his suppressed handgun at anything moving in the car.

"When I say so, fling your door open, Cass," Johnny ordered, "but stay down. Don't get out whatever you do." Cass grunted some form of response.

Two more bullets tinged through the glass and shredded the top of the front passenger seat.

"Now!" Johnny yelled and Cass shoved on her door.

Immediately, bullets tore through the metal as Baldy's fire was drawn to the motion and AJ watched Johnny rise above the dashboard. Two deafening shots cracked from his gun and he wiggled himself up until he could step over the passenger door which refused to open.

AJ risked a look and saw Baldy on the ground by the front corner of the SUV. Danitess was climbing into his vehicle, but Johnny was on him before he could close the door, pulling him back out and dropping him to the tarmac with a knee in his back.

"Everyone okay?" AJ shouted, her hearing numbed from the gunshots. She looked down and saw blood on her right arm, but couldn't feel any pain. Rosie was still bent double, keeping his head down, and she put a hand on his shoulder, pulling him upright.

"Oh shit," he muttered, and she immediately realised he'd been hit.

Noise began growing from around the car park, but AJ blocked it all out. "We need a cloth to stop the bleeding!"

Cass looked back. "Rosie! You've been shot!"

"I'm aware, hon," he groaned.

Emily handed AJ a wadded-up shirt which she pressed against the wound in Rosie's left shoulder. She quickly tipped him forward again and looked at his back. Not seeing any blood, she rocked him upright.

"Shit, AJ, what are you trying to do to me?" Rosie complained.

"Sorry, mate. Looking for an exit wound." AJ glanced over at Emily. "You okay, Em?"

Emily nodded, and AJ realised she was sitting there in her bra. She'd taken off her shirt to use on Rosie. "You trying to impress Johnny with your knockers?"

Rosie looked to his right. "Good Lord. That's some good nursing care right there."

"Hey!" Cass yelled. "Get your eyes off her, you dirty old man."

AJ grinned. "I think he's going to live, Cass."

"Everybody put your hands in the air!" came a voice AJ thought she recognised.

They all looked up to see there were three sheriff's patrol cars around them. Officer Reid was behind the middle car with his service weapon aimed at Johnny. Two more officers were behind the other two, both with weapons drawn, using their cars as shields.

Johnny had his hands in the air, but a foot still resting firmly on the base of Danitess's back.

"We need an ambulance here," AJ yelled. "Gunshot wound."

"Sir, slowly put the gun down, step away from that man, and lie face down on the ground with your arms out wide," Reid yelled. "We have an ambulance on its way, ma'am, but first we need to secure the scene. Stay in the car."

Johnny looked at Reid and then the other two officers.

"Do as they say, Johnny," AJ shouted. "No way all three are Danitess's men."

"I assure you, we're the good guys," Reid responded. "The officer you're referring to is in the back of my car, ma'am." He turned his attention back to Johnny. "Sir, you need to comply. Right now."

Johnny let the gun hang loosely between his fingers and stepped away from Danitess, moving towards the first police car. He looked directly at Reid again. "You'd better be legit." He reached down and placed his weapon gently on the ground, then took several steps backwards to keep himself between Danitess and the weapon. He lay down with his arms straight out from his sides.

"Any weapons in the car?" Reid directed at AJ.

"No, sir," she replied. "But there's a man down on the other side of the Beetle who was armed, and the one you can see beside the SUV. But I don't think either will give you any trouble."

The nearest officer stepped around his cruiser and picked up Johnny's gun, then Baldy's, which was next to his body. The officer dropped the magazine from both and cleared the chambers before placing everything on the roof of his car. He then approached Johnny and, taking his hands one by one, cuffed them behind his back.

Reid came out from behind his car, leaving the third officer with his gun on the Beetle. He walked over to Danitess, who began picking himself up off the ground.

"Stay down, sir," Reid ordered, but Danitess continued getting up.

"I said stay down!"

Danitess looked at him with disdain. "I'm gonna call the Governor right now and put you on the phone with him. These people have something that belongs to me, and they killed my bodyguards. I'm gonna shoot that son-of-a-bitch and get my shit back."

"Sir, I'm only going to say this once more. Get back down on the ground and spread your arms wide."

"Do you know who I am?" Danitess yelled, spittle flying from his mouth. "I'm getting my cell phone from the car, and if you want to keep your badges and your precious pensions, you'll back away."

Danitess grabbed the handle and swung the driver's door open as Reid stepped forward, pulling the Taser from his belt.

"Not another step, sir!" Reid yelled, and the two men stared at each other as everyone else fell silent.

A door opened on one of the cruisers. "Can I see if Rosie's okay?" Poppers shouted and Reid took his eyes off Danitess for a moment.

The Miami mobster reached into the van and when his left hand reappeared, he held up a mobile phone, but hidden from Reid, his right quickly followed with a gun. The policeman pulled his focus back to the suspect, and instantly realised he was a step behind. Before he could react with the Taser, he had a gun barrel pointed at his chest. Danitess spun back against the side of the SUV and slumped to the floor as two gunshots echoed around the car park.

Reid took a step back and caught his breath as the third officer stepped from behind his car, sidearm still aimed at Danitess on the ground. But he needn't have bothered. Both shots were on target.

37

SATURDAY

AJ sat in an interview room with Officer Reid and another policeman whose name she'd missed. She was on her third interview. After she had repeated the same details for the umpteenth time, Reid finally sat back in his chair and looked at the other officer. If they exchanged a signal, AJ didn't notice, but she was struggling to keep her eyes open.

"We're going to release you, but you need to delay your return to the Cayman Islands, Miss Bailey," he said wearily. It had been a long night for him too.

"For how long? I have customers all week. They're expecting me Monday afternoon."

"I'm sorry, miss, but we can't have you leaving the state until we're completely satisfied we have all we need in this case. There are still several areas where you broke the law. There may still be charges."

AJ sighed. "Can I ask you a few questions?"

Reid paused for a moment. "This concludes the interview, at…" He looked at his watch. "Oh-five-hundred, fifty." Switching off the recording, he turned to the other officer and nodded. The man stood and left the room. Reid waited until he'd closed the door before turning back to AJ. "I'll answer if I can, but there are many details of an open case I can't disclose."

AJ nodded. "I understand. I wanted to know how you knew to come to the church?"

Reid furrowed his brow and thought carefully before replying. "Let's just say we've had an eye on a certain officer within the ranks whose behaviour had raised some flags. That officer arrived at Mrs Lee's house as we were loading up the armed gentlemen you'd encountered. He offered to transport them to the station for us. We needed a second vehicle, as we also had Mr Garrison."

"Who's Garrison?" AJ asked, trying to recall who else had been at the house. The whole thing felt like it had taken place days ago.

"The man everyone calls Poppers."

"Of course, sorry."

"So we let the other officer take the two suspects while we transported Garrison, who began telling us who these two men worked for. He was quite agitated about it and concerned about all of you. All our cars have trackers, so I notified the sergeant to keep an eye on where the other officer went. He drove to the station, but made a stop along the way, spending ten minutes at that church. Poppers was just a witness, so we had no reason to hold him, but he was keen to stay with us. We were now looking for all of you, so I dropped my partner off at the station to process the suspects, and Poppers stayed with me.

"A few hours later, my sergeant called me by cell, and told me the officer we were tracking had returned to the church. It wasn't unusual to pull people over at that spot, but he hadn't radioed anything in, which is standard procedure. It was all on a hunch, really, but Sarge called two other cars to the scene, and while we were sitting by the road, assessing the situation, we heard gunfire."

AJ sat there, stunned for a moment. It had been by the slenderest of circumstances and fortunate decisions by others that the police had arrived when they did. Her group may well have survived, having already taken out both bodyguards, but if Danitess had escaped, or lived, none of them would keep breathing very long. As it was, they'd be praying his next in line was happy to move on and not seek some form of revenge.

"I'm really sorry we didn't trust you all along. Please pass on our thanks to the other officers and your sergeant."

"You had good reason not to trust the uniform, as it turned out, so the resisting arrest charges will go away. Currently, the only pending issue, unless something else surfaces you've neglected to tell us, is the business with the body at the *Spiegel Grove* wreck. The Coast Guard will be the ones to follow up on that."

Reid stood. "Let me escort you to the front desk and we'll get your personal effects returned."

AJ followed the man to the front of the small station and was relieved to see Cass and Emily waiting for her. The three women threw their arms around each other.

"You saved my bacon," Emily said, squeezing them both tightly.

"You saved all our arses, love. Johnny was right, they'd have shot every one of us," Cass added.

AJ tried to thank them, but the words wouldn't come out. It was all for the right reasons, but she'd killed a man, and she'd have to live with that. While it was certainly better than dying alongside her friends in a Volkswagen Beetle in a church car park, it wasn't a burden she'd be able to shake easily.

They finally separated. "I heard Rosie was taken to Mariners Hospital," AJ said, still sniffling. "Can we go straight there?"

Cass wiped a tear from her eye. "We've just been waiting for you. One of the coppers offered to drive us."

"Sorry about the love bug, Cass," Emily said with a hand on her arm. "Poor little bugger has a few holes to mend."

"Give my sorry excuse for a husband something to do when he gets home."

"Nice shirt," AJ said, looking at the Monroe County Sheriff's Office T-shirt that almost hung down to Emily's knees.

"Wait till Boone sees my souvenir. I'll have him begging to know who the hunky copper was that gave it to me."

AJ grinned. "I doubt it."

"I know," Em conceded. "He's a joy vacuum when it comes to jealousy."

An officer had AJ sign for the few items she had with her and they walked towards the door. "Does that mean Rosie gets to stay in the house for a while?"

Cass laughed. "Until he drives me bananas and I send him back to the doghouse."

Opening the door to the outside world, AJ was surprised to see a glow from the east as the new dawn approached. "What day is it?"

"Saturday, I think," Em replied, slipping her bright green sunglasses on despite the early hour.

AJ groaned. "The conference, Em. We're supposed to be there in just over an hour or so."

"Sod that for a game of soldiers," Em mumbled. "Maybe we can join them for the afternoon?"

"Or cocktails this evening," AJ suggested upon further reflection.

"Now you're thinking."

All three turned at the sound of a voice nearby.

"Hey Cass," Poppers said, getting to his feet from the bench where he was seated. "I was hoping I might come with you to see him?"

Cass put her hands on her hips, and AJ wondered whether Poppers was about to get a tongue lashing or an invitation.

"Tell you what," Cass said. "It's about three miles to the hospital. That gives you five minutes to explain yourself, and we'll be at the right place if I don't like what I hear."

Poppers looked tired, black eyed, and very worried, but he agreed. "That's fair."

Officer Reid appeared at the door. "Looks like I'm your ride. I have the keys to one of the SUVs so we can all fit."

"Hey, what about Johnny?" AJ asked. "Has he not been released?"

Reid shook his head. "No ma'am. We need to hold him a little longer. He has representation coming down later this morning."

"Is he being charged with anything?" Emily asked.

"Not currently, but his story didn't perfectly match up with all of yours, and he was involved in a fatal shooting."

"So was I," AJ said, shocked by the words leaving her own lips. Fatal. Dead. I, Annabelle Jayne Bailey, killed someone.

"Not true, at least so far," Reid replied. "First of all, your man, Mr Cash, claims he shot both men, and secondly, the one you shot is still alive."

AJ felt her legs go weak and a range of emotions overwhelmed her. The news that she hadn't taken a life was a relief, but on the flip side, the bastard had been about to kill Emily without hesitation. Thinking he was dead felt awful, but now knowing he would live felt almost as bad. He certainly didn't deserve to live. She would have plenty to talk to her friend Nora about when she got home. The police constable could relate.

"That's nice of him to take the blame for them both, but I shot the first man with Johnny's gun, as I explained."

"Wait, did you say Mr Cash?" Emily asked.

"That's the name on his driver's licence, Jonathan Cash."

"No shit?" Cass laughed. "He wasn't kidding."

"He has parents with a sense of humour," Em added.

Reid resumed walking towards a white SUV decked out in sheriff's livery. "Both shootings appear to be justified, but that's not my call. We have detectives taking over this morning. I'm sure they'll get everything straightened out. We did call the gentleman in South Africa who claims he can prove the diamond is his property, and that he hired Cash to retrieve it. My guess is we'll cut him loose when we receive verification."

He opened the doors, and they all piled in, Cass insisting Poppers take the front seat.

"You're sure the gemstones are safe at the station, officer?" Cass questioned, seemingly not for the first time.

"I assure you they are, Mrs Lee. We will track down the rightful owners today."

Cass sat back, but didn't look relaxed. Her husband in hospital and a night without sleep were probably more significant contributors than the gems.

Reid was barely out of the car park when Poppers turned and began pleading his case.

"It started when Rosie wouldn't tell me what he'd found, Cass. He was being all weird about it. I've never known him to be that way. He ended up giving me this shiner, and you know that's not like him."

"He was probably trying to protect you," Cass retorted. "Did you ever think of that?"

"Well, later, yeah. But at the time, it just seemed like he was being a dick about it all. I mean, why tell me he'd found something big, and then clam up?"

"Okay. So you were being a major pain in the arse, and Rosie clocked you. What's next?"

Poppers fidgeted in his seat and stammered a few times to get the next part out. "So then, you see, this guy Johnny shows up, and he's looking for Rosie. Except he doesn't know anything about him, 'cos he says he's looking for Rodney Lee. I told him I don't know anyone by that name, but he keeps on at me. Says someone told him we were friends. I got to thinking, maybe if I get in with this guy, I can steer him away from Rosie, you know?"

"Poppers, if you started with three lives, you're two down. Johnny offered you money. That's why you agreed to help him."

"Ouch," Emily commented under her breath. "ER's about to get more business."

Poppers frowned at Emily before continuing. "Fine, so I was mad at him and the guy was throwing money around, but I never told him anything useful, I swear."

"Why were you arguing on the phone with Rosie?"

"Which he also lied to us about," AJ pointed out, then felt a little guilty for piling on the guy. He was already losing his appeal.

"Someone must have told Rosie I was helping Johnny. He called and chewed me out. I tried to tell him I was steering the guy all over town, wasting his time, and he finally calmed down."

"Did he tell you where he was at the time?" Cass asked.

"No, and I didn't ask him. It would have sounded like I was trying to give him up, you know?"

"Fine, so tell us why you let Johnny kidnap and hold Emily all afternoon, huh?"

"I didn't know who she was, and he said he wasn't going to hurt anyone," Poppers said feebly. "I made sure she was treated nicely as best I could. There was no opportunity to slip her away or I would have done it."

Reid shook his head. "Are you sure you don't want to press charges, Miss Durand? We can still prosecute the man for kidnapping."

"Who? Me?" Poppers blurted in surprise.

"You would be an accomplice, sir."

"Nah," Emily responded. "He was useful in the end, so it seems a little ungrateful to nick him now. I might have another shot at his goolies though, as a deterrent, you understand?"

"To be honest, I don't understand a lot of what you ladies say," Reid admitted without taking his eyes from the road.

38

SATURDAY

He put the indicator on for the left turn into Mariners Hospital.

"Hey Cass, any chance we could run by the Cuban place just up the road?" AJ suggested. "I could murder a coffee and a pastry."

"Good idea, love. Silly sod will be fine without us for a few more minutes. They still haven't called to say he's out of surgery. Mind you, I'm not sure there's enough coffee in Colombia to keep me awake, but we'll give it a try."

Reid indicated right and moved out of the turn lane. Five minutes later, they stood in the early morning light outside Sunrise Cafe Cubano, waiting for their order.

"Did Rosie say anything about Phil?" AJ asked Cass quietly, off to one side. "Did he ask him to dive the *Spiegel*?"

Cass shook her head. "No." She took AJ by the arm and led her a few more steps away from the others. "Phil dropped Rosie off at that old derelict boat that's moored off the north end of Rodriguez Key. Told him to hide out there, left him with two bottles of water and a bag of crisps, and Phil said he'd go find out what was going on. He'd told Rosie about Poppers going off with Johnny, so Rosie called Poppers from the boat, which is the call Stubby overheard.

"He said he was going back and forth with Phil over text and on the last one he received, Phil said he'd be out to pick him up in the morning with food and what-have-you. Then Rosie's phone battery died, so he was stuck there. Phil never came back. Rosie wasn't worried until mid-morning, and then he didn't want to make the swim in daylight as he knew someone would see him."

"So Phil knew what Rosie had found? He knew he had the gems?"

"Oh yeah. Phil took him out to dive the wrecks and hide them. But Rosie never told him exactly where he'd put them."

"Phil found one, so he must have figured it out."

"Rosie said Phil had acted a bit weird from the get-go. After they figured out they had the stolen painite stones with a reward, he promised Phil they'd split the money. But he said Phil kept telling him he didn't want all that money, he just wanted enough to get to Tahiti with the missus. When they saw Johnny breaking into his truck at Harry Harris Park, they were on their way in from hiding the gems. After that, Rosie had Phil drop him at the house. Told him to come back in a couple of hours. That's when he left all the clues for me in case things went pear shaped. Didn't tell Phil about any of that either."

"I still don't get how Phil knew where to find the diamond?"

"I'm getting there, love," Cass said, catching her breath. "Rosie said he let one thing slip after he came up from the *Spiegel*. He freaked himself out a bit on the dive and when Phil asked him how it went, he told him he almost forgot how to find the engine room. They were tied on the 4 ball, so it was obviously the port engine."

"He must have used too much gas searching the engine room," AJ said glumly.

"Ol' Phil hadn't made a dive like that in donkey's years. He probably fumbled around trying to find his way. By the time he did, I bet his dive plan had gone to hell."

"He was on air," AJ pointed out. "He could well have got narc'ed enough at 130 feet in the engine room to get disorientated. Made it up to the passageway and ran out of gas there. Poor bloke. Horrible way to go." AJ shuddered at the thought. She'd been close to running out of gas at depth before. It was a memory that stuck with her.

Then a thought hit her. "Oh bugger," AJ gasped. "He was on his way out to the *Spiegel* when we passed him Friday morning."

Cass's face dropped. "I bet you're right."

The young woman called from the window, so they wandered towards the desperately needed caffeine. AJ couldn't get the vision of Phil's lifeless body from her mind. She knew he'd been dead for hours by the time she'd arrived, but she'd botched the recovery and cast him loose across the ocean. If he had any family, they may never have a body to bury, cremate, or mourn. A few minutes ago she'd been ready to eat half the display cabinet of pastries, but now the guava pastelitos in her hand seemed unappetising.

Officer Reid drove them back down US1 to the hospital and surprised them by parking the SUV and getting out.

"If you don't mind, I'd like to make sure your husband's okay," he said.

Cass smiled. "I don't mind at all."

Once inside, it was back to waiting. As they walked into the small hospital, Cass got the call that Rosie was out of surgery, but it would be a while before they could see him in recovery. Hospital coffee wasn't nearly as good as the Cuban brew they'd arrived with, but if nothing else, it gave them something to do while they waited. Except for Emily, who curled up in a chair and went to sleep. AJ snapped a picture of her with her head slumped back at an awkward angle, mouth open, and a small rivulet of drool running down her chin.

Cass was finally allowed to see her husband in recovery, and once they moved him to his own room, the others were invited to visit. Emily was emitting low, rumbling snores, so they left her sleeping. AJ was surprised how sprightly Rosie appeared to be, sitting up in bed and chatting with Cass. The pain meds lingering in his system from the surgery were likely playing a part. After all the pleasantries were spoken, Officer Reid bid his farewell and began to leave. Before he reached the door, his mobile buzzed in his pocket and he continued into the hallway to answer the call.

"I don't know what to say," Poppers said, standing nervously at the foot of the bed. "I should have just stayed out of everything. I'm really sorry, Rosie."

"Water under the bridge," Rosie replied. "I owe you an apology. I had no business smacking my best friend."

Popper's relief was unmistakable as a broad smile lit up his tired and weathered face. It only lasted a moment. "I can't believe what happened to Phil," he said, his voice cracking. "What the devil was he thinking?"

Rosie shook his head. "I reckon we all went mad around those gems. He didn't want anything to do with the reward money. Said it was all mine, but he was obsessed with that diamond. He kept on about it, wondering where it had come from and how much it was worth. I should have known something was up when he left me on that old boat. When he was leaving, I told him to be careful. He looked at me and said, 'When all this is over, promise you'll come visit me in Tahiti?'"

Cass squeezed Rosie's hand and Poppers ran a hand through his messy hair. "What did you say?"

Rosie looked up at Cass. "I told him we'd all come spend a week or two with him."

"That's what we should do then," Poppers blurted. "Take Phil and his missus to Tahiti. We can spread their ashes somewhere nice."

"That's exactly what we should do," Rosie replied, but Cass turned to AJ, who was looking at the ground. The room fell quiet as everyone realised the problem with that plan.

"I never should have involved any of you in all this," Rosie said. "Or better still, I should have left well alone in the first place."

Poppers struggled for a moment to get the words out, finally asking the question still burning in his mind. "Why include Phil but not me, Rosie? I know you and Phil were close lately, but Rosie, we go back forever. It really hurt when you chose him over me."

Rosie shook his head and sighed. "That wasn't a choice I made, my friend. Phil was on the boat with me Tuesday morning. He was there when I found the gems."

The room fell quiet once more.

"Sorry to bother you again," Reid said, appearing in the doorway. "But I thought you'd like to know. The Coast Guard retrieved a body a short while ago. They believe it to be Phil Giles."

AJ immediately looked up, and Rosie gave her a smile. "Better plan some time off for a trip to Tahiti, my dear."

"You lot left me sitting out there," Emily mumbled, bumping past Reid as she entered the room with her hair ruffled and eyes barely open. "I was just catching forty winks."

AJ grinned. "Did I tell you I saw the gnome?"

"Huh?" Em replied sleepily, looking around the room. "Do I know him?"

ACKNOWLEDGMENTS

My sincere thanks to:

My wife Cheryl, my family, and my wonderful friend James, for their support, advice, and encouragement.

My fellow author and great friend, Nick Sullivan, for allowing me to borrow his wonderful Emily Durand character. If you haven't read Nick's Deep Series, you've been depriving yourself!

Phil Giles, the winner of a character contest I ran through my monthly newsletter. When I began writing, I wasn't sure where I was going with Rosie's friend, Phil. By the end, when things didn't go too well for poor ole Phil, I was committed to the name and it felt weird to change it! Now the real Phil Giles has quite the story to tell down the pub!

My superb editor Andrew Chapman at Prepare to Publish. My novels are always improved in his hands.

Shearwater dive computers, whose products I proudly use.

Reef Smart Guides whose maps and guide books make my research so much easier, and for allowing me to include their wreck maps in this novel.
They're also kindly offering a 20% discount to my readers on their

waterproof map cards using the code AJBAILEY when ordering directly from their site at www.reefsmartguides.com

The Tropical Authors group for their magnificent support and collaboration. Check out the website for other great authors in the Sea Adventure genre.

Drew McArthur, Chris Buckley, Andy Marquez, Gene Clingan, and Ashlee Jergens for their tech and wreck diving help. If I failed to portray a diving detail accurately it is purely my error as their guidance was faultless.

Florida Keys fishing help from my friends Nolan and Olivia Wilson, owner operators of Miss O Sport Fishing.

REEF and the Coral Restoration Foundation who are both real entities doing marvellous work to preserve and protect our precious oceans. Discover them online.

My advanced reader copy (ARC) group, whose input and feedback is invaluable. This group pushes me to be a better writer, for which I am eternally grateful. It is a pleasure working with all of you.

Above all, I thank you, the readers: none of this happens without the choice you make to spend your precious time with AJ and her stories. I am truly in your debt.

LET'S STAY IN TOUCH!

For more info or to join my Newsletter, visit my website
www.HarveyBooks.com

For fun AJ Bailey merchandise, visit my online store
www.AJBaileyGear.com

If you enjoyed this novel I'd be incredibly grateful if you'd consider
leaving a review on Amazon.com
Find eBook deals and follow me on BookBub.com

Visit Amazon.com for more books:
AJ Bailey Adventure Series,
Nora Summer Caribbean Suspense Series,
and collaborative works;
Graceless - A Tropical Authors Novella
Timeless - A Tropical Authors Novel
Angels of the Deep - A Tropical Christmas Novella

ABOUT THE AUTHOR

Nicholas Harvey's life has been anything but ordinary. Race car driver, adventurer, divemaster, and since 2020 a full-time novelist. Raised in England, Nick now lives next to the ocean in Key Largo with his amazing wife, Cheryl.

A motorsports career may have taken him all over the world, both behind the wheel and later as a Race Engineer and Team Manager, but diving inspires his destinations these days – and there's no better diving than in Grand Cayman where Nick's *AJ Bailey Adventure* and *Nora Sommer Caribbean Suspense* series are based.